# THE THREE HARES
## B L O O D L I N E

# THE THREE HARES

## B L O O D L I N E

## GEOFFREY SIMPSON

Published by thewordverve

www.thewordverve.com

The Three Hares: Bloodline / by Geoffrey Simpson — 1 ed.
Published in the USA by thewordverve
www.thewordverve.com

www.geoffrey-simpson.com
www.facebook.com/The3HaresSeries/

Issued in print and electronic formats
ISBN 978-1-948225-18-2 (pbk)
ISBN 978-1-948225-17-5 (ebook)

Library of Congress Control Number: 2018900836

Summary: Best friends uncover a lost secret society and are hurled into a
desperate race to save their dying city from dystopia.

YAF001020 YOUNG ADULT FICTION / Action & Adventure / Survival Stories
YAF042000   YOUNG ADULT FICTION / Mysteries & Detective Stories
YAF062000   YOUNG ADULT FICTION / Thrillers & Suspense

To my dearest Lili and our boys Jonathan and Henry—

Many years ago, I knew that I would never become an author. With your inspiration and support, there will never be another *never* again.

This adventure is for you.

Chapter One

# From the Wild

E than Drake clutched the damp stone tethered with a frayed rope. His fingers ached. A drip of sweat flung from the tip of his nose as he leaned back and launched the contraption high into a dead, gnarled tree.

The stone devastated small twigs in its path and screamed back to earth only inches from his friend's feet. "Watch out, man! You almost got my shoes dirty," Jacob Carter said.

"Nailed it." Ethan pulled back on the rope, retracting the extra slack.

Jacob grabbed the bound stone and walked over to where Ethan stood with the other end of the rope in his hands. "Finally." He whistled loudly. "I thought we might need to burn the park bench tonight."

It had been raining for days, and the only dry wood for their campfire was high off the ground.

Ethan tightened his grip on the rope, his muscles

exhausted from repetitive stone chucking. "Your pile yesterday wasn't any better."

They each wrapped an end of the rope around their hands, standing beside the other. Knuckles white, scraped, and raw. "One, two, go!" Jacob said.

Together they sprinted away from the tree. The rope elevated quickly until the point of impact.

Ethan winced in pain as the rope's fibers ripped across his raw palms. Fingers strangled from blood. The dead branch shattered into the air as the thickest part projected in their direction. They dove for cover.

"That'll burn nicely," said Ethan, lying on the damp forest floor as the branch landed between them. A grin shone through the gritty, smeared dirt on his face. When he was immersed in nature, he was happy.

They collected the scattered scraps of their success from the ground. For nearly a week, they had been camping in the forest just outside Winslow Falls. Something they often did to fill the void of summer break.

"That's enough wood," Ethan said. His stomach grumbled for nourishment, anxious to move on.

Jacob gathered a pile of branches in his arms, "Yeah, let's go back to camp. See if we can scare up something fierce for lunch."

They had become quite proficient outdoorsmen, despite being fourteen with no real guidance from their parents, or any other adults for that matter. The school library had a survival manual, which Ethan had checked out, and conveniently "lost." It was more than a manual; it was their guide through the wilderness, a definition of their being.

"Let's check out Bullfrog Lake. I bet we can find some luck," said Ethan. He piled the remaining branches in his worn-out arms.

The boys made their way back to the camp, positioned on the bank of Norfolk Creek. Each summer, they continued to build their masterpiece, Fort Tomahawk. Heavy rains through the spring of '92 nearly washed them out. But their best work had been during the two years since. Their skills were sharpening.

As they approached their camp, the air dampened and cooled. Although very wide through this stretch, the creek was shallow. Trees loomed over the banks, leaving only a sliver of visible gray sky. The flats were filled with boulders, which they'd used to build their encampment.

Ethan unloaded his quickly weakening arms just in time. The wood tumbled onto the sparse pile. "Gotta move. Fish aren't gonna wait," he said, thoughts still on his stomach.

Jacob allowed his stack of branches to fall to the ground, and the boys grabbed their rods and bikes, charging up the small hill, back into the dark forest.

"I'm starving, man. I could eat the rump of a rhino," Jacob said.

Ethan enjoyed his buddy's ridiculous comments. Unfiltered and free. He wished he, too, could blurt out such things, but something always restrained him. That said, he did *not* envy how often Jacob spent in detention for this particular talent.

Not only did they respect how critical nourishment was when living off the land, they also realized how much more energy they spent doing so. Finding food was a daily quest, but they did keep some basics stocked at their camp, just in case. Snacks, canned ham, and beef jerky. After all, they only pretended to be survivalists, fur traders, or whatever random idea they had on any given day.

Bullfrog was only minutes away and their preferred location for bass fishing. "I'm gonna check the new habitat off Point Gore," Ethan said.

Jacob slumped his shoulders, "Hey, I wanted to start there."

"Let me have a few casts first. Then you can do whatever your princess heart desires."

Jacob grinned. "Fine, but watch out for Uncle Harold."

"You ever gonna drop that?"

"How could I? You whining like a little girl, '*Get it out, get it out. It hurts,*'" Jacob mimicked, while rubbing his eyes, pretending to cry like a baby.

The previous year, just before they closed up their summer camp, Ethan had attempted to set the hook on a tasty lunker. It was their long-sought "Uncle Harold," a largemouth bass that could rival a Range Rover. But Uncle Harold got the best of him, as he always did.

Harold had broken the surface like a cannonball, gobbling the lure, performing his best tail walk in the process. Ethan hammered back on the rod to set the hook. In slow motion, the fish grinned at him with a taunting wink, spit the hook out just as the line jerked tight, and Ethan's favorite Jitterbug lure charged back at him with the speed of a bullet. Both treble hooks buried themselves deep into his upper arm. Point Gore had been born that day, and Jacob thought it was hilarious.

"I want revenge," Ethan said. He had nightmares about that dumb fish.

They abandoned their bikes at the edge of the forest. Cautious to not startle the fish, they carefully walked out onto the small peninsula.

Days before, Ethan and Jacob dragged a thick tree branch into the water and built a submerged stone wall. The long, deep underwater shadow was the perfect bass habitat, and Uncle Harold was the mark.

Ethan bit his lip. Partly remembering the hook in his arm and partly dreaming about catching the Range Rover. His rubber worm was Texas rigged, and he tossed out a precise cast. Just below the water's surface was their homemade stone wall. The worm settled perfectly upon it. He offered the gentlest tug to bring animation to the worm. It hopped off the ledge, suspended in the crystal-clear water, and slowly dove into the deep shadows below.

The water was still, except for the gentle ripples left from the lure. A low fog eerily hung, slowly burning off as the sun's rays pierced the surrounding trees. It was beautiful, peaceful, and it was all theirs.

The line instantly tightened and shot to the right as it pulled a trail through the mist. Ethan reacted like a pro. He swung left, tip low, and set the hook. Hard. The line zipped off the reel. The fight was on.

Jacob jumped to attention and grabbed the net. "Harold?"

"Dunno. But he's huge." Ethan planted the butt of the rod just above his belt and pulled up. As he lowered the tip, he reeled hard. Repeat. Each time the fish went right, Ethan pulled left, and vice versa. He battled with the fish, inching him closer and closer to the shore.

Ethan already fantasized about telling the story of how he'd caught Harold on the first cast . . . in their own homemade trap.

Jacob lurched into the water without hesitation. He swooped the net over the beast. "Not Harold, but nice fish, man," he said.

Uncle Harold had a belly like a blue whale. This guy didn't. Although slightly disappointed, Ethan knew this one belonged high on the all-time record list.

"First cast, dude." Ethan said. He thrust his fist into the air in celebration, laughing out loud. "You can have Point Gore now."

Jacob glared back at him with narrow eyes and tossed his friend a smirk. "Thanks."

Shoving his thumb into the fish's mouth, Ethan clamped down on the lower lip and heaved the beast high into the air. It was a fine specimen indeed. "Nice," he said.

Jacob nodded. "Yeah, I gotta say, that's a good start. But we got more work to do."

The fish was bagged, and they began their routine. They inched all the way around the cove through the rest of the morning. Strategically launching lures toward the edge of submerged logs, seaweed lines, and rocky outcroppings. Their fishing skills were polished and entirely self-taught.

Fishing was a necessity to their camping trips, but it was no chore. Many days, when there was no treasure map to chase down or a new improvement to their camp to build, they would fish for the pure joy of it, often shifting to just catch-and-release.

Today, they had other plans.

"I'm done. Let's get back to camp and gobble these guys down. I'm starving," Jacob said, then he waggled his eyebrows in excitement. "Plus, I wanna start the treasure hunt."

Last night, Ethan had created the treasure map. At dusk, he had gone out on his own and buried an old wooden box beneath a spooky old tree. What was inside the box was always the same, but that didn't matter; it was about the hunt. Ethan drew up the map with clues, pirate style. Distinguishable trees, rocky features, and even self-made stacks of stones were all clues to the puzzle. There were no rules, but a big red X had become tradition.

As he ignited a stack of fresh, dry wood in their riverside fire pit, Ethan said, "You're gonna like this one. I wrote it in code."

Jacob cocked his head, glaring at his friend. "I hate riddles, man. Tell me you didn't do it in your dumb riddles."

Ethan laughed. "Fine. If you wanna lose, don't try to figure it out."

"It better be good. I don't wanna follow riddles and have it turn out to be a lame hunt."

Each of them carved up their own fish. Guts removed, heads chopped off, and scales cleaned. The fire was hot, and Jacob broke down the burning logs with a long stick. Ethan laid the old cooking grate over the fire. The fish met the grate with a fierce sizzle.

"Oh, it's good, dude. It's always good," Ethan said, concluding with a wink and conniving grin.

They devoured their fish, still a bit raw, but their hunger stole from their already limited patience. It was shortly after eleven. They were well-fed and ready to hunt treasure.

Ethan went inside their homemade hut. Its walls were built from stacked boulders with wooden support beams and mud mortar. The slanted roof was made of thick logs first, then stacked with smaller and smaller sticks. A layer of clay mud was caked over the top, making a great waterproof shelter for two. He returned with a map rolled up like a scroll.

Jacob, with outstretched hand, beamed in anticipation. The map looked authentic; it was crusty and aged yellow. A technique they used by squeezing lemon juice on cheap printing paper, which was then held over the heat of a candle. Jacob unrolled the crinkled map.

The chase was on. Jacob read through the clues and took to the forest. First, he found a stack of sticks on the ground, assembled as a large arrow pointing due north. He counted twenty paces.

A rope dangled from a tree above. At the end was a large stick with a V-shaped tip. He followed the clues step by step, which led to each homemade contraption. Ethan followed him through the forest for nearly two hours before Jacob managed to find his way to the final clue.

Jacob chuckled when he found the disturbed ground beneath the spooky, old tree. He dug at the loose dirt until he hit the hard wooden box. "I win!" he said, jumping in celebration.

Feeling a sense of pride, Ethan laughed with his friend. It was a good map. Their goal was to make it as hard as possible, but not impossible. If you could find the treasure, you win. If the map proved to be faulty, or impossible, you were deemed "Bad Pirate" and were forced to clean fish for the next two days. It all made sense. To them, anyway.

Jacob pulled the box from the earth, dusted off the dirt, and opened it. Lying inside was a six-inch hunter's knife. It was always the hunter's knife, rusty on the sides but sharp as a razor.

They spent that evening by the fire on the banks of Norfolk Creek. It was tradition after a hunt to tell ghost stories. They each took a turn progressing the story down various twists and turns, most of which were some level of disgusting.

Jacob gazed deep into the flames. "I wish we didn't have to go back tomorrow."

"I know. Dad said I gotta be there," Ethan said, shrugging his shoulders. "Besides, we can get some good home cooking."

"And a shower. Pee-yew," Jacob concluded.

They'd both grown up in Winslow Falls and really knew little outside its borders. It was once a thriving iron town, but not in their lifetime. Remaining fragments from its boom era still existed, but even those last artifacts struggled to survive.

The city drifted toward a permanent slumber. Students of Winslow Falls High who did not leave town after graduation were considered certain failures among their fellow classmates. Really, who would stay in such a tortured place?

The next day, Ethan and Jacob rode back to town on their bikes. They stank like rotten fish with undertones of dirt and stale sweat. They had till dinnertime to get home and shower, so they didn't rush.

Jacob had been invited to Ethan's house for dinner, which happened often, and he frequently accepted. His own family was so dramatic about everything, especially over the past year.

Tonight, however, was a family announcement from Ethan's dad. The boys' interest was piqued.

During the past months, Ethan's dad had been acting very strange and on edge. He hadn't always been that way. He cherished his son and always had time for him. Ethan was an only child, unlike Jacob, who had a big brother away at college. Ethan's parents welcomed Jacob into their home; in fact, he was treated like a second son.

When the boys entered the house, Ethan's mom had the table stacked with food. A pork roast was the centerpiece, steam billowing from the brown-crusted beast. Smashed potatoes, steamed broccoli with garlic, and fresh bread from the local bakery completed the meal. Mom was not a fancy chef, but she undeniably had skills in the kitchen.

Dinner was always casual, and everyone was encouraged to discuss their days. Each of them dove for the food, slopping heaps of potatoes and broccoli on their plates. Ethan's dad had his trusty carving knife out from the wooden box. His special set. Pinning the roast down with a serving fork, he sliced into the juicy meat.

As he carved, he cleared his throat and said, "Well, this new guy running for mayor is really stirring up the town." A slab of meat flopped over, splashing some juice on the table. "He is twisting everything and everyone around. If he gets elected, it'll be a major setback for Winslow Falls."

Ethan's mom lost her cheerful enthusiasm. "Is he running now?"

"Yup, it's official."

Earlier in the summer, a man came to town from a glorious distant land of success and prosperity. He instantaneously gained a following of social elites. They saw hope in his large stature, broad shoulders, and mysterious aura.

But it was not just those things that carried him into the hearts of the people. His fiery words and gestures had captured the frustrated public's attention. He radiated confidence.

At the time of his arrival, the presiding mayor, who looked like he might have been the local barber, was running for reelection unopposed. Despite his limitations, the town was complacent. The people preferred to *complain* about unemployment than to actually *do* something to improve it, Ethan's dad had often said. To some extent, blame became their culture . . . their identity.

Dad cleared his throat again. "I decided to quit my job."

Now he had everyone's undivided attention.

"Actually, I've been working with a private group over the past month. We're running a counter-campaign against this new guy. But despite our best efforts, he keeps on coming."

"Quit! What do you mean you're gonna quit? How will we pay the bills? Our mortgage?" Mom's complexion shifted to a shade of red.

"Honey, let me finish. The campaign has donation money set aside. Besides, if this guy wins the election, there'll be bigger problems than the mortgage."

Dinnertime was soon filled with a tempered debate, only because Mom restrained her rage. "Why didn't you ask me first?"

"Because I knew your answer, and it wasn't what I wanted to hear."

Her eyes widened as she swallowed in disbelief. "So you just do it?"

Ethan hadn't seen Mom so pissed before. She could burn holes into Dad's forehead with her wickedly intense glare. This was way worse than when he'd set the toaster on fire.

Their debate escalated as Ethan and Jacob looked on. Dad struggled to explain how he must do this for the greater good.

Ethan's parents didn't fight often, but when they did, it was somehow controlled and civilized. Probably due to Mom's extraordinary patience. The boys finished their meals while still hot, but Mom's and Dad's dinner slowly cooled in the midst of the heated argument.

"I need to head out to the campaign office tonight. We're planning a big rally, and they need my help."

Mom, though concerned about the ramifications of the decision, eventually chose to support Dad. She always supported him, and he usually gave her good reason to.

Dad ultimately skipped dinner altogether and headed out into the summer night.

After the dust settled, Ethan said, "Come on. Let's go to the attic."

"Thanks, Mrs. Drake," Jacob said as he pushed back from the table. He was rough around the edges and crude, but when Jacob was in Ethan's house, he was an angel. He appreciated Ethan's family.

The boys had a small desk in the attic, which they used to plot treasure maps, plan pretend fur-trading adventures, or design new construction projects for Fort Tomahawk.

"That's crazy stuff, man," Jacob said. "My parents just sit around and bitch about things. Your dad's actually gonna do something about it."

"I know. He's been acting more and more upset about this guy running for mayor. I'm not surprised he finally blew a gasket."

They spent hours goofing around in the dusty attic with no regard for how late it was.

The phone rang downstairs, and Ethan's mom answered. They could only make out her side of the conversation, of course, and even that was quite muffled. "Hello, Drake Residence." She paused for the response.

"What? Police?" Her voice spiked. "What happened?"

Her breathing quickened. "No. Oh no . . . no. There must be a mistake!"

The boys looked at each other with terror-filled eyes. Ethan's heart plummeted with uncertainty. All they could do was listen. Something terrible had happened.

Mom began to sob. It wasn't crying; it was utterly out-of-control sobbing. As the boys charged down the stairs to find out what had happened, she dropped the phone. Small shattered pieces danced along the tiled kitchen floor. She collapsed in much the same way. Her shattered pieces were everywhere.

That moment would change the boys' lives and their friendship forever. It changed everything.

Chapter Two

# The Map

The following June, one year after the dreaded phone call, school had let out for the summer. Ethan and Jacob had no plans, and their initial excitement had already begun to fade. As boredom crept in, they decided it was time for an adventure.

The school year had been terrible. Ethan was constantly distracted, his grades suffered, and the summer could not have come soon enough. Everyone at school knew about the accident, and rumors spun like drunken spiders. He either received unwanted and overwhelming sympathy or was teased by the shallow jerks who commonly lurked the halls of the ninth grade.

His dad had died that warm summer night, leaving him and Mom in a tailspin. Family should be a rock, a foundation from which life flourishes. Ethan's strong, confident, and patient mom had become useless. Ethan was lonely, and if he planned to do anything with his life, he would need to do it on his own.

One thing of significance dawned on him that year. Humans are emotional morons.

"Mom's driving me nuts," Ethan said as he rummaged through an old box in the attic. "This morning, a light bulb burned out, and she started crying."

Jacob was just out of sight, obscured by the chimney. "Don't know, dude. She's getting worse, isn't she?"

Ethan tossed a few things from the box onto the attic floor. "Doesn't she get that I don't wanna be reminded of everything Dad used to do? Like screwing in some stupid light bulb? Who's the adult, anyway?"

Jacob poked his head around the corner and threw an old teddy bear at him. "Not you!"

Ethan sneered at his friend but knew he was only trying to cheer him up. "I don't know . . . we gotta find something to do."

Jacob was shoulders-deep in the oldest of the boxes, mostly filled with Ethan's baby things. They often searched the attic for old stuff to use in their adventures at home or at Fort Tomahawk.

The spacious attic was directly above the bedrooms and mostly used for storage. A writing desk and a bookshelf stood by the window overlooking the front yard. Natural lighting spilled in through the unadorned window. Ethan and Jacob had played in that attic even as toddlers. Several structural posts ran along the center of the room, and at the far end was where the fireplace chimney came through.

The boys sorted through boxes of old toys, books, and useless trinkets saved by Ethan's parents. One stack was off limits. They were filled with his dad's things. Simply looking at them dampened his mood. His mom had asked a friend to move some of Mr. Drake's stuff into the attic so she didn't have to be constantly reminded of his death. Those boxes were the only new ones, and their crisp appearance alone was a reminder of how fresh the scars were in Ethan's life—barely scabbed over.

Ethan's head snapped up when he heard a loud cracking noise followed by a crash. "Be careful, man! I don't need Mom snooping around up here."

After a moment of silence, Jacob—still obscured by the chimney—said, "Whoa, what the…? You gotta see this!"

Ethan poked his head around the corner to find his buddy kneeling on the ground over a broken floorboard. "What did you do?"

"I shoved the boxes out of the way and saw this symbol burned into the floor." Jacob lifted a short plank, which indeed had a branded triangle on it. "When I was looking at it, I leaned on the bottom half, and it squeaked. So I pulled, and it just popped right off."

Ethan hovered directly over his friend's shoulder, looking down into the space that had once been covered by the plank. "What's down there?"

He could only see the top of the object, but it was made of old leather and was heavily cracked. Looked like a bag of some sort, but he couldn't be sure. Ethan wondered how old it must be with such a thick layer of dust covering it.

Jacob reached down to pull it out. Ethan considered the possibility it was his dad's and pulled back on Jacob's shoulder. "Hold on a minute," he said, quickly grabbing the mysterious bag for himself. "I wanna look first."

He dragged what turned out to be a leather satchel from the dark chamber. The flap was brittle and had two tarnished clasps. A cloud of dust hung in the room, each particle illuminated by the beams of sunlight.

Jacob shifted his attention toward Ethan, whose eyes were blank and consumed by distant thoughts. He leaned in toward his buddy, placed a hand on his shoulder, and whispered, "Come on. It's okay. Let's open it."

Ethan regained focus and glanced up at his friend. He knew it was way too old to be his dad's, and so really, there was no reason for caution. He flipped the two clasps, yanked the straps through, and opened the leather flap.

The bag was unexpectedly lightweight. It quickly became obvious that it was empty. Ethan dug through the side pockets, which produced nothing more than old dust. He was overwhelmed with disappointment, desperately needing a distraction from life. The emotional roller-coaster ride was exhausting.

"Let me look," Jacob said as he snatched the bag from Ethan's loose grip. "We'll *make* an adventure out of this."

Jacob impatiently yanked the flap open. The stitching, aged and fragile, tore away from the deteriorated lining.

Ethan winced.

Without hesitation, Jacob grabbed the tattered edge and crudely pulled it back, yielding a loud zipping noise.

A shiver ran down Ethan's spine, partially because of the sound of the stitching being torn apart, but also because of what was revealed. A thick folded parchment was hidden behind the lining.

Jacob's eyes nearly popped from his skull. "Holy crap!"

Ethan was motionless in anticipation. Everything in the world faded. There was no attic, no Winslow Falls, no jerks at school, and no sad memories of his father. At this exact moment, there was only one thing that existed. A golden parchment.

Delicately, Jacob pulled the paper from its leathery tomb. Folded several times, it was thick and obviously very old.

The corner behind the chimney was dark, but the light beaming onto the desk from the window was the ideal place to inspect their newly found discovery.

The parchment folded out several times until it was nearly two feet by three feet. In unison, they cheered, "Treasure map!"

"Did you plant this?" Ethan asked.

"Hah," Jacob said, surprised at the accusation. "I wish I could make something like this."

Ethan knew their skills were limited to printer paper stained with lemon juice. But if not Jacob, then who? "How old do you think it is?" Ethan asked. "It looks like a real ancient pirate's map."

"Don't know, but the ink's all faded." Jacob ran his fingers along the text. "Doesn't look like a normal treasure map, either. More like a puzzle."

The boys loomed over the warm, sunlit desk, inspecting the text and images, trying to understand what it all could possibly mean.

"Look here," Jacob said, pointing to a line of elegant handwriting stretching in an arch across the top of the document. He slowly read it out loud, enunciating each word.

*"Those who have desire to find change, in a place which is rooted in evil, will search till the ends of the human condition."*

Ethan realized he'd been holding his breath. He inhaled deeply then let it out in a loud huff. "What the heck does that mean?"

Jacob pointed to the middle of the map. "Here. Doesn't that look like a cave? What do you think?"

Ethan's enthusiasm turned a corner as he contemplated the map's origin. "Do you think Dad hid this in the attic? Maybe Grandpa?"

"Don't know, but we're not asking your mom till we've inspected it more," Jacob said, thumping his hand on the desk. "If she gets pissed, she might take it away."

Ethan nodded, never lifting his gaze from the map. "We won't tell a soul," he whispered.

Jacob sucked air through his teeth before suggesting, "Not anyone . . . except your grandma."

Ethan snapped his head up. "Shut up! That's not funny."

"Hear me out," Jacob said, hands up defensively. "Maybe she'll recognize it and tip us in the right direction. It's not like she's gonna tell anyone."

Ethan squinted in disbelief. "She's in the late stages of dementia. How's she gonna 'tip us in the right direction'?"

"You know. She brightens up sometimes with old memories. She even mumbles things sometimes. Who knows what'll happen?"

"No!"

"Come on. We gotta try!" Jacob looked pitiful in his pleading.

"No. We're not bringing this to Grandma, end of—"

Ethan's mom called from the bottom of the steps, her voice lacking any discernable energy. "Dinner."

"In a minute, Mom!" Ethan shouted. He turned to Jacob to conclude the discussion. "We're not taking this to Grandma, no way! Let's hide the map so we can look at it in the morning."

Nearly pouting, Jacob folded the map back into the satchel and tucked it under the floorboard once again. They headed down the rickety attic stairs one after another.

"Would you like to stay for dinner, Jacob?" asked Ethan's mom in her monotone voice.

"My mom's expecting me, Mrs. Drake. My brother Mike and his girlfriend just got home from college for the summer. Thanks for the offer, though." Jacob had always been uncharacteristically polite with Ethan's parents.

"Next time," she replied with a hint of disappointment.

"See you in the morning, dude," Jacob said as he punched Ethan in the shoulder with an extra burst of energy. Their faces glowed with their secret and the possibility of a great adventure.

Ethan washed up and joined his mom for the usual silent meal. Both lost deep within themselves, they rarely exchanged a word beyond the essential "pass the salt please."

Ethan was buzzing with thoughts of the map, the satchel, Dad, and Grandma. He was more distracted than usual and completely missed his mom asking about what they were up to in the attic.

"Ethan, did you hear me?" She obviously had picked up the change in his disposition. "You feeling okay?"

"Yeah, Mom, everything's fine," he said, surprised at her question. He had no interest in talking right now. "May I be excused? I wanna go read."

"Of course." Her shoulders sagged. "Say goodnight before you go to sleep."

Ethan brought his dishes to the kitchen and climbed the stairs without another word.

Hours later, after watching a series of droning TV shows, she poked her head into his room. "I'm going to bed now. Don't stay up too late."

Ethan was in bed, leaning against the wall with his pillow behind him. The book in his hand meant nothing to him; it was just a prop.

He tended to avoid conversations with his mom. What words of wisdom could she possibly provide without being the dreaded hypocrite? She had nothing to offer, which infuriated him. He had held her on such a high pedestal before, and now he couldn't help but be disappointed in her. He was lonely and felt abandoned by her.

"Night," Ethan mumbled, giving her a quick glance with his sharp green eyes.

He decided to wait until his mother was fast asleep, and then he would ascend to the attic and study the map. It wasn't like sleep was on the agenda tonight, anyway.

Nearly an hour later, the house was motionless and silent. He tiptoed just down the hall to his dad's old office to grab the flashlight. Placing one foot cautiously in front of the other, he winced as the stairs creaked slightly under his weight. By the yellowish glow of the flashlight, he steered his way to the back corner of the attic.

Kneeling beside the secret compartment, the light flooded over the floorboard, illuminating the branded triangle symbol in the wood. His heart pulsed at the sight.

Shadows danced through the room as he lifted the board. Extracting the satchel from its tomb, he carried it to the desk by the darkened window. He glanced outside, but with the glowing flashlight, the window acted as a mirror concealing the dark world beyond. A face he hardly recognized stared back at him: his own reflection.

Ethan unfolded the map and carefully arranged it upon the old writing desk. He balanced the flashlight on some old books, allowing its beam to wash across the ancient paper. He was ready. Finally, he could study its contents.

It was beautiful and intricate. *A master must have created this artwork*, he thought. No ordinary pirate with a peg leg could have imagined such a perfectly balanced thing. A patch on an eye would dissuade such depth of purpose.

His fingers trailed over the map, picking up a distinct texture. The document was embossed with a complex image. He had noticed some edges earlier, but thought nothing of it. Now, in the harsh, contrasting glow of the flashlight, the ridges became distinct and formed an intriguing pattern.

He grabbed the light from the top of the books and shined it at a shallow angle to intensify the contrast. Still, the pattern was impossible to decipher. He knew the markings were absolutely added to the map with intent.

He leaned over the desk, stretching to the small but fully stocked bookshelf behind him, and grabbed paper and a red pencil from an incomplete and mostly broken set of coloring pencils. His dad once taught him how to make copies of graveyard headstones. The thought of using the trick now was an unsettling thought as visions of his dad's tombstone flickered through his mind.

Ethan carefully laid the paper over the impression. He lightly swiped the side of the pencil lead back and forth until the image transposed.

"Whoa." The image became defined for the first time. Sketched in red on the paper were three rabbits chasing each other in a circle. The rabbits' ears formed a sort of triangle in the middle. Ethan considered the branded floorboard, wondering if there was a deeper meaning to the triangles.

He looked back at the original parchment and bravely decided to use the edge of the pencil directly on the map. Carefully he colorized the high points, and the three rabbits eerily formed over the other markings. He had originally thought of the map as a masterpiece, but this undeniably took it up a notch.

The embossed rabbits aligned with the old, faded, inked-in images. The cave Jacob mentioned was directly centered within the inner triangle of the rabbit's ears. Ethan thought the cave must be the final destination. What long-lost treasure could possibly be found there?

On the lower left side of the map was a simple image of a rising sun. A half circle beaming with rays of light sat on a horizontal line, which represented the ground. At the top of the page, under the text Jacob had read earlier, a full, round sun was depicted at high noon. Finally, on the lower right, the same sun was setting.

Inside the imaginary arcing sun's path were the three rabbits, now highlighted in red pencil. Each rabbit soared over a specific image. Ethan leaned in more closely to examine those images.

Within the first rabbit, on the top left of the circle, was an open book with illegible text. The second sketch, on the top right, was an image of a powerful waterfall tucked into a forest scene. Finally, the one on the bottom was a stone, castle-like watchtower. Each image was accompanied by a short, cleverly written riddle.

Deep into the early hours of the morning, Ethan pored over the details, trying to comprehend what he was looking at, but there was only one thing that became clear to him: he was utterly exhausted.

✳ ✳ ✳

Ethan jerked his head off the desk, awoken by a creaking noise. A string of drool, slowly sagging, connected him to the desk. He was disoriented and realized he had fallen asleep while studying the map. Anxiety rushed through him. *Is that Mom coming up the stairs? Am I about to be busted?*

Ethan slowly turned toward the hatch door leading into the attic . . . and saw Jacob's head pop up.

*Not mom.* He breathed a sigh of relief and wiped the drool from his mouth.

"You're already here?" Jacob asked as he inspected his friend's weird expression. "Seriously, dude, are you drooling?"

Ethan just looked at his hand, now wet with slime.

"You *slept* with the treasure map? Why didn't you wait for me?"

This was the earliest Ethan had ever seen Jacob. *Probably couldn't sleep last night, either.* Ethan scratched his head, tousling his messy, brown hair, and wiped his eyes. Deliberately ignoring the question, he said, "Come on. You gotta see what I found."

Jacob moved over to Ethan's shoulder, peering down at the red rabbits. "What's that?"

"That's what I want to show you," Ethan said, grinning as he looked up at Jacob's astonished expression. "The map had an embossment, which I traced."

"Cool beans!" Jacob said, running his finger across the page. "You're not nearly as dumb as you look."

"And the pictures. I think they're clues that lead you through the forest to the cave pictured in the middle of those rabbits." Ethan moved his finger across the map. "The treasure has to be buried in the cave."

Jacob smirked. One thing was certain: they would no longer be bored this summer.

For hours, they hung over the map. Necks stiff, eyes blurry, but determined. Despite finding many interesting elements on the map, they had no idea where to begin in terms of understanding what it all meant. Excitement and anticipation became overwhelming.

Ethan had been considering something for hours, but finally pulled himself over the line. Seemingly out of nowhere, he plainly said the word, "Okay."

With narrowed eyes and a crinkled brow, Jacob looked at his friend and said, "Huh?"

"We'll go," he said, intentionally not clarifying his point. Jacob's eyes went wide. "Do you mean . . . ?"

"Yup. Let's show it to Grandma."

"Yes, yes, yes!" Jacob jumped from his chair, his fist held high in victory. His sudden movement knocked the chair backward, sending it to the floor with a loud crash.

"Shhh. Mom's gonna come up here and find out what we're up to," Ethan hissed. Just at that moment, they could hear her shuffling at the bottom of the steps.

"Ethan!" she yelled. "What are you doing up there?"

He glared at his friend as he shouted back, "Jacob's here. We're just hanging out."

The steps began to squeak as she ascended toward them. Ethan's heart skipped a beat in anticipation. "Have you guys seen that box of old toys?" she asked, her voice closer now. "The Millers down the street asked for them."

They quickly grabbed the map, folded it, and tucked it away on the nearby bookshelf, out of sight. Just in time. Her head, then upper body, appeared through the opening as she climbed the last few steps.

"What've you guys found up here that's got you so excited?" she asked. Her tone was brighter today.

No quick words came to Ethan as his brain stalled without an answer. Jacob jumped in. "Um, well, we're just pretending to plan a mystery," he said off the cuff.

She chuckled and offered a rare smile. "You guys and your adventures. Don't stay up here all day. It's too dusty."

Ethan saw her looking at their feet and realized he had dropped the etched picture of the rabbits under the desk. His stomach dropped.

She turned, grabbed the old box of children's toys she had come searching for, and headed back down the steps. Halfway down, she said over her shoulder, "Have fun, boys."

They waited until the coast was clear. "Did she see it?" whispered Ethan, already knowing the answer.

Jacob nodded. "Definitely." He picked up his chair and returned it to the desk. "You think she knows what it is?"

Ethan shrugged his shoulders, hoping that would be the end of it. Besides, there was nothing they could do about it now.

A brilliant smile returned to Jacob's face as he shifted the conversation back to where it had been before the intrusion. "Let's go see your grandma."

"Now?"

Jacob raised his eyebrows in a taunting encouragement. "Yup."

Ethan grinned and nodded. He placed the treasure map and sketch within an old folder from the shelf, and the empty satchel was returned to its dark enclosure beneath the floor. Not a moment was wasted as they left the attic, with Ethan carrying the folder concealing the most prized possession—their first real pirate map.

"Bye, Mom. Off to plan our mystery," Ethan shouted as they both ran outside, leaving no time for her to respond. They had a mission, and their excitement was rabid.

Chapter Three

# A Break in the Silence

Hands gripped around the vibrating handlebars, Ethan charged down the choppy, dilapidated road. "I can't believe you talked me into this."

"You know it's our best shot," Jacob said, huffing between words.

Ethan lived on a rural road on the outskirts of Winslow Falls. It was once a farming community just outside town, but as the city's borders expanded years ago, the land was sold to housing builders. Still, much of the area remained undeveloped. His street was one that was nearly vacant except for the few scattered old farmhouses.

The death of the town's growth had left scars on the road from the long-departed construction vehicles which once tirelessly roared through the neighborhood.

"You really think Grandma's gonna say something?" Ethan asked. He already knew it was a fat chance and didn't know why he'd bothered to ask the question.

Ethan drifted back into his memories of her first days in the nursing home years ago. She incrementally became less capable of living alone, sliding deeper into her lonely, dark world. Her dementia was stifling, a barbaric process to watch unfold. He hoped she couldn't recognize the downward slide herself. He was never sure about that.

Grandpa had passed away before Ethan was born, and he was often told how they would have been two peas in a pod. Their looks and personalities were profoundly similar, according to Grandma. "Cut from the same mold," she would say.

Ethan often daydreamed of spending time with his grandpa—so much, in fact, that he unintentionally manufactured fragments of memories only existing in fiction.

"Forgot to tell you," Jacob said as they pedaled. "We finally got our new neighbors. They got a daughter!"

Ethan's head snapped around. "Yeah? And?"

"She's soooo hot, dude!"

Ethan knew he wasn't kidding. He hadn't seen Jacob so excited since he'd locked lips with his first girl, Samantha the Smoocher. Something still on Ethan's own to-do list. "What's her name?"

"No idea. I only saw her from a distance."

"Well, if you wanna cuddle, you probably gotta learn her name." Ethan's bike swerved with his exaggerated laughter.

"Shut it. Focus on the mission," Jacob said while veering his bike toward Ethan and joining in on the laughter.

Ethan nearly hit the curb as he pushed Jacob away from him.

"I bet that cave's out in the pines past the old quarry," Jacob said. "That area's filled with rocky formations just like the picture."

"Nobody goes out that far. Gotta be thousands of acres out there." Abandoned fields whizzed by them on both sides of the road as their bikes rattled on the choppy street. "How are we ever gonna find it?"

"Don't know. But if we find the cave and the treasure . . . man, this is gonna be a rad summer!"

Ethan thought that if Jacob had a wagging tail, he could be a stand-in for an excited puppy. His own enthusiasm wasn't much milder. "Absolutely!" he said. "A summer for the record books."

As their fantasies ran wild about long-lost treasure, they reached the nursing home sooner than expected. It was a somber sight. A prison shielding them from the gloomy secrets of loneliness and misery awaiting them in their own final hours. Each time Ethan gazed upon that transitionary house, he gravitated toward the opinion that the worst years are the last years, and life is better when we ignore our imminent fate.

The distinct smell of cleaning agents hit them with force as the automatic sliding doors opened. Of course, there was that other smell, one which Ethan could never quite put his finger on. *If you condense and bottle sorrow, does it have an odor?*

They registered at the front desk then proceeded to Grandma's room. It was creepy walking through the halls, passing the occasional half-dead human. Hollow and lonely was a terrible way to end a full, vibrant life . . . or even an uninspired one.

They finally approached room 223. It was the medical side of the nursing home, so the sparse apartments were more like hospital rooms. Most of Grandma's belongings had been moved to storage. Only essentials and a few mementos remained to spark distant, slowly slipping memories.

The boys entered the room just as the nurse was finishing up Grandma's sponge bath. An invasive sight indeed. Grandma trembled, her expression numb, void of awareness. Even as the boys stood there, quietly hovering by the door, she had no reaction whatsoever. The nurse seemed pleased to see them, waving them in as she completed her task.

"Well, Mrs. Drake, your grandson Ethan has come to see you today," she said with a well-rehearsed upbeat voice.

Ethan pushed aside the awkwardness that he'd come to expect with these visits. "Hi, Grandma. It's Ethan. How are you feeling today?" He paused for a moment, allowing her time to process everything. "Jacob came to see you today as well."

On cue, Jacob tossed her his best exaggerated smile.

Ethan approached his grandma, hugged her frail bones, and planted a gentle kiss on her hanging, toneless cheek. Jacob followed suit. Ethan knew that Jacob, too, had wonderful memories of her from his own childhood.

Grandma Drake was well known for spoiling the boys. Since Ethan was her only grandchild, he got it all. When the boys were younger, it was always cookies and candy, reading books way past bedtime, or letting them splash around in the muddy puddles. She loved Ethan unconditionally, and Jacob, too—he was no less than her own flesh and blood.

Grandma's hazy eyes looked upon the boys, her hands trembling uncontrollably. She tightened her lips in her best effort to smile. She was happy to see them.

Ethan eased his way in with small talk. He filled her in on all the things happening around town and shared how Mom, her daughter-in-law, was doing.

He didn't dare tell of Mom's deepening depression. It was a burden he wished not to unload on her.

Growing impatient with small talk, Jacob elbowed his buddy in the ribs, encouraging him to cut to the chase.

Ethan glared with squinted eyes, feeling it was too intrusive. The reality was that he, too, was anxious to get started. He exhaled a quiet sigh and moved into the subject slowly. "Grandma, we were playing in the attic and found something really cool." He paused between sentences, hoping it would improve her ability to follow. "We're curious. Maybe it was left in the house from when you and Grandpa lived there?"

At the mention of Grandpa, she became a bit more alert and, by a fraction of a degree, dialed in to the discussion.

Jacob, twitching and unable to contain his eagerness, said, "It's a map! Hidden under the floorboards."

Ethan's eyes burned into Jacob, and he gave him a "slow down" gesture with his hand, something he often had to do with his friend, who always seemed to be straining at the leash. Ethan returned his gaze to Grandma and said, "There was an old leather bag hidden under the floorboards behind the chimney in the attic. There was a map inside of it."

The boys looked at each other as Grandma offered no sign of recognition.

"There's a triangle symbol burned into the floor where it was concealed," Ethan said as he pulled the folder out of his bag and opened the parchment.

Air softly vented between her blue lips in the form of a long sigh.

"Have you seen this before, Grandma?" Ethan hoped with all his might that, somehow, they were connecting with her.

Grandma extended her hand and slid her fingers along the red-shaded embossment. Her hands had nearly stopped shaking. She then closed her eyes and retraced the entire image with her boney fingers.

"Grandma, was this Grandpa's?" Ethan stared at her closed eyes and could see rapid movement behind her eyelids, as one would have during a dream.

Jacob was silent as they watched her climb from her dark chasm.

Grandma Drake finally looked up at Jacob with an expression of concern, then slowly panned to Ethan. She took his hands and placed them within her own. He kneeled beside her. With all her strength, she squeezed, yet so delicate to not harm a cracker. A single tear streaked down her cheek as she locked eyes with her one and only grandson.

Ethan noticed how dull and faded her eyes had become.

After a fleeting pause, she nodded in confirmation. Her hand sluggishly rose and pointed to the closet across the room. "There," she said.

The boys gawked at her in awe. She had not spoken an intentional word for months.

Ethan regained his composure, unsure of what to make of the request. He looked toward Jacob, who was fixated on the closed closet door. The objective was now clear. Gently placing the hand that still held his upon her lap, he stood and began moving toward the closet, his footsteps soft, almost gliding across the floor. He pulled on the wobbly handle, opened the door, and then looked back at his frail grandmother. "What do you want me to get?"

She delicately rotated her wrist, pointing toward the upper shelf, and whispered, "The box."

Ethan's heart raced in anticipation as he turned his sights back to the closet. Resting on the top shelf was an antique wooden box, lightly covered in dust. "This, Grandma?"

She confirmed with a simple nod.

*She almost looks haunted*, Ethan thought, and he shivered a little bit inside as he reached for the box.

Overly cautious about dropping it, he returned to his Grandma's side and held it out to her. She placed her hand upon it and, once again, closed her eyes.

She began to stutter, but stopped to compose herself. In a faint, fragile voice, she finally said, "Open it."

Ethan looked to Jacob for encouragement, but he sat speechless, watching the event unfold. He returned to the box and slowly flipped the latch, opening it.

Inside the small, unmarked box was a tattered, burgundy cloth concealing and protecting an object within. He looked again at Grandma, who sat stoically, unmoving except for one nearly imperceptible nod. Ethan folded back the soft cloth and unwrapped the object—an antique gold pocket watch with a cover that flipped up to reveal the watch's worn face.

But it was the symbol on the cover that harpooned the boys' attention. Three rabbits chased each other in a circle across the surface. The exact same symbol that was on the map.

Ethan and Jacob glanced at one another with wide eyes; neither spoke. Grandma seemed frozen, perhaps lost in memories rocketing to the surface from the dusty, dark corners of her mind. Ethan could only guess at the history of the timepiece and the untold effect it may have had upon her life.

After an eternal moment, she broke her trance. She reached out to Ethan, grabbed his fingers, and cupped them around the watch.

"For me?" Ethan asked. The metal was cool; the sensation penetrated deep into his flesh.

In a slow, hollow voice, she said, "This is yours, my boy. It always was." She hesitated to catch her strained breath. "Use your time wisely."

Her hands began to tremble once again. As quickly as her senses had sharpened upon seeing the map, they receded back within herself. Her gaze became distant as she drifted away from them. She had apparently rallied her last bit of energy to present the watch to Ethan. It was as if the effort had taken everything she had left in her.

Uncountable questions burned within him. Was the watch Grandpa's? What was the meaning of the map? What did the riddles mean? Why was this so important to Grandma? But the truths remained veiled in shadow. She withdrew into her solitary darkness and was no longer able to engage the outside world. She was alone once more, and her secrets were buried in the impenetrable chamber within her. Ethan had seen it before.

Their hands still clasped within one another's, Ethan exhaled and then gently broke the bond. The boys offered their best goodbye hugs and kisses. A feeling of guilt mixed with excitement washed over Ethan as they left her room.

In their possession, they held a new puzzle piece. *A golden pocket watch with the three rabbits embossed on the cover.*

They charged away on their bikes, riding back through the fields from which they had come. Jacob abruptly took the lead and veered to the left, off the main path, down a bumpy, overgrown trail toward the forest's edge. A single tree grew apart from the rest at the back of an old, abandoned farm field. A large old oak, one they'd frequently climbed throughout their childhood.

Ethan followed him down the trail without hesitation. The purpose was clear.

The tree stood as broad as it was high, towering over the edge of the field, casting a wide shadow. A weathered picnic table resided beneath the looming canopy—it had been there for as long as the boys could remember, but newer at one time, of course. Now the decomposing boards could tell the story of their lives.

They tossed their bikes against the tree's trunk and sat down on some large boulders, cool in the shade. Sheltered from the intense summer sun, they were ready to study their new prize.

Ethan grabbed the box with his sweaty fingers and carefully extracted the watch. "Look. There are initials between the rabbits' ears."

Within the inner triangle, framed by the three rabbits' ears, the initials were worn and hard to decipher. Ethan stood from the boulder and found a ray of sunlight piercing through the tree's canopy. The markings were illuminated and became legible.

Jacob hovered over his shoulder, and they read the inscription simultaneously. "E Z D."

Articulating each letter, they sharply snapped their eyes toward one another. Jacob's were nearly popping from his head. "Those are *your* initials!" he said.

Ethan stared at the three worn letters. His thoughts spiraled out of control.

"Ethan Zephaniah Drake," Jacob said.

Ethan shook his head in disbelief. "Yeah, but this watch is much older than me. It could be a hundred years old or something. Besides, Dad and Grandpa don't have my initials."

"You have ancestors with these initials?" asked Jacob.

"Don't think so. Years ago, Dad showed me our family tree. He told me I should be proud of the Drake family history, and I should carry the name with honor. I don't remember anyone else with my initials."

Jacob jumped to his feet like a hound in hot pursuit of a fox. "Where's it at?"

Ethan shrugged. "He used to keep it hidden inside an old book in his office, but I have no clue which one. I haven't seen it in forever."

The boys continued to examine the watch, comparing it to the map. They searched for any connections beyond the image of the three rabbits.

Ethan realized something about the map and lurched forward in excitement. "Look at the three suns."

Jacob leaned in as Ethan's finger glided across the map along the imaginary arc of the sun.

Ethan read aloud the text that accompanied each position of the sun. "The sunrise says, '*Within time is a path.*' The full sun says, '*For the hunter.*' And the sunset says, '*But the hour is getting late.*'"

Jacob picked up on the idea and said all of it as a single sentence.

> *"Within time is a path for the hunter, but the hour is getting late."*

Ethan clapped his hands together. "This has to be a clue about the watch."

Jacob flipped open the cover again and looked at the clock's face. "Maybe there's something here . . . like, maybe something's gonna happen at some specific time, sometime late?"

Ethan fought back a smirk—Jacob's idea was a little ridiculous, since the watch wasn't actually ticking—but he didn't want to discourage him. "Uh, yeah, but it's not actually keeping time. I don't think it's gonna tell us anything."

"We need to wind it, dude," Jacob said as he grabbed the tiny dial between the tips of his fingers. "Crap, it won't budge. I think it's broken."

Ethan reached out to try his luck. "Let's see."

"Try to open the watch itself," Jacob said. "Maybe there's something stuck inside."

Ethan inspected the watch's structure, but there was no obvious way to open it. Not a hinge or screw could be found, just a narrow groove running around the entire circumference.

"Okay, maybe you have to twist the entire housing," Jacob said.

*Now he might be on to something.* Ethan palmed the watch. He squeezed it between his sweaty hands and attempted to rotate the back cover, like one would a jar of pickles. His palms slid across the surface with no chance of gaining traction.

Jacob vigorously wiped his hands on his jeans and grabbed the watch from Ethan. He pressed his palms hard against either side of the watch and gave a firm counterclockwise twist. The back panel broke free of its long-withstanding grip, and the entire housing began to unscrew.

Ethan sucked in a breath. "You got it!"

With only a few complete turns, the back panel separated from the main body. Jacob grinned as he held up the two pieces. "Of course I did."

Their enthusiasm welled up as Jacob flipped over the parts to inspect the inner guts of the timepiece. "Wow, look at those gears and springs," he said. With the parts only inches from his nose, he inspected them like he knew what he was doing.

"That's awesome. How the heck does it work?" Ethan's inner geek rumbled to the surface. The intricacies, materials, gears, and springs were fascinating. It was unbelievable to him that the watch had once kept accurate time *without a battery*.

Jacob scratched his nose. "Looks clean, though. Don't know if it's jammed, but I can't see anything."

"What's that inside the casing?"

Jacob adjusted his gaze. "Is that another engraving? I was looking at the gears and didn't think to look there." He used his fingernail to scratch at the inscription. "I can't tell what it says."

Ethan took the watch back to the lone ray of light beaming through the tree's branches. The sun, once again, illuminated the way. He read the text out loud.

*"The direction of your entry runs counter to your path. Pursue this Hare with caution."*

"I hate riddles!" Jacob said, throwing his hands in the air. "I just wanna find the dumb treasure cave."

Ethan laughed at his impatience. "Deal with it, man! That's half the fun of a treasure hunt. Besides, there's no way we'll find the cave without solving the riddles."

"What's it gotta do with someone's hair, anyway?"

Ethan enjoyed pushing his buttons. "It's spelled H A R E, as in rabbit."

Jacob huffed at the teasing. "If you're so smart, what's the answer to the riddle?"

Ethan tightened his lips. "Maybe it's telling us which way to follow the rabbits around the circle." He realized his suggestion was nothing more than a wild guess, but better to guess than not.

The boys flipped back to the map. Ethan delicately traced his finger along the arc from the sunrise to the sunset. "But the hour is getting late," he repeated as his fingers settled upon the sunset. "Look at the hands on the watch. It shows about 4:20. That's about where the sunset is on the map."

Jacob rolled his eyes. "So we start at the sunset? Dude, that doesn't tell us anything."

"Hold on. The text says, 'The direction of your entry runs counter to your path.' To get into the watch, you had to rotate it counterclockwise to unscrew the cover. So . . . does that mean counter to counterclockwise? Meaning clockwise?" Ethan realized he now sounded ridiculous. *It sounded better in my head.*

"Beats me," Jacob said, grasping his hair with both hands. Then his frustrated expression shifted toward one of enlightenment. "But what if it *does* mean clockwise? The first sketch is the stone tower at the bottom of the map, clockwise from the sunset. So, we start with the tower!"

Ethan knew it was nothing more than a shot in the dark, but he'd take it. "Sounds like our best guess."

Jacob spanked the boulder with his hand in a drumroll of celebration.

Ethan looked around and noticed the real sun had begun to set. "We should stop for the day. I told Mom I'd be back for dinner."

"Yeah, it's getting late," Jacob admitted, but his enthusiasm didn't dwindle one bit. He was literally bouncing on his toes. "Same time, same place tomorrow. I can't wait!"

They packed up and rode to the main trail in the golden glow of the summer evening. Jacob lived clear on the other side of town, so at the main intersection, they went their separate ways.

Ethan and his mother were watching a comedy show when the phone rang in the kitchen. He hopped up to grab the cordless phone and noticed the caller ID said it was from the nursing home. He handed it to his mom. He thought it might be about their visit earlier today, but why?

She muted the show and, without checking caller ID, answered with a polite, "This is Mary."

She listened for a moment, and then her expression slipped from nearly cheerful back into sadness. She nodded, following the voice on the other end. After several minutes, she asked, "Will she be okay?"

Another elongated moment passed, and she finally said to the person on the other end, "We'll come by tomorrow morning to see her. Thank you for calling."

She didn't tell Ethan what the phone call was regarding; instead, she embraced him in a deep, sorrowful hug. He could feel her warm tears against his neck. He knew Grandma had slipped deeper into her cavern of solitude, or perhaps something worse. His tears intertwined with his mother's as he considered the possibilities. An eternity hung in their embrace. Only the occasional sniffle broke through the thick silence of their living room.

As the flickering glow of the TV splashed upon the wall, Ethan's mind ran wild with images of Grandma from that very morning.

There would be no more comedy tonight.

Chapter Four

# Castle Tower

As he lay in bed, Ethan's thoughts were consumed with concerns for his grandma and about his visit with her yesterday. How she had momentarily broken free from her mental prison to pass along the antique pocket watch. He wondered if he was responsible for her turn for the worse.

Unanswered questions riffled through his head. Had she hung on to her last stream of consciousness so she could pass along the watch? Had she cried because she knew she was ultimately saying goodbye forever? Why had she looked at Jacob as if she feared for him? None of the questions would be answered, but they hung heavily around Ethan's shoulders.

The early dawn transitioned toward daylight. Ethan could hear Jacob's old bike rattle down the street and finally turn into his driveway. He went to the window and in a low voice instructed his friend, "Stay there. I'm coming down." He pulled on his jeans and shirt from yesterday, flew down the stairs, and flung open the front door.

Jacob stood there. Ethan motioned for him to stay silent and led him around the corner to the barn.

Jacob looked around curiously. "What is it? Why are we in the barn?"

In a somber tone, Ethan said, "Last night, Grandma slipped further away. This morning, Mom and I need to go over to the nursing home to discuss the situation with the doctors and decide what to do next."

Jacob was silent as his face twisted with sorrow.

Ethan put a hand on his friend's shoulder. "I know, I know . . . this is all very weird."

Jacob was able to finally choke out, "I'm sorry, man. Are you okay?"

Ethan knew Jacob was thinking not only of Grandma, but the fact that Ethan had just lost his dad as well.

"I guess. I don't really know what to think," Ethan said. "I spend more time thinking about the connection between Grandma and the watch than I do about her actually getting worse. It really hasn't sunk in yet."

"Oh, man. I wish I knew what to say. Do you want me to come with you guys?"

He shook his head, and his breathing trembled. Before he got any more emotional, he quickly said, "Naw, I think it's best that Mom and I do this together, just us. But we should start looking into the castle tower when I get back."

"Do you mind if I borrow the map while you're out? Maybe I can get us going with a good lead."

"Yeah, that's a good idea. Let me grab it."

Ethan tiptoed into the house, so Jacob did, too. "Why are we being so quiet? Where's your mom?" Jacob asked.

"She's still sleeping. Last night's news sure didn't help her depression. I mean, Grandma wasn't her mom, but they were close."

"If you need anything, you know . . ."

Ethan turned to look at his friend, who was being uncharacteristically empathetic. "Yeah, I know. You'll be here for me."

Jacob nodded.

"Thanks for that," Ethan added.

Jacob nodded again and looked away for a moment, swallowing hard.

Ethan snuck up the stairs and snagged the map. When he returned to the front door, he handed it to his friend. "Okay, so I'll call you when I get back. Find something useful on the map, will ya? I need a good distraction about now."

Before he woke his mother, Ethan slipped into his dad's office, hoping to find the family tree. The office was small with a simple desk and a couch that could fold out to a spare bed. The bookshelves along the wall, from the door all the way to the back of the office, completely overpowered the space and were crammed with books. So many books.

Ethan looked at all the books and let loose a sigh. He had a great memory, but it was many years ago when Ethan had last seen the family tree, and he really had no idea where to begin. So he just . . . began. One by one, he looked through the books, until finally he came across a thick, green book with gold-trimmed pages. Something about it seemed familiar.

His memories rushed back to the day his dad went through the detailed notes within the family tree. He quickly fanned through the pages, but the document was not there. No document, and no one to tell him the stories of his ancestors.

Despite a sense of loss and disappointment, he continued to flip through a few more books. Nothing. Dejected, he left the office.

Ethan woke his mom so she could start getting ready for their trip to the nursing home. No telling how long it would take her to just get out of the house. Some days, it was a lengthy and complicated event.

This time, though, she popped up and got busy, much perkier than he had expected. Ethan suspected it was just an act for his benefit, maybe hers, too. She repeated a few times through the morning, "It's the natural process of life, however sad it is."

At the nursing home, they had a private meeting with the doctor, who explained that Grandma had slipped into a coma. There was still a chance that she could fight back, but the odds were against her. The doctor recommended they give it a little time and see how things progress. Ethan could read between the lines, however. Grandma was in her final hours.

✳ ✳ ✳

After a lot of paperwork and more discussions with the doctor, Ethan and his mom finally returned home. The mood was somber, and Ethan was anxious for a reprieve. He called his best friend as soon as he walked into the house.

"It's me. I'm back. You find anything?"

"Yeah, I think I got something. Meet me at the Old Watermill," Jacob said cryptically. "How soon can you leave?"

"Give me ten minutes to get changed, and I'll head out."

"Cool. Oh, and bring your telescope and compass." Jacob hung up before Ethan had a chance to respond.

Ethan smirked. Jacob was so dramatic sometimes. But Ethan didn't question the request and immediately set to changing his clothes and gathering up the watch, telescope, and his dad's compass. He literally ran out the door, yelling to his mom, "Off to Jacob's!"

The Old Watermill was about a half mile past the big oak tree where they'd investigated the inside of the watch. It was an abandoned stone building in the process of being swallowed by surrounding vegetation. A small stream was diverted to a dammed pond, which now acted more like a mosquito farm than anything else.

Ethan arrived to find Jacob already snooping around. He was walking around the building, inspecting the walls, both high and low.

Without taking his eyes off the building, still scanning up and down, he said, "Come here. I found something interesting."

Ethan hurried over.

"My dad has a book on Winslow Falls history, so I did a little research on castle towers in the area."

"Jacob, this isn't a castle tower!"

"Hold on, listen. I read there were three watch towers built on the edge of town along the edge of the forest. Mostly, they were there to protect the town against thieves," he explained. "Over the years, the towers became obsolete and eventually were torn down. The stone from one tower was reused to build this watermill."

He now had Ethan's attention.

"Soooo, this is the old watchtower," Jacob said as he gestured to the stone walls.

He stepped away from the building and laid out the map on a nearby wooden bench. "Look here." He pulled out his small children's magnifying glass, which looked quite silly in his hands. "If you look here at the map, at the shading on the stones of the tower, there's a pattern."

Ethan leaned in to get a clear view of what Jacob was showing him.

"When you look close enough, one stone toward the top is a different shade," he said as he pointed with his finger. "And on that stone, there's an eye, an arrow, and the number 248 engraved on it."

Ethan snatched the magnifying glass, scrunching his nose at the silly little device. He was glad nobody was around to see him using it.

"Wow, you're right," Ethan said as he inspected the stone on the map. He kept moving the magnifying glass away from the map and then back again. "Without the magnifying glass, all that stuff just looks like part of the stone's texture or whatever. Good job, man." He was impressed at Jacob's find.

They searched the perimeter of the building, looking for some sort of special stone with markings on it. Soon, Jacob broke the silence. "Look!" He pointed high up on the wall. "That one over the window doesn't have the same color mortar around it."

Ethan came around to his side. "Which one?" He craned his neck, looking up to where Jacob was pointing. "I don't see it."

Without answering, Jacob began scaling the wall, using the windowsill as his initial foothold. His arm was fully extended, and he nearly fell. "I can't reach it." He exhaled in frustration and hopped back to the ground.

Ethan focused on the targeted stone, not sure if it was "the one." It had no eye, arrow, or number on it, but it certainly looked out of place. He looked around, focusing on the bench where all their things were. Suddenly, he had a plan.

"Let's flip the bench up against the wall as a ramp."

Jacob snapped his fingers and pointed at his friend. "Good idea."

Together they positioned the bench at an angle under the stone of interest. Ethan grabbed the bottom of the bench to brace it from falling, and Jacob took the lead. He gripped the sides with his hands and climbed up the bench until he was able to perch upon the bench's thick leg, high above the ground.

Now face to face with the unique stone, he began inspecting it. He scratched it, then pushed on it. "This thing isn't moving!"

Ethan handed him a rock from the ground. "Hit it. Maybe it will break the mortar."

Jacob carefully gripped the wobbly bench with his left hand and swung the rock hard against the stone block.

It moved. Only a half inch, but it moved! Then a loud, metallic, clicking noise rang out from inside the watermill.

"Yeah, baby!" Jacob exclaimed.

"Yeah, baby is right! Come on, get down," Ethan said.

Jacob climbed down halfway, then jumped to the ground. His grin matched the excitement in his voice. "I think I unlocked something."

"Definitely sounded like it."

The boys stepped back and considered their options. The window that Jacob had earlier attempted to climb was barred over—no chance with that. They continued around the building to a reinforced wooden door.

Ethan pushed and pulled on it without success. In frustration, he threw his shoulder into it. The door popped open into the darkness beyond. Unprepared for the movement, he tumbled to the ground.

Jacob stepped past him. "Whoa."

Streaks of daylight spilled through the opening. It was probably the first light the interior had seen for a century. As they slowly entered, their eyes adjusted. They could make out the interior of the main room now, a rectangular shape. Other than a pair of old tables in the corner, it was completely empty. Not including the thousands of cobwebs, of course. From the left side of the room, narrow stone steps led to a wooden hatch in the ceiling.

They made their way up the steps and pushed the hatch outward onto a viewing platform. Short walls around the perimeter prevented the view of the platform from the ground. "The watchtower!" the boys said in unison.

In the center of the roof was a wide but short pedestal with a large, metallic, circular plate on top. The plate had incremented tick marks representing the 360 degrees of a circle. Within the center of the plate was a round piece that rotated. It had a line drawn through the center, tipped with an old Native American arrowhead.

"Be back in a minute," Ethan said as he bounded down the steps to grab his dad's telescope from the ground where the bench had been. He returned just as swiftly, taking two steps at a time. He placed the tripod of the telescope on the rotating pedestal and aligned the telescope with the arrowhead. Ethan pulled out his compass, and identified the appropriate mark for 248 degrees. They rotated the plate and telescope until the arrow pointed directly at that exact tick mark.

"You wanna look, or me?" Jacob asked.

"You got us here; take the honors." Ethan bowed and made a sweeping gesture with his arm.

Jacob climbed onto the pedestal, confirmed the alignment, and peered through the eyepiece of the telescope. It was pointed downward, toward the fields below. He then elevated the telescope toward the horizon, and paused. After a moment, he said, "You gotta see this!"

Ethan joined him and took control of the scope. He gasped when he realized 248 degrees looked directly at the front drive of the mayor's office. "What's that mean?" he asked in disbelief.

"Don't know, but look at the text around the outer edge of this pedestal." Jacob squatted down, pointing out the faint words carved circumferentially around the outside of the stone pedestal. He read them aloud.

*"The tower of corruption can only be seen through special glass, as its cast dark shadow blankets the mass."*

Ethan climbed down to look at the inscription for himself. "What's this map getting us into?" he whispered. "Remember the inside of the watch? *Pursue this Hare with caution!*"

Jacob scratched his head, his hair a crazy mess, as usual. "The mayor is one sleazy guy. At least that's what I've heard."

Ethan nodded. "My parents always got upset when they would talk about him. My dad used to say, 'Voting for Maxwell Hofner is like asking a fox to tend your chickens.' For some reason, Dad seemed almost ashamed that the mayor had gained so much popularity."

Jacob looked out over the fields with his naked eye, able to see the mayor's office in the distance. "Well, there's no way this map is about Mayor Hofner. He hasn't been around as long as the map has."

"I agree, but the warnings do sound like things people say about him. Did you hear how he started to bus the poor and homeless people out of town in the middle of the night?"

"Yeah, my parents couldn't stop talking about it for a week." Jacob shook his head. "Then again, a lot of people cheered him for doing that. Like he was cleaning up the streets, or whatever."

"Yeah, pretty weird," Ethan said, because, in his mind, he couldn't understand how people could be like that.

The boys grew quiet for a moment. The mayor's office was definitely in the line of sight

Ethan thought: *Are we now chasing down Mayor Hofner?*

Strange for two fourteen-year-old boys to be talking about politics, but it was the way of things now, almost like a survival skill, to understand what they could, to be in the know about what was happening to their future.

Winslow Falls had witnessed the last of their iron foundries falling victim to the changing times. Doors were closing, and unemployment was breaking record highs. The loyal citizens had nowhere to turn until Maxwell Hofner walked into town last summer.

He came to Winslow Falls with a promise. The promise was simple: he would turn back the clock and bring the town to its former glory.

Desperation hung thick, and he offered a solution to the people's problems. His victory was a landslide but not without protests. The community began to divide, crumbling in on itself.

In retrospect, the people of Winslow Falls didn't stand a chance.

Chapter Five

# A Book of Golden Deeds

Neither Ethan nor Jacob had been so dedicated to a cause in their lives. Chasing through riddles and finding this mysterious cave was not just a distraction from the all-too-often boring days of summer; it was also a distraction from mourning.

All they could think about was yesterday's discussion at the top of the Old Water Mill—their newfound interest in the mayor's activities. Was this strange treasure hunt somehow significant to the way their city was being run?

Ethan's memories of his father hung thick, constantly eating at him. The coincidence of his dad's death, which occurred during the transitional days of Maxwell Hofner becoming mayor, and this treasure hunt with the mayor as a key puzzle piece were hard to ignore.

Bright and early the following morning, the boys met at the old oak tree on the edge of the forest instead of at Ethan's house. It was a shorter ride for Jacob, and Ethan was trying to avoid discussions with his mother about Grandma.

Generally speaking, they avoided Jacob's house altogether. Not because his family didn't want them around, but because every time they were there, it was one sad story after another. It was a constant assault of complaining and blaming, which the boys simply couldn't stand to listen to. Ten minutes, fifteen minutes, okay. But an hour of the same argument except with different words . . . really? Who has time for that?

Ethan had arrived before Jacob. He was perched on the picnic table as the morning sunlight provided a gentle, golden hue across the adjacent fields. The ground was damp with dew, the air still as a painting and crisply cool.

In his hand, he had his own magnifying glass, definitely a more adult-like version than Jacob's, hovering over the map as he searched for more clues. Specifically, he was looking at the image superimposed over the second counterclockwise rabbit at the top left of the map. At first glance, the picture was of some old book lying open on a table.

With the magnifying glass, he could see that the text of the book was intentionally indecipherable, although there were a few exceptions. Some of the letters could indeed be identified. The corner of the page on the right was bent down, as if it had been earmarked for future reference.

Ethan heard Jacob approaching on his bike. He glanced up from the map and watched as his friend slammed on his brakes, driving a cloud of dust into the air. "My parents forced me to stay for breakfast today," Jacob said, breathing hard from the bike ride. "It's

Saturday, so everyone was home. Blah, blah, blah." He rolled his eyes.

"It's Saturday? Hm. I had no idea," Ethan said. "With no school and my mom not working, days just run together, I guess."

Jacob shrugged as he approached the picnic bench. He flung his backpack onto the damp ground and peered at the map. "So, what did you find?"

"Well, after looking at this image of the book, I can see some actual letters within the scribbles." Ethan pointed to a few. "I haven't pieced them together yet."

Jacob reached into his backpack and pulled out a piece of paper and pen. "Okay, what's the riddle?" His eyes could not have rolled farther back into his head.

Ethan read aloud the text under the image of the book, carefully enunciating each word.

*"Mind your concentration on concentricity, for the waves are in rings of three."*

"Oh, brother." Jacob shook his head in disgust, exhaling loudly, but played the game anyway. "You find any concentric rings? Maybe the open pages of the book are like a wave?"

"Maybe," Ethan said as he contemplated other solutions. "I don't see any patterns with the letters, though. There are twelve of them. They gotta mean something. I mean, you can't make out anything else *except* those few letters."

By this time, the boys were both hunched over the map trying to read the letters through the magnifying glass together. As they began to lean on each other, Ethan blurted, "Back up, dude! I can't breathe, let alone concentrate."

Jacob pushed back from the table, noticeably irritated. "Just let me look. You've been staring at that dumb thing all morning and still don't have a flipping clue."

Ethan ignored his friend's frustration. "Wait, maybe the waves are like when you drop a pebble in a pond?"

"What the heck are you talking about?" Jacob snapped.

"Look." Ethan pointed directly at the center of the book, even though Jacob would not be able to see it without the magnifying glass. "If you start here and draw three increasingly larger circles, four letters appear inside each of those rings—three rings, twelve letters total." When he looked up, Jacob was rolling his eyes at him.

"You mean, like, *concentric*? That's exactly what I told you to look for."

Ethan frowned, realizing something was off with his friend. "Who pissed in your cereal this morning?"

"It's nothing!" he blurted out, seeming even more ruffled for the confrontation.

Ethan knew for sure now that something was going on. He waited for an explanation. While he wanted to get back to the map, he knew they couldn't concentrate until Jacob let go of whatever crap was bothering him.

Finally, Jacob sighed and said, "It's just...well, my dad told us this morning that he and a bunch of other guys have to cut their hours at the factory. There's some dumb law that says if an employee isn't full-time, then the company doesn't need to pay for health insurance." He stuffed his hands in his hair and pulled. "Whatever. I had to listen to all that this morning."

The reality was that Jacob's dad always had problems with work. It really didn't matter who the company was or what the economy was doing—he was just not very employable. He spent more time complaining and blaming, than he did working hard. Ethan knew this, and he knew Jacob knew it, too. That was why they avoided Jacob's house, and his father, as much as possible.

Ethan's face softened, and he said, "Yeah, my mom is having a terrible time finding work right now. Seems like there aren't any jobs out there. Must be the work of our great mayor, Maxwell Hofner." He laughed, trying to break the tension.

"What a . . ." Jacob smirked as he put his fist to his mouth and coughed over his next word: ". . . tool!"

The boys laughed away their families' dysfunctions and let their frustrations fade. Now they could focus.

Ethan returned their conversation to the map. "Okay, so the letters seem to fit in *concentric* circles," he said, jokingly overemphasizing the word "concentric."

Jacob waved his hand dismissively and then picked up his pen and paper. "Okay, read me the letters in each ring, and I'll write them down."

"Outer circle is O-O-K-B. Middle circle is O-L-D-G. And the inner circle is E-E-D-D."

Jacob tried reading the letters out as words. "What does 'Ookb Oldg Eedd' mean?"

"Beats me. Maybe it's a word scramble.

"That's even worse. Wait, where did you start on the circle?"

Ethan pointed to the upper left corner of the book. "On the left. Why? Where should I start?

"Let me try something." He rewrote the letters, his tongue sticking out of his mouth as he concentrated. "Ha! I got it! If you start from the bottom, the words are BOOK, GOLD, DEED."

"Awesome. Okay, now we're getting somewhere. I didn't think about starting at the bottom—the same place as the rabbit, and the book, and the riddle itself. Okay, so . . . what the heck does BOOK GOLD DEED mean?"

"Um, uh, I'm guessing it's a . . . *book*," Jacob said with a goofy expression on his face.

"Very funny." Ethan shook his head, smiling at his friend's sarcasm. "Um, okay, so, do you think they have, like, *books* at the *library?*" he added to continue the foolishness.

They both burst into laughter and started packing up their things. They were headed to the public library.

*** *** ***

Once their bikes were parked, they headed up the steep steps leading toward the main entrance of the neoclassical library building.

Ethan looked way up to the top of the columns as he climbed the steps. "I haven't been here in years."

"I've *never* been here," Jacob said with a proud chuckle, as if it were a badge of honor.

Jacob pulled open the massive, heavy front door. When the door shut behind them, the rattle of the old latch echoed throughout the vast, quiet room, announcing their arrival. The boys instinctively winced at the sound.

A few people turned their heads, but quickly returned to their readings.

Ethan whispered, "Come on," and they proceeded through the large room to the farthest back corner. They sat across from each other at a solid wooden table with two green banker's lamps on top.

Jacob leaned forward and whispered, "Okay, so . . . where do we start? It's gonna be impossible to find this book—never mind what the actual title is—with all these *books* in the way." He snickered as he gestured at the rows and rows of shelves surrounding them.

Ethan rolled his eyes; Jacob really had no idea how to use a library. He nodded toward a nearby computer terminal. "The computer, dude."

"Right."

The boys moved over to the terminal. One of the librarians approached them, probably noticing that they were uncomfortably out of place. Not a single person in the library was their age. "Can I help you find something?" she asked kindly.

"Nope," Jacob blurted out, not even looking at her.

"No, but thank you, ma'am," Ethan said, smiling sweetly at the librarian. She nodded and then shuffled off. He turned to Jacob. "Try to be nice."

Jacob looked at him innocently. "What? We got this." He grabbed the mouse, and the black screen flickered with illuminated green text. "Whoa. Such new technology," he snorted.

Ethan smiled, and the boys began to search for their mysterious book, using different variations of the words. Just when they thought there was no hope, they almost jumped out of their chairs when they saw a distinct possibility appear on the screen. It was the title of an old book published in 1864 by Charlotte Mary Yonge—*A Book of Golden Deeds*.

"This has gotta be it!" Ethan said, slapping the table with enthusiasm.

"Dude, shhh. But I think you're right."

Ethan scribbled the information about the book's location on a scrap of paper near the terminal.

Now, they could search the library. The process took them entirely too long, but eventually they found the right section. Ultimately, they came across the book, wedged between two larger books on the top shelf. It was green with gold letters down the spine—and much smaller than Ethan had expected.

Before going for the book, they looked at each other.

"Ready?" Jacob asked.

"As always."

Jacob reached up high and pulled the book out. They performed a rough external investigation. It was definitely old but in decent condition. As Jacob slowly flipped through the book, Ethan noticed that one of the pages was creased—at one time, it had been folded over. He grabbed Jacob's arm to stop him from continuing.

"Hey, flip that page over so the creased corner is on the top right, just like it is on the map."

Jacob did just that, and they scoured the text for special clues.

"It looks like someone erased some underlined words here," Jacob said, pointing to the area.

The faint markings were nothing more than an impression left by the pencil, but it was visible enough. Ethan read the words that had been underlined:

*"While men and women still exist who will thus suffer and thus die, losing themselves in the thought of others, surely the many forms of woe and misery with which this earth is spread do but give occasions of working out some of the highest and best qualities of which mankind are capable. And oh, young readers, if your hearts burn within you as you read of these various forms of the truest and deepest glory, and you long for time and place to act in the like devoted way, bethink yourselves that the alloy of such actions is to be constantly worked away in daily life; and that if ever it be your lot to do a Golden Deed, it will probably be in unconsciousness that you are doing anything extraordinary, and that the whole impulse will consist in the having absolutely forgotten self."*

They read it together several more times, trying to understand what it meant.

Ethan attempted to summarize. "So, it's saying that a golden deed is the truest and deepest glory. But it will only happen if someone absolutely forgets themselves . . . every day."

"I don't know what the heck that means," Jacob said. "So, first the map tells us how dangerous it is to pursue the tower of corruption. Now we need to forget ourselves to perform a golden deed? Kinda crazy, right? What does it all mean?"

Ethan chewed on his lower lip for a moment. "Honestly, I don't know." Shaking his head, he looked at his friend. "I just don't know."

Jacob started to put the book back on the shelf, but Ethan stopped him. "Hey, I'm gonna stay a bit and do some, uh, light reading."

Jacob gave him a wide-eyed look and nodded at the book. "Really? This?"

"Yeah, the underlined text talks about being inspired by the stories within the book, and now I'm kinda curious."

"Whatever, man. I gotta get back home. Mom's making me do some chores. When do you want to start digging into the third rabbit?"

"Come over for dinner tonight? I think we're ordering pizza. We can take a look at the map after we eat. Come over around six."

"Cool. See you then. And have fun reading," Jacob said; then he laughed, which sounded like a weird, whispery cackle, and headed for the door.

Ethan found his way back to the table with book in hand. He stayed in the library for several hours, burning through much of the afternoon. It was hard reading, but he was indeed inspired by what he read.

All the short stories and poems described characters who had achieved truly selfless acts of goodness. The time frames and settings covered anything from ancient Rome all the way through the colonization of America. As Ethan's eyes began to tire, he found himself simply gliding over the words without really understanding them any longer. It was time to wrap it up and head back home.

He wasn't sure why really, but he chose not to register his name with the library by checking out the book. He went back to the shelf and placed the book where they had found it.

As he was leaving the library, two well-dressed gentlemen were standing by the checkout line, and both seemed to be watching him. One whispered to the other as Ethan passed. *Business suits on a Saturday?* Ethan thought that was odd, but he avoided eye contact and kept moving.

For a moment, he wondered if he should be worried. Had they really been watching him? And why? He shook it off. There was no reason to believe the men in suits were spying on their investigation. Besides, nobody knew they were solving the map's clues. In fact, nobody even knew they had a map. Without giving it any further thought, Ethan left the public library and headed home.

Chapter Six

# Erosion

Down went their pizza. They couldn't wait to start investigating the third and final rabbit—the waterfall. The final step of the outer circle was on their agenda tonight. Seriously, who could remain calm?

Nearly no dialog occurred at the dinner table. Mom was withdrawn, as she frequently was. The only subject the boys wished to discuss was not for her ears. Their tongues burned in anticipation. In fact, their tongues burned from the pizza sauce, too, as they had no patience to wait for it to cool.

Devouring the last remaining slice, Ethan asked with his mouth still full, "May we be excused, Mom?"

She stared blankly at her dinner plate. A half-eaten slice of pepperoni pizza stared back. She softly responded, "Sure, boys, but not too loud. I am not feeling so well this evening."

Jacob stood. "Okay, Mrs. Drake. Thanks for dinner."

She merely nodded in response. The boys took their plates to the counter, then dashed up to the attic, which they now referred to as their "war room," bounding two steps at a time.

At the desk by the window, Ethan pulled the map out of the folder and unfolded it carefully. They immediately hovered over the map, eyeballs focused on the third image surrounded by the final rabbit.

A fierce waterfall projected out over a rocky cliff and plunged into a pool below. Large pine trees spanned the surroundings, and a creek flowed from the pool of water.

Ethan's finger shot to the map, pointing to the riddle included under the waterfall image. He read it out loud:

*"Erosion is a conflict of friction, which merely exposes deeper and hidden layers. Cleansing the earth will never rest, until the core has been met."*

They looked at each other then back at the text.

"Dude, I'm glad this is the last one. No way could I take any more of these ridiculous riddles," Jacob said.

Ignoring the comment, Ethan picked up his magnifying glass and started perusing the image for any clues or hidden messages. He noticed some shadows inside the pool of water, starting at the outflow of the creek and heading directly into the center of the roaring falls. "Look at those shadows." He pointed to each of them, drawing a squiggly line with his finger through the water. "Do you think it wants us to walk directly into the center of the waterfall?"

"Yeah, well, I'm not a big fan of walking into the middle of a waterfall, but that doesn't really matter 'cause we don't know *where* this waterfall is," Jacob said. "There are a ton of waterfalls in the pines; I have no idea where to begin."

Ethan abruptly stood and said, "Wait here," and then he tore down the steps. Several minutes later, he was back with a different map. "This is my dad's map of the forest. It doesn't show the actual waterfalls, but it does have all the rivers and creeks. Maybe we can find some places to start our search."

"Ah, sure," Jacob teased. "That won't take all summer or anything."

"Come on, stop complaining. It's worth a shot."

The boys spread out the new map and traced through all the streams and rivers they could identify. They disregarded any areas where the water went through an open field, since the image on the ancient map clearly showed pine trees and rocky cliffs. This helped to narrow down the possibilities, but there were still uncountable options. After reviewing the map of the forest for two hours, they sat back, exhausted.

Jacob stood up from the desk and rubbed his eyes. "I'm going home, dude. We're not gonna solve this one tonight, if ever. Nothing makes sense right now. Maybe some sleep will help."

"I agree," Ethan said through an exaggerated yawn. "There are just too many streams to make a good guess. But I'm gonna look a little more. See you tomorrow."

They high-fived each other, and Jacob headed down the stairs.

It didn't take Ethan long to realize he could no longer focus on the map. He joined his mother for a TV show to distract him from the investigation. *Nothing like brainless entertainment.*

After an hour, he and his mom headed for their bedrooms. But Ethan wasn't as tired as he was before. He had gotten a second wind. He waited until his mother was fast asleep and headed to the war room for another round.

Situated in front of the two maps, he mumbled, "There has to be something here . . ." He went from the old parchment to his dad's forest map—back and forth repeatedly. Over time, the images were burned into his mind. He had a strange sense that there was something in common between them, but he couldn't lock down the connection.

Finally, he gave up for the night and folded the maps. With the last of his energy, he headed back down the stairs to his room to get some much-needed sleep.

Despite his intense exhaustion, his sleep was restless. Images of rivers, ponds, pines, and rabbits chased through his mind, and of course, the waterfall. It was frozen in time in his shallow dream, the water hanging mid-air. Something familiar appeared to him within the falling water.

"That's it!" He shot up in his bed, heart racing. Quickly, he slid from beneath the covers and padded up the attic stairs.

The desk was softly illuminated by the moonlight coming through the window. He didn't flip on the light but instead walked to the window and looked out. It was a beautiful night. He used to love looking up at the stars as his dad told him stories of the constellations.

Suddenly, he saw movement under a tree near the barn. *What the . . .?* Whatever it was, it was pretty big. His heartbeat pulsing more quickly, Ethan lowered himself so only his eyes protruded above the windowsill.

No further movement came, however. Had his mind been playing tricks on him? In his exhausted state, he knew that was possible, but still . . . the ominous feeling stuck with him. He tried to push it to the back of his mind.

He returned to the desk. Instead of turning on the light, he allowed caution to prevail and grabbed the maps, heading back to the closet of his bedroom with a flashlight. His clothes dangled above his head on their hangers.

Maybe it was the fact that he was looking at the maps in a new place. Maybe his racing heart had caused him to view certain elements with a keener eye. Maybe he was just lucky. But as soon as Ethan had once again compared the two maps, a surge of energy rushed through him, erupting into a controlled, quiet laughter. "I got it." With great satisfaction, he refolded the maps and climbed back into his bed, falling into a deep, well-deserved slumber.

Ethan ended up sleeping in much longer than he'd planned and was running late—almost an hour late. He peddled his bike feverishly to get to the old oak tree where he and Jacob had agreed to meet. In his mind, he could already see Jacob's impatient expression and stance.

When he pulled up, Jacob was pacing along the edge of the woods. "Where have you been? You said you'd be here an hour ago!"

Ethan ignored his friend's dramatic greeting. He hopped off his bike and parked it at the trunk of the old tree.

"Whatever. Dude, I got it!"

Jacob held up his hands. "Don't even tell me. I don't want to know. Listen, we're stopping our investigation."

Ethan looked at him with wide eyes, shocked at his friend's sudden U-turn. "Huh? What are you talking about? I found the path to the waterfall, man!"

Jacob looked at his friend with a pained expression, then glanced around, as if he were afraid someone might be listening. "No, seriously, someone followed me home last night. I eventually lost him, but it creeped me out. I know it's about the map. I don't know. Look, I just don't want to get in too deep with this. It's . . . well . . . it's getting way too real. It's just not, uh, fun anymore."

Ethan's forehead crumpled as he watched Jacob struggling with his concerns. He looked toward the edge of the forest, and something came to him. "It must have been the library. I saw two strange guys whispering about us yesterday . . . well, it seemed like that, anyway. And—"

"What? Why didn't you tell me this last night?"

"It slipped my mind. Plus, it didn't really mean anything to me—not until just now, when you told me you were followed."

"Come on, Ethan. I wanna find the cave, too, but we don't know the first thing about these people! We have no idea who's watching us. They may even be the people who killed your dad." Jacob quickly covered his mouth with a hand and then slowly brought it back down. "Sorry, that didn't come out right, but seriously, it's something to consider."

Ethan was not really shocked by the statement. He, too, was considering that possibility. Perhaps it was more of a motivation than a deterrent to him.

Ethan thought about telling Jacob about the movement in the shadows by the barn last night, but he wasn't even sure it had been real. Besides, Jacob was jumpy enough. It would certainly add the last nail in the coffin to the treasure hunt, which Ethan wasn't prepared to do just yet. "Listen, at least let me tell you what I found."

"Fine," Jacob said, still on edge. "But then we end this."

Ethan ignored the last comment and laid the maps on the picnic table, side by side. "Look at the rivers on the forest map." Ethan took his finger and traced several branches of the river system. "Now," he shifted over to the waterfall image, "look at the patterns within the waterfall itself."

"What patterns? I don't see anything."

Ethan traced his finger along the flow lines of the water falling off the cliff. "Do you see it?"

"Are you saying there's a map or clue or something inside the waterfall?"

Ethan slapped him on the back. "Exactly." He watched as his friend gravitated from hesitant to intrigued, oscillating between the maps, comparing patterns.

When he finally spoke, it was with reverence. "Dude, how did you find this? I mean, wow. You're like a real detective or something."

Ethan grinned. "You're never going to believe this, but . . ."

"But what? What?"

"I saw it in my dreams!"

Jacob pulled his chin back and frowned. "Uh, yeah. Right. Your dreams."

"It's true!" Ethan couldn't help himself; he started to laugh. He had to admit it sounded crazy, no matter how real it was. He stopped laughing abruptly when he saw the look on Jacob's face. *Oh no, he still wants to quit. Oh no, no no.* "Come on, man. Were so close."

"I don't know. It's way too weird. All of this."

Ethan gave him a nudge. "We just gotta be extra careful and watch each other's back. We'll make sure no one sees us. We can't stop now. We won't be able to think of anything else, anyway."

"Yeah, yeah." Jacob waved him off and looked at the waterfall again. "Well, I do see the pattern in there, but really, what does that tell us about how to find it?"

"I wasn't sure, either. After looking at the tall trees on the treasure map I noticed four really dark spots, which looked out of place. See? If I make a cross between those dots, it makes an exact cross right here." He snapped his finger down on the corresponding location on his dad's forest map. "The line intersects with an area that is full of trees and exactly where the elevation changes. Certainly a perfect place to investigate. What do you think?"

"Mmm, as good a guess as any, I suppose. But that's way out there in the forest. It'll take us all day to get there."

Not willing to let a little hard work interfere, Ethan persisted. "So? X marks the spot, right? We gonna do this?" He raised his eyebrows in encouragement.

"Jerk." Jacob grabbed his bike and darted off down the trail leading into the forest. "You coming or what?" he shouted over his shoulder.

Ethan smiled, shoved everything in his bag, and peddled hard to catch up with his friend. They followed the path through a mixed forest, including maples and oaks. They headed in deeper. Pine trees started appearing along the path, until eventually there was no other type of tree to be found. The lowest branches of the old pines were high enough so that all they could see were the trunks scattered off into the distance. The dead-calm air hung thick upon the fern-covered floor; the forest was hauntingly beautiful.

As they rode, it became darker and cooler, even at high noon. Immersed in shadows. As beautiful as it was, Ethan had to admit it was also somewhat creepy.

After half an hour, Ethan shouted from behind, "Hold on, Jacob. I need a break." His muscles burned as the terrain changed from flat to rolling.

Jacob slowed down a bit, breathing equally hard. "The trail should meet the river soon. Then it'll run alongside until we reach the waterfall. We'll stop when we reach the river; it should be about the halfway point."

"Argh. Halfway?" Ethan hadn't considered just how far away this waterfall might be—and then they might not even have it right. It could be a dead end. Was it worth it? Of course it was. "Fine, a little farther."

After another fifteen minutes, the trail finally swung around a small, rocky slope and came up alongside the river. The boys, enthusiastic about reaching the milestone, got off their bikes onto their wobbly legs, and rested on a boulder near the water's edge.

The river was relatively shallow, but wide and filled with boulders. The noises of nature filled the air—the gurgle of water dancing along the rocks; the birds chirping; the steady breeze swaying the tops of the pines.

The boys slowly regained a normal heart rate. They looked at the forest map together, analyzing how much farther they needed to go. It became clear that Jacob's estimate was quite a bit off. They were only about a third of the way to their destination. The map showed switchbacks on the trail; they were heading for some serious uphills.

"If we want to get there and back before dark, we gotta keep moving," Jacob said. "Maybe we should slow down a little, so we don't wear ourselves out. Those hills look brutal."

A twig cracked in the forest behind them. They snapped their heads around to look over their shoulders, but they saw nothing.

Ethan looked at Jacob. "Okay, let's get outta here."

It was a mission now, and *he* certainly wasn't going to be the one to quit.

The boys continued their journey deep into the pines; the river came and went from the trail's edge. Their conversation had dwindled to zero as they followed the increasingly difficult trail. Somewhere along that trail, they'd transitioned from determined to survival mode.

Nearly an hour and a half later, they could finally hear the roaring sound of a waterfall in the distance. The air was cool and damp. The trail had been narrowing for some time now, battling the encroaching undergrowth, so they rode in single file. Jacob shouted, "I think we found it."

Ethan didn't respond—*couldn't* respond. His lungs burned. But he was excited. Over one last hill, they came zipping down with gravity's encouragement toward the plunge pool at the base of the waterfall. They jumped off their bikes, letting them collapse on the ground, and walked closer to the roaring waterfall. Their legs were wobbly from the long ride, and it felt as if the ground was moving.

"That's pretty cool," Ethan said as they gazed at the roaring water before them. The waterfall was larger and more violent than Ethan had expected. The entire area was damp with mist.

Hands on his hips, still a little short of breath, Jacob nodded in the direction of the waterfall. "We're supposed to walk into *that*?"

"Well, if we're at the right place, I expect there'll be some stepping stones, so we can walk directly through the pool into the center of the waterfall."

"Yeah, but that water will toss us right off the stones. It's seriously fierce."

Ethan laughed. "It's only water." But he had to admit, it seemed like an impossible task. He pulled out the map, looked at the shadows in the water, and headed to the shallow end of the pool. "I can see a couple boulders just under the water's surface in a zigzag pattern, like the drawing. Look." He pointed at an area in the water.

"Good luck," Jacob mumbled as he sat on a boulder at the water's edge. "This ought to be entertaining."

Ethan started down the path of rocks, which were about ten inches underwater. With each step, he noticed that the water's current increased, making it difficult to keep his footing.

At the same time, the water became deeper, and when a large fish startled him, Ethan slipped off the stone and landed directly in the deep water. He slammed his elbow on the stepping stone, hard enough to draw blood, and released a yelp just as his head went beneath the surface. A mouthful of water rushed in.

He'd never been more thankful to see Jacob in his life. His friend had apparently jumped to action in order to help, diving into the cold water for the rescue. By the time Jacob reached him, which was only a blink of an eye, Ethan had his head above water, coughing and shaking his wet head.

"Crap, that hurt," Ethan said as he swam back to where he could touch. He heaved himself up on an earlier stone and immediately began to retrace his steps toward the falls. Diluted blood trickled down his forearm.

"Yeah, you're welcome," Jacob said as he followed Ethan into the deep.

The boys continued along several more stones, carefully navigating each and every step. Finally, they reached the waterfall. Ethan's last step, directly in front of the roaring waterfall, caused the stone beneath him to sink slightly. He nearly fell again. Water began to rain down on him from above. It was then that he realized a large object protruded through the waterfall, dividing the water and creating a tunnel into an inner chamber. The object was a gigantic stone, cantilevered from behind the falls.

"You're not going to believe this!" he yelled to Jacob over the sound of the rushing water. He looked back and grinned at his friend, who had just stepped up behind him. Jacob's eyes were wide, as was his grin. No sign of regret for continuing the journey could be seen. They quickly took the final steps through the watery tunnel onto a ledge behind the falls.

"Wow, that was freaking awesome!" yelled Jacob.

"YEAH!" screamed Ethan at the top of his lungs as an uncontrollable surge of energy rushed through him.

They were soaking wet, panting like dogs, and looking at each other in disbelief. Jacob began laughing like a hyena, and Ethan joined in.

Once they'd settled down a bit, their eyes begin to pan around the dark chamber hidden behind the waterfall.

Ethan reached into his pocket, pulled out his small flashlight, and clicked the *on* button. Water began dripping out of the casing. He released a sigh as Jacob smiled at the misfortune.

"It's not so dark. Look," Jacob said.

Opposite the waterfall, they could make out some shapes painted on the natural stone wall. As their eyes began to adjust to the moderate darkness, they could see the shapes were actually paintings, like one might find in a Native American cave.

"Wow, look at these!" Ethan walked up to the wall and inspected the paintings.

He could make out an image of a red fox howling at the top of a hill. Behind the fox was a pine forest, and peering out from behind the trees were dozens of rabbits. All but three were cowering. Those standing tall were next to each other with their ears bolt upright.

The three rabbits stood in front of a cave.

Ethan placed his hand on the cold stone wall, where the drawing of the cave was. "Here. The cave. I think it's identical to the one from our map."

"It's gotta be. Now, how are we gonna find it?" Jacob asked as he looked further down the wall. "I bet there's something here that'll tell us."

They continued searching the painting for clues.

"It looks like there's writing on the wall over there." Ethan pointed to the far end of the ledge. They walked together and stopped at where the writing was. Ethan noticed the ledge continued downward into a steep, vertical fissure, deep into the shadows. Jacob squinted in the dim light, and read the words on the wall:

*"Descend into darkness and a choice from two shall be made. One will shed light upon your way, the other, darkness will forever stay."*

"Really?" Jacob said, backing away slightly. "No way am I going down some crack into the darkness."

"You don't have to, Jacob. I will. Something about this place is pulling on me. I can't explain it, but I somehow feel . . . obligated." Ethan's words were calm and even.

"No way. I'm not gonna be the one to explain to your mom that I lost you in a crack behind a waterfall. Especially because we were chasing some treasure on some dumb map!"

Ethan looked at his friend, then back toward the crack in the wall. "It's okay. I'll be right back." He felt excitement, intrigue, perhaps a sense of destiny, but there was a void, where he should have felt fear.

Without hesitation, he put his hands out in front of him for guidance and shuffled his way down the steep, narrow fissure. It was narrower than his shoulders, requiring him to turn his body to fit. The path continued at least a hundred feet, when suddenly Ethan could no longer feel the walls. The path had leveled out and widened considerably, but he only knew this by his sense of touch.

It was absolute blackness. He could hear his heart rhythmically thumping. There was no difference when his eyes were open or when they were shut; he felt as if he had been swallowed. It was a darkness he had never before known.

Ethan scrambled to recall the riddle from the map. *"Erosion is a conflict of friction, which merely exposes deeper and hidden layers. Cleansing the earth will never rest, until the core has been met."* He stood at the edge of the crack, making sure with his foot that there was still solid ground ahead.

He continued to talk out loud to himself. "What does it mean, 'until the core has been met'? What are my two choices?" He pondered some more. "One, follow the edges around where I can touch the walls, or two, step straight out into darkness to find the core? Crap, I have no idea what it means." Ethan wanted to return to Jacob and the comfort of light, but he felt more compelled to proceed.

He took a long, deep breath. With his right foot, arms extended directly in front of him, he stepped forward into the abyss. He didn't fall to his death, so he took another step. Then another. He began to worry that if he got too far from the crack, he may not find it again.

Other thoughts raced through his head. Why was he here? Was the map intended for him? Why had his grandmother feared for Jacob? Why had she cried?

Ethan stepped forward again. By now his eyes were closed; it was inconsequential for sight, but somehow it helped him focus. He remembered hearing something about how black is not a color but, rather, the absence of light. Ethan now understood.

Just when he thought the weirdness couldn't get any weirder, he felt himself rise above his physical body. His decisions were no longer his own, and he mentally began to walk forward until he heard a metallic clicking sound underfoot.

He abruptly stopped. All around him, he could hear a hissing noise, almost like gas. "Oh, crap. This is it. This is the end," Ethan mumbled. His only thought was what his death would do to his poor mother, as regret filled his consciousness.

Somewhere in the darkness, one metallic click followed another. *Click, click, click*—it went on for a few seconds. Then, fifty feet out in all directions, gas torches burst into flame.

Ethan let out a gasp as he was finally able to see what surrounded him—a large, domed chamber—and he was right in the middle of it. He turned and saw the narrow crack from which he had come, and from that crack was a path that led directly to the center, where he now stood. The path was a bridge, and the center plate upon which he stood was a narrow column descending into the infinite darkness below.

He looked up at the dome as it flickered in the torchlight, and his mouth hung open. Painted upon the natural stone of the dome were three rabbits chasing each other—the rabbits from the map and the watch. Each were about a hundred feet long, and, together, they circled the dome. Inside the triangle created by their ears was another painting of the cave, also depicted on his map, but this time, the Castle tower, the *Book of Golden Deeds*, and the waterfall were all missing. In their stead was a detailed trail map, winding its way through the forest to the cave's entrance.

Written under the rabbits circumferentially around the entire room were these words:

*He who seeks The Three Hares shall see through shadowed deception, reside within deeds of golden, and wage war upon the unjust.*

"JACOB! Get down here!" screamed Ethan, hoping his friend could hear him. He needed help memorizing the riddle and the trail map. Besides, Jacob needed to witness all this for himself.

At that moment, one of the torches burned out. Followed shortly by another.

"Crap." Ethan looked up at the ceiling and scrambled to memorize the path, the words. Another pair of torches burned out. He stepped on and off the plate with no effect. The final torches started burning out more quickly than the predecessors.

Ethan charged forward, back to the crack in the wall. He did not want to get caught out in the darkness. Ten feet before reaching the crack, the final torch was extinguished, and his final strides were guided from the latent image within his eye. He looked back over his shoulder into the total darkness. He wished he'd had more time. Ethan steadily climbed back up the fissure, where he could hear Jacob climbing down in response to his scream.

"Turn around. We'll talk when we get out of here," Ethan shouted.

As the boys climbed back up, Jacob explained that the blockade through the waterfall was gone; it had apparently returned to its original position. There was no longer a tunnel through the water.

"And there is something else I need to tell you," Jacob said with a hint of embarrassment in his voice.

Before he could explain, Ethan saw it.

A girl was standing there on the ledge. Pretty, shoulder-length blond hair, and wearing shorts and a t-shirt.

Ethan was shocked. "Who the heck are you?"

A broad, glowing smile crossed her face as she took a couple steps forward to shake his hand. "Ah, you must be Ethan. I'm Elizabeth Walker, Jacob's charming and wonderful neighbor."

Ethan, although furious for the intrusion, shook her hand. Her handshake was firm and confident.

"That's what I was trying to tell you," Jacob said. "This is Liz, my new neighbor."

She looked over at the painting on the wall. "So, what is this place?"

Ethan stared at Jacob in complete confusion. He had no idea what was going on. He would soon have his answer.

Jacob shuffled his feet for a moment then angrily flipped around to address his new neighbor. "Did you follow us here? I told you . . . you can't tell anyone!"

"I didn't tell anyone," she said, looking offended by the accusation. "I saw you get on your bike this morning and just had to follow you guys. I'm bored out of my mind in this lame town!"

Ethan's eyes narrowed. He couldn't believe what he'd just heard. "You told her about our adventure?"

"Well, um, yeah. She's been watching me come and go all day every day," Jacob said sheepishly. "Look, she doesn't know anyone in town, and she was so insistent. I don't know. I just told her." He glared at her. "And now I wish I hadn't."

Ethan shook his fists in the air, frustrated. "Geez, man. We should discuss these things first, dontcha think?"

Liz was apparently unfazed by the discomfort between the old friends. "Phew, I'm exhausted. I didn't expect you guys would go so far out of town. So, was this place on your treasure map?" After an awkward pause without an answer, she said, "It's cool. Your secret is safe with me. What is this place? It's really unbelievable!"

Jacob cleared his throat. "Uh, yeah. The map had a few puzzles on it, which we solved over the past days. The clues showed us how to get here and how to get through the waterfall." He glanced at Ethan, who was eyeballing him. Jacob rolled his head in exaggeration. "Come on. I'm sorry, okay? I had to tell someone, and she doesn't know anyone here, so I figured our secret would be safe."

Ethan said nothing, laser beams still shooting from his fury-filled eyes.

Jacob shifted his attention to the waterfall. "Look, can we move past this? I think we should get back to dry land. Not sure what the best way is, though."

"Fine," Ethan said, throwing his hands in the air. Really, what could he do about it now? *What's done is done*, he thought. He looked around and considered their options. Grinning, he pointed at the waterfall. "We go right through it. The water should be deep enough down there."

Jacob nodded, a smile forming on his face as well. Without another thought about it, the boys simultaneously got a running start and launched themselves into the waterfall. The crushing cold water smashed them into the pool below. After tumbling a few times in the deep, turbulent water, they both resurfaced without harm.

"Oh yeah!" Jacob shouted, pumping his fist triumphantly.

Ethan was about to do the same when he realized that Liz had not followed. "Where is she?" He felt responsible for her safety, even though he was still a little angry that Jacob had betrayed their secret—and to a girl, no less.

A shout from above them, and there was Liz, midair, in a graceful dive through the waterfall. She disappeared beneath the water and then surfaced directly between them. "That was a rush!"

Jacob and Ethan stared at each other, then laughed. Liz joined in. Maybe Liz wasn't so bad after all, Ethan had to admit. Besides, having a cute girl tagging along wasn't the worst thing he could think of.

The three of them made their way back to the riverbank and stretched themselves out on boulders to dry off as much as possible. As they lay there, Ethan told the story of his descent into darkness. He explained the map, flickering in the torchlights, on the domed ceiling. He tried to be as detailed as possible, hoping that between the three of them, they could figure out the path to their ultimate destination—the cave with three fearless rabbits standing in front of it.

The hour was late, though, and they had a long ride home.

Their damp clothes were cold and uncomfortable, but they hopped on their bikes and pressed forward. It was nearly dark as they emerged from the forest near the old oak tree.

Ethan had already decided to forgive Jacob for his big mouth. Before the three parted ways, he officially welcomed Liz to the team. They agreed on their next meeting time and place for their final quest: the search for the mysterious cave.

Chapter Seven

# A Bridge of Opportunity

Reacting to the latest rumors, the streets of downtown Winslow Falls were in an uproar. It was not uncommon to see protestors join the crowds since Mayor Maxwell Hofner had taken office, but this particular day was extraordinary.

People crowded the elaborate stage in front of the town hall. Decked out in his tailored blue suit and red tie, guarded heavily by security, Mayor Hofner stepped out of his limo, walked up the steps, and approached the podium. The audience was restless. He raised his arms and gestured for the crowd to quiet down. Hushing sounds circulated amongst the spectators, and as simply as that, the floor was his.

In a booming voice, he said, "Good people of Winslow Falls, I stand before you with yet another promise achieved." His eyes seemingly addressed each and every individual personally. "Jobs have arrived at our doorstep, and now it is upon *us* to open the door to our future."

He took his time. He allowed his words to sink in. He built his momentum. "I have negotiated with Teumessian Industries to come to our fine city. They have agreed to open their next major project within our borders, on underutilized land."

His audience was now captivated. He was speaking of a monumental change to the city, and the people knew it. "Over three hundred jobs will be created, and we will be able to welcome this great opportunity for only a small cost."

The mayor was handed a stack of paperwork by one of his advisors standing behind him. He waved it in the air for everyone to see. "This bill is to build a new bridge across Norfolk Creek. Its purpose is to support the heavy equipment required by Teumessian Industries to start building their facility, as well as to support your daily commute to your new jobs. I have signed this bill, and one of our very own construction companies will build the bridge in record time."

"And what exactly does this Teumessa company do?" shouted a defiant protestor.

The mayor responded with confidence. "Our partner, *Teumessian Industries*," he emphasized the pronunciation of the company's name, "is an environmental company which specializes in nature's energy."

Another protestor shouted from the back, "Who will pay for the bridge contract?"

The mayor smiled. "We have leveraged existing funding from previously-approved projects. Those projects, which were granted by your last mayor, proved to show absolutely zero growth for our fine city. We will simply rearrange the funding.

"In addition, we will add only an insignificant incremental tax to a few very specific luxury items. With these small, barely noticeable steps for funding, we will be able to achieve our dreams!"

He owned these people now. He was a master of his craft.

"I promised you that we would return to our days of glory, and today, for Winslow Falls, the wind has changed direction in our favor!"

A smirk ran across his face as the crowd cheered. "What was it that I told you during my campaign? Ah, yes. I told you that such a beautiful city should have a very lovely voice, since the people are so wonderful. Please sing with me in celebration."

The crowd began to cheer, louder and louder. So much so, that they drowned out any attempts to ask further questions of the mayor about the taxes, the bill, the funding, and anything else critical to this deal and the city. But with the promise of new jobs, nothing else seemed to matter.

The mayor allowed himself a moment to bask in his fans' adoration. He raised his hands into the air once again. He declared, "Our future is here!" and then stepped away from the podium.

Security rushed Mayor Hofner to his waiting limo. The crowd continued to roar in celebration, with only a few still in defiance. Then, as quickly as he had arrived, the mayor left the scene.

While he was being shuttled away from the town hall, he dialed his phone and grinned as he said, "It's done! Our plan is officially in motion."

"Very good," said the grizzly voice on the other end of the line. "I knew you would be the right guy for the job. I expect you will follow through on, shall we say, stifling the bidding process for that bridge, yes? I can't emphasize enough how important the contractor selection is to me. Don't let me down now. We are only beginning our master transformation of Winslow Falls."

Maxwell Hofner replied with confidence, "We will go through the proper selection process for the bridge to avoid the appearance of scandal, but let's just say, there is no doubt in my mind that the results we seek will be achieved."

"There is no room for error on this, Maxwell. Do not screw around with it. This bridge is only the beginning. Teumessian is our future. The transformation of Winslow Falls begins with this first strategic project. Imagine, low wage workers pumping out massive cash flow."

"It is all taken care of, Ezra. It's—"

"Do you know you have already gained a defiant audience?" snapped the man on the other end of the line. "Never allow them to see your cards."

"Of course I have a few protestors, but they have no idea what is really going on. The vast majority of people are singing my song. Besides, who's going to turn away three hundred jobs during these hard times?"

"Do not underestimate what you do not understand. I will do my part, but you must not let your arrogance drag us down. Watch yourself, Maxwell."

The line went dead.

Ezra Reynard returned the phone to its cradle and sat back, taking in the immensity of his opportunity, the immensity of his life.

His vision of the master plan was beginning to form, and he was bold, confident, and proud. It was a vision that would place Winslow Falls on the map as a haven for the wealthy and elite. Social order, roles defined and enforced, and a vault of money, the likes of which had never been seen before.

People knew Ezra as the leader of the Red Fox organization, which had a centuries-long history of corruption and deceit. But it was time to make his own mark, have his name burned into the history books, to be known as the greatest leader of Red Fox . . . of all time.

Ezra looked out his window across the courtyard of his mansion, grinning at the idea of becoming a living legend.

*** * ***

Jacob met Liz between their houses, and they rode their bikes over to the old oak tree, where Ethan was waiting. They spent most of the morning preparing for their trip to search for the cave.

Sitting at the picnic table, they reviewed their notes about the watchtower, the *Book of Golden Deeds*, and the descent into darkness behind the waterfall.

Liz was fascinated by what the boys had already achieved. "This is unbelievable," she said. "How did you guys figure out all these clues? It's much more elaborate than I expected."

Jacob started filling her in on all the nitty-gritty details, but Ethan stopped him. "We gotta start from the beginning, right?"

Jacob grudgingly agreed. Neither Jacob nor Ethan had ever had a girlfriend. In fact, Liz was the first girl they'd ever really hung out with. Ethan sensed Jacob liked her, and honestly, Ethan liked her too—she was charming, yet full of unharnessed personality.

Ethan described how the adventure had begun. "We found this old satchel under a floorboard in my attic with the map hidden inside. We're guessing my grandfather put it there a long time ago. Grandma recognized the map and then gave me this." He handed her the pocket watch, and as she studied it, the boys studied her.

While Liz ran her finger along the edges of the watch, Ethan continued. "As you can see, the same three rabbits that are on the map are there on the cover of the watch. Oh, and initials are engraved here." He pointed to the letters "EZD."

Liz looked at him with bright eyes. "Wow, Ethan, this is really all about you, isn't it?"

Ethan, nervous by her overt interest in him, shifted the subject back to the task at hand. "Uh, okay. So, the map to the cave. We need to sketch what I saw yesterday—you know, the stuff on the dome inside the waterfall—onto this forest map."

Ethan did his best to recreate what he had seen. For the most part, he was pleased with the result.

They then agreed to prepare for a full-blown camping trip starting early the next day, complete with sleeping bags and essentials, since they weren't sure how long they would be gone. Ethan and Jacob knew their parents would be fine with it because they camped out often. Liz didn't seem to think her parents would care—she'd said something about how her parents never knew where she was anyway, which Ethan thought was strange. He never really considered that parents could be so detached from their kids. Despite his own mother's depression, she would still freak out if he disappeared for a couple days without knowing where he was.

They also agreed to be as careful as possible that they were not tailed. The fact that Liz had followed them into the forest and they'd been completely unaware didn't sit well with Ethan. They had to be extraordinarily on the ball.

They were so close now . . . Ethan could almost see the treasure chest buried deep inside the cave. Glistening gold, rubies and other gemstones, ancient coins and artifacts. An adventure of a lifetime.

When he finally climbed into bed that night, his imagination ran wild with the possibilities.

Chapter Eight

# Rabbit Hole

A t the trusty old tree, they met at the break of dawn. Everyone was on time with their backpacks loaded and sleeping bags strapped to the back of their bikes.

Jacob was visibly excited about the adventure. He hopped off his bike and swung his backpack off his shoulders. "This is going to be awesome!" he said. "I packed some serious gear, a *fresh* flashlight, and some sandwiches."

"Nice! Okay. Let's quickly review our plan and get outta here." Ethan spread out the topographical map of the forest, which included the sketches he'd done from memory yesterday afternoon.

Jacob and Liz gathered closely around him.

"So here we are, at our oak tree," he said. "We'll take this main trail out a few miles. Once it comes alongside Norfolk Creek, we'll take the second footbridge to the west. After a quarter mile, we'll enter Mogao Nature Preserve." Ethan traced each segment with his finger.

"This is where we'll exit the trail and off-road it toward our destination. It seems we'll need to head northwest to this ridgeline." Ethan pointed out the topographical feature on the map. "And follow the western edge up to here." His finger landed on a cluster of hills.

He leaned back and said, "I really don't remember *exactly* where in those hills, but our cave should be tucked in there somewhere."

Jacob was ready to go, already flipping his backpack over his shoulders. "Not as far as yesterday, but still a buttload of hills. I'm ready."

Ethan folded the map and stuffed it in his pack. Almost in sync, they jumped on their bikes to begin their quest.

Liz took off with a burst, and Ethan shouted, "Hey, take it easy. My legs are killing me from the last ride."

She laughed. "Yeah, yeah. Not so tough, are you?"

Jacob edged up next to him and helpfully added, "Even a girl's outpacing you, dude." Then he roared with laughter.

"Shut it, man. At least I wasn't afraid of that dark hole."

"Yeah, well, I *should* have been afraid of the dumb crack. Only a lunatic would go down there."

"Whatever." He eyeballed Liz, still a ways ahead of them. *Mrs. Flash.* "By the way, did you hear about the new project Mayor Hofner announced yesterday?"

"My parents were there and couldn't stop talking about it all evening." Jacob rolled his eyes. "I guess he's got some environmental company coming in to set up a factory or something on the other side of the creek."

Ethan worried about their little slice of heaven. "Do you know if they'll be knocking down some of our forest?"

"My dad said he cleverly avoided *any* details about the plan. He did mention they'll get funding from . . . I don't know, somewhere. Some kind of redirection of funds from other projects. They'll also increase taxes on some stuff."

Liz had slowed a bit and was now just slightly ahead of them. Apparently, she'd overheard some of the conversation. "I don't trust that guy. I bet you anything he'll chop down the whole forest for this stupid factory."

Neither Ethan nor Jacob argued the point.

Despite their recent biking adventure and sore legs, the boys were fueled by their anticipation of finding the cave. Liz remained fresh as a daisy, and Ethan could have sworn he'd heard her humming a few times. The cool morning air became even chillier as they pedaled deeper into the forest.

They stopped short when a black bear and a cub appeared near the edge of the trail ahead of them.

"Should we wait for them to leave?" Ethan whispered.

"Stop whispering, for Pete's sake. They aren't that close. We can just get up our speed and blow by them," Jacob said, and had already begun increasing his pace.

"Oh crap," Ethan muttered and pumped hard on his pedals, tucking up close behind Jacob, Liz at the back of the pack. Ethan held his breath as they blew past the mother and cub and didn't let it go until they were far past the beasts. He nearly had a heart attack when the mama bear stood up on her back legs when they whizzed by. Too close for comfort, as far as he was concerned. He knew how protective mama bears could be.

On the other hand, Jacob and Liz were laughing and taunting each other, apparently unfazed by the potential danger. Ethan joined in halfheartedly, keeping his eyes on high alert for similar dangers as they headed toward the footbridge that crossed Norfolk Creek.

Norfolk Creek ran through the forest and was more of a river than a creek. The main part wrapped around the north side of town, heading east, right around where the new bridge was planned. The creek was fed by many side streams and rivers, like the one produced by yesterday's waterfall.

The three of them rested on the reinforced wooden footbridge, which spanned almost twenty yards in length. It was primarily made to support the hiking trail system. Even though the river wasn't that deep, it was wide and windy, creating large bars filled with boulders. For years, the boys had played in and around these waters, building forts and rafts and fantasizing about being fur trappers in the wilderness.

After a short break, they were back to the pedals. Now deep within the pines again, they were heading to the Mogao Nature Preserve as their final stop before the trip turned into an off-road adventure. The terrain was increasingly hilly, and they had to walk their bikes occasionally to breach the top of some of the steepest hills.

Once they approached the nature preserve, the forest opened up to a beautiful, expansive meadow. In the springtime, it was always packed full of wildflowers. However, It was early summer and only a few flowers remained, the field mostly filled with tall, grassy plants swaying in the breeze.

"Okay," Ethan shouted as he brought up the rear. "Let's pull over up here. I wanna take a quick look at the map again. And we should probably start looking for deer trails or something to help us get through the fields."

When everyone had stopped, they straddled their bikes and took a long look at their surroundings. The field was teeming with insects buzzing and humming. Large grasshoppers bounded through the grass; butterflies bobbed in the air; and dragonflies darted around them. Any other summer day, they could spend all afternoon here, but today they were on a mission.

The ridgeline they were looking for was nowhere in sight.

Ethan pulled out the map and spread it across his handlebars as best he could so they could all three inspect it. "The ridgeline should be somewhere over there." He looked up and pointed in a northwesterly direction.

"We're probably close, but this meadow is gonna be tough to get through on our bikes. We need a deer trail or something. Let's keep going, see if we can find one farther up," Liz suggested.

They rode a couple hundred yards more, searching for some sort of path through the meadow—to no avail. Frustrated, they dismounted their bikes.

"I guess we're just gonna have to bulldoze our way through this field on foot, then," Jacob said, swatting some bugs buzzing around his face. "We'll leave our bikes here; no one will see them with all these weeds." He led the way through the tall grass, pushing the thick weeds down with his shoes. "This is gonna suck," he grumbled.

Ethan and Liz were able to follow with relative ease since Jacob was basically creating a path for them. Ethan didn't know if Jacob realized it or not, but he wasn't going to mention it. He was just grateful he wasn't the one in the lead at the moment. Then he saw the tree line off to the left, and a thought occurred to him. "Hey, head over to those trees. It'll be easier to walk once we're near the tree line."

"Yeah, well, that's brilliant," Jacob said, and then pointed at a deer trail carving a path straight for that very tree line. "Looks like you weren't the first to think of it. Besides, I was just about to tell you to take the lead. You lucked out."

"No arguments, boys," Liz chimed in, her face now covered with grime and sweat. "Let's get to it." She charged ahead of them to take the lead, as they looked at each other, mocking her bossiness.

Once they reached the edge of the forest, the grass disappeared, and they had greater freedom of movement under the tall pines.

Ethan scanned the area. "Okay, we need to look around. There should be a ridge somewhere ahead, and we've gotta stay to the right of it. Otherwise, we'll be heading farther away from the patch of hills we're looking for."

"You know, we should mark our trail," Liz said. "We could get lost trying to find our way back."

Jacob said, "I was just going to suggest that."

Ethan rolled his eyes and let out a snicker. "Yeah, that would really be a crappy way to end our adventure. No way back, dying with our cold, glistening treasure in hand."

Liz bent down and stacked three small stones on top of each other in front of a tree. "There. I'll do this every twenty yards or so. When we head back, we can follow them right back to the meadow and our bikes."

Ethan smiled. "You're a good addition to the team, Liz. Where would we be without you?"

She beamed from the praise, while Jacob mumbled, "Like I said, I was just about to suggest it. But yeah, good job."

Suddenly they heard a *snap* from behind them. All three whirled toward the sound and then froze.

"What was that?" Ethan whispered.

"Who's out there?" Jacob yelled, startling Ethan and Liz so that they literally jumped.

"Holy crap, Jacob," Liz said, glaring at him.

They waited quietly for a response or any new noises, but the forest remained silent. "Maybe it was a squirrel?" Ethan offered.

"Fat squirrel, but probably something like that," Jacob said, but it was clear he didn't really think so.

Chills ran down Ethan's spine. He reached out for Liz's arm and grabbed it gently, steering her away from the sound. "Let's just keep moving. Keep your eyes peeled." He looked back at Jacob, who was still staring into the forest behind them. Finally, he turned to follow them, which greatly relieved Ethan.

The three of them were now moving at a good clip across the forest floor, amongst the ferns. Every so often, Liz would stop to create a trail marker. Slowly, the ground began to slope upward. Ethan let loose a huge sigh of relief when he saw the ridge. "Finally."

"Let's follow it around," Jacob said.

The ridge was rocky, and as they walked farther, it grew taller and taller into a full-on cliff looming overhead. Several areas looked like caves but were no more than recessions in the stones. They knew the cave they were destined for was still up ahead, according to the map, but each possibility still sent a charge of enthusiasm through the group.

"Hang on, everyone." Ethan stepped to the side near a large boulder and pulled out his map again. "Look over there." He pointed to the right, opposite the cliff. "That looks like this hill here on the map, the first one before we get to the cluster."

Liz put a hand next to one side of her mouth and whispered in mock suspense, *"The cluster."*

Ethan gave her a blank stare. "Whatever." Of course, Jacob snickered.

Keeping the map in hand, Ethan proceeded along the cliff's edge until he saw several large, rounded hills ahead of them. When the others had caught up, he said, "This is it."

There was a cluster of five rounded hills, seemingly arranged in a circle. The three adventurers headed toward the center of the hills and then proceeded to encircle each hill, looking for any sign of the cave. Due to the large size of the hills, this research proved to take quite a bit of time, but they were determined.

By the time they'd completely rounded the third hill, however, their confidence was beginning to waver. "It has to be around here somewhere," Ethan said, tossing his hands in the air. "The cave was definitely a part of the map on the ceiling under the waterfall."

"I don't know. I'm not seeing anything that looks like a cave around here," Jacob said.

Liz was more encouraging. "Aw, come on. Let's keep looking. We're not done yet."

And so they headed for the fourth hill. The inward-facing side of the hill was the rockiest of all the hillsides so far, more like the cliff on the ridge than anything else. Ethan's heart rate picked up. "This is interesting."

Jacob eyeballed the craggy hillside with an intense glare. "Definitely," he said. Then he gasped and pointed at a narrow path between a pair of massive jagged rocks. "That's it! Has to be."

Liz and Ethan looked in the direction he was pointing, and then the three slowly crept toward the crevice.

"Are we going in?" she asked.

Ethan took a deep breath, debating the wisdom of entering yet another potentially dangerous situation. Images of a dragon guarding the treasure crept across his mind.

Jacob nudged him, smirking. "No turning back now."

"Yeah, yeah," Ethan said as he began to walk between the rocks, followed closely by Liz and Jacob.

Inside the crevice was a heavy wooden door. Jacob jerked on the handle; then, realizing no hinges were showing on the outside, he pushed. "Locked. Maybe just jammed. But it won't open." All three then pushed on the door simultaneously. It wouldn't budge.

Liz wiped her hands on her shorts. "Well, that sucks. What now?"

Ethan looked around, and in the shadows he saw three circular metal plates protruding from the stone wall. It was too dark to make out any details. "There's something over here."

Jacob yanked off his backpack and riffled through his bag for the flashlight. Nothing.

"You said you brought a fresh flashlight. Right?" Liz asked.

"Yeah, it's here somewhere. I know it is." Jacob stopped suddenly. "Oh crap. I think I left it on my bed."

Ethan lowered his head and closed his eyes. "Come on, man. Really?" Liz simply shook her head.

"Wait!" Jacob said as he dug into the side pocket of his backpack. He pulled out a lighter. "Here." He struck the wheel; sparks dashed, producing a small radius of flickering light.

Liz let out a sigh. "Better than nothing, I guess."

"Bring the lighter closer," Ethan said, gesturing at the plates on the wall. "See? They each have a different symbol." He swept his hand across their surfaces, feeling the texture. "A rabbit, a fox, and a pair of swords crossed."

Jacob said, "There weren't any clues on the map for this. What are we missing?"

Ethan thought for a moment. "Maybe it's a combination lock? You know, push them in the right order and the door opens?"

"Really?" Jacob wore a doubtful expression and let the lighter go out for a moment. "Are you just guessing? What do you think the symbols mean, anyway?"

"Could they be connected to the watchtower, the book, and the waterfall?" Liz asked.

Ethan bit his lower lip, contemplating the suggestion. "Good guess."

Jacob flicked the lighter back on. "Well, which one is the rabbit, then?"

Ethan shrugged as he focused on the plates. "Not sure. I guess the watchtower could be the fox. My dad used to say that electing the mayor was like asking a fox to tend your chickens."

Jacob nodded, letting the lighter go out again, adding, "And didn't you say that the words in that room under the waterfall said something about waging war upon the unjust?"

"Yeah, so the waterfall is the swords."

Liz joined in on the puzzle solving, her voice pitched higher with excitement. "That means the rabbit is the golden deed!"

Ethan threw an idea out there. "Okay, so, we need to push the fox, then the rabbit, and then the swords?"

Jacob responded with a touch of sarcasm. "*If* it's a combination lock, *if* the symbols mean what we think they do, and *if* that's the correct order, then, yeah, I agree." He flicked the lighter back on and gestured Ethan toward the plates. "Your honors, dude."

Ethan stepped forward, and Liz and Jacob took a step back. "Thanks for the support," Ethan muttered.

"Hang on," Jacob said, letting the lighter go out once more. "I can't keep this thing on forever. It burns my thumb." He waited a moment, then flicked it back on. "Okay, go."

Ethan placed his hand on the fox, looked back to his friends, and then pushed hard. The disk slid into the wall, making a hollow thumping sound, once fully depressed. He did the same with the rabbit and then settled his hand over the swords. But he did not push.

"The suspense is killing me, man. Just push it!" Jacob said. Ethan closed his eyes and took a deep breath. "What's wrong, man? We're so close?"

"I'm just wondering if this map, the watch, and now this cave are really intended for us," Ethan said in a soft voice.

Out went the lighter.

Jacob spun in a circle, frustrated. "Well, we're not going to know until you open this stupid door so we can investigate."

"And it's pretty obvious you are connected somehow," Liz added.

"I know. I get what you two are saying, but I think we all realize by now that this is not a *treasure* map, right?"

Jacob said, "Yeah, I've been kinda suspecting."

Liz simply nodded.

"Okay, are you ready?" Ethan turned back to the last plate, and Jacob flicked the lighter.

Jacob joked, "What's behind door number three?"

Ethan pressed hard upon the pair of swords. A third and final thumping sound announced itself. Suddenly a heavy *thud* sounded behind the door.

The three of them crept back to the door. Jacob extinguished the lighter and put it in his pocket so he could use both hands to work the door. Ethan joined him, and together they pushed on the heavy, reinforced wooden door. It slowly creaked open into the darkness.

Jacob relit the lighter, but the room was way too large to be impacted by such an insignificant flicker. The ambient light spilling in from outside was limited, but just enough to see four wide stone steps heading downward. They cautiously took them one at a time.

When Ethan stepped onto the main floor below, a familiar hissing sound blasted from all directions. Jacob and Liz froze in their positions on the stairs.

Ethan turned to his friends, "Don't worry. That's—" Repetitive clicking sounds then could be heard, and torches ignited around the room. He grinned and finished his sentence: "That's the gas torches lighting."

Jacob held his palms up, looking at his friend in disbelief. "How the heck do you know that?"

Ethan shrugged. "Happened in the domed room, by the waterfall."

"Look at that," Liz whispered, awestruck, her eyes scanning the ceiling of the massive room, which was now fully illuminated. The boys followed her gaze. Ethan immediately recognized the hares chasing each other around the perimeter of the dome—a near replica of the domed ceiling under the waterfall, only immensely larger.

"Crap," Jacob murmured. His jaw hung open as he looked around.

Ethan suddenly felt a creeping chill run up his spine. "You know what, guys?" he said. Liz flipped him a look. "Sorry, *and* ladies. Anyway, I think . . . well, I think maybe we shouldn't be here."

Jacob moved toward the center of the room. "Come on, dude, the coast is clear. We gotta look around."

Liz grabbed Ethan's arm. "Yeah, come on. We came too far not to check it out."

Of course, Ethan was curious, but he couldn't shake that weird feeling. Ultimately, he allowed Liz to lead him farther into the room. *This girl is gonna be the end of me,* he thought. At the center was a group of six red leather couches, all facing each other, in a large circle. In the middle of the circle was a detailed tile mosaic embedded in the stone floor—an old but still vibrant mosaic of the three rabbits chasing each other.

Off to one side was what appeared to be a study area, with four wooden desks. Each of them was empty, with the exception of an occasional pen. Past the desks, toward the back right of the room, was a huge table made of wood. At least twenty chairs stretched around its perimeter. Apparently, an eating area.

Directly opposite the main entrance door, an elaborate, multilevel library filled the wall space all the way to the ceiling. The elaborate bookshelves were packed full with old books. Several red, leather lounge chairs were sporadically placed around the area, obviously for reading pleasure.

The library was so impressive, they stood for a moment just absorbing its beauty. It would take a few lifetimes to read all of the books, Ethan guessed.

Just behind the library were stairs going down to a dark hallway.

The three of them descended the stairs to find a short hall with several doors on each side, and one door directly at the far end. They tested each one, but all of them were firmly locked. "These locks are just old-fashioned lock-and-key stuff," Jacob said. "I wonder where the keys are."

Since no one had an answer for that, they returned upstairs, moving past the library to find another astounding piece of work. It looked like a wrestling ring of some kind, with the floor a dark burgundy and three black rabbits running around the outer edge. They stared at it in silence, looked back toward each other, extending mutual shrugs, then walked back to the middle of the room. Liz plopped down on one of the couches, letting her blond hair bounce.

The boys each settled into a couch of their own. Ethan said, "They're certainly obsessed with these rabbits." He let out a light chuckle.

Liz gazed up at the exquisite mural. "They are truly fascinating." Then she added, "This is like . . . a secret society."

And with those words, Ethan understood the wariness he'd felt earlier. He had been thinking the same thing, only just now realizing it.

"Yeah, without any members," Jacob scoffed.

"I wonder if my father knew about this place." Ethan's tone sounded sadder than he'd intended. Looking at his friends, he shrugged.

Liz's face crumpled into a look of confusion. "What?" She looked from Jacob to Ethan.

"His dad died last year."

Ethan, avoiding eye contact, let his eyes wander around the colossal underground chamber as he spoke. "My dad was killed last year in a car crash, but, really, it didn't seem as simple as that. The police report at first said the accident was a result of foul play, but later the report was changed. Said it was caused by my father's reckless driving. Things never really added up, but Mom and I . . . what could we do? I think it was a hit-and-run. My dad was hardly a reckless driver. I guess the police simply didn't have a clue about how to investigate, so instead of pursuing it, they just changed the report and closed the case."

He paused, and his friends waited him out, gave him the space to let things sink in. "As I sit here, I'm just thinking about how my dad was connected to this place. I mean, the map probably belonged to my grandfather, but was my father connected as well? Was he also associated to these three rabbits? Does it relate to his accident?"

Jacob and Liz sat motionless, just listening to Ethan express his inner thoughts.

"Why did my dad act so ashamed of himself when Maxwell Hofner was elected mayor? And now, during our research into the puzzles, we find out the mayor is one of the major clues. I only have more questions and less answers with every step we take. Here we are at the end of the treasure hunt, or whatever you want to call it, and we find out that's not what it is at all. *And* we still have no answers as to what it really means."

All three of them sat in silence for a long time, absorbing the ambiance of the room, lost in thoughts and curiosities. "It's getting late," Ethan finally said, standing, groaning like an old man. "We should head back home. This has been nothing more than a wild goose chase. I'd really hoped that the cave would bring us some sort of resolution, even if it wasn't a treasure. Some sort of answer." He was overcome with dejection, and he realized he sounded like a whiny five-year-old. But he just couldn't help it.

"Oh, we're definitely coming back. This is way too cool. We can—" Jacob stopped when he saw Liz glaring at him; Ethan caught the look between them. "Uh, yeah, okay. Let's get out of here." He grabbed his backpack and threw it over his shoulder.

"I'm sure there is more to this place than what we found today." Liz stood and placed her hand on the small of Ethan's back.

"I wanna know what's behind those locked doors downstairs," Jacob said as he joined them, and the three adventurers headed out of the domed room.

They all paused at the top of the steps. The torches had started to burn out.

They rode in silence all the way back to the old oak tree.

Jacob spoke first. "So, what's up for tomorrow?"

Ethan looked at him and then Liz. "I need some rest. I'm just gonna chill out and watch TV tomorrow, I think. You're welcome to join me. Both of you."

"Okay, I'll call you." Jacob said.

Liz gave a double thumbs-up. "Whatever you guys want to do, I'm in."

Jacob and Liz headed back to their neighborhood, and Ethan followed his path back home.

As Ethan rode on alone, he had an overwhelming sense of being lost in the world. His father was gone, his grandparents were gone, his mom was hardly hanging on, and he now had more questions than answers to the puzzles that had recently consumed his life.

Pulling into his driveway, he could see his mother through the window, watching TV in the dark. The flickering colors flashed around the room.

All he could do was drive his feelings deep down inside himself, and join his mom. He knew that she, too, was at the end of her ability to understand this wicked life.

"Hi, Mom. I'm back," he said as he entered the living room and turned on a lamp.

"No camping tonight?"

"Jacob wasn't feeling well, so maybe another time."

For the first time, he felt a sense of responsibility for what was left of his family. He and his mom began to talk late into the evening, the TV volume on low, the shows forgotten. They had not spoken so openly since his father's death, and it felt good to reconnect. Still, Ethan never mentioned the map, the adventure, or the cave.

Those were his secrets.

He wouldn't soon forget them.

## Chapter Nine

# Rise Against Tyranny

Kicking through an intermittent sleep, Ethan dreamed of the three rabbits. His dreams—or probably more accurately, nightmares—were about finding the hidden cave and coming across a dangerous secret society that lived within. The secret clan was protecting the lost treasure buried deep inside the bowels of the earth.

He was abruptly woken from his dream by a large hand firmly smothering his mouth. The unidentified person pulled him up to a sitting position, and then a gag was stretched around his mouth and tied tightly. Before he could see the perpetrator, a dusty burlap bag was jerked over his head and tied around his neck. He could see nothing. The person then bound his arms and yanked him out of bed.

Ethan's screams were muted as he was dragged from his home. His efforts to alert someone, anyone, were pointless—he could barely hear his muffled shouts himself. His feet kicked behind him as he could feel the overgrown grass of the front lawn. They were heading to the street. The kidnapper wrapped his arms around Ethan's torso and lifted him into a vehicle. Once the door closed, the engine started. Then there was a calm and steady voice.

"We have been watching you for some time now. It seems we need to talk. Do not resist; we will not harm you unless you give us cause."

Fear gripped Ethan's soul. Thoughts of his friends dashed through his mind. The cave. Who had seen them at the cave? Had they been followed? He attempted to respond, but the gag would not allow a decipherable response.

"Shhh. You will have your time to talk, young man. Be patient."

The creepy voice accelerated Ethan's heartrate even more. The car drove for maybe fifteen minutes until the paved road turned to gravel. After a much longer stretch of time, they finally pulled off the road and parked the car.

During the drive, Ethan had regained some control of his racing heart from the initial struggle. He chose to spend his energy processing the possibilities of his current situation. He feared for his friends' safety. Had they been captured as well? Was this the shadowy figure in the bushes near the barn? Had Jacob really lost the person tailing him that night? Perhaps these people also knew where Jacob and Liz lived. How could he warn them?

"Come with me," the man said, eerily cool and calm. His strong hand grabbed Ethan's arm, pulling him to his feet outside the car. "I recommend you walk on your own. I am not in the mood to drag you."

Ethan mumbled a few vowels and began to walk in the direction his host established. They went inside a building, which smelled of old, damp wood. The smell was familiar, but Ethan couldn't place it.

"Sit down," the kidnapper said. He pushed Ethan down onto what he guessed was a couch.

He could hear other people mumbling, probably through gags. His heart sank. He knew those voices, even if they were muffled. When the kidnapper removed the bag from his head, Ethan's fears were confirmed.

There sat Jacob and Liz next to him on the couch, burlap bags on their heads.

His gag remained as the kidnapper removed the bags from his friends' heads.

The three of them stared at one another. Terror dominated their expressions. Ethan had never regretted his curious spirit more than he did right then. Sneaking into that cave had taken their adventure too far.

Their kidnapper was in his late fifties. Only an average-sized man, despite his immense strength and obvious fitness. He was lean and wiry with buzz-cut, white hair. His white beard was also neatly trimmed short. He wore a tight, long-sleeved black shirt and jeans.

"You three have been snooping around a lot recently," the man said. "I will take off your gags if you promise not to scream."

All three nodded in confirmation.

"Good."

Their gags were removed.

"Who are you?" Jacob blurted out.

"I will ask the questions, Jacob. Not you. And I expect answers."

*He knows our names*, Ethan thought.

Liz was silent, looking petrified.

Jacob never could fall into a role of obedience, never knew when to keep his mouth shut. "How do you know my name?"

Ethan grimaced but was surprised when the man actually answered the question.

"I am the Protector. My responsibility is to ensure the secrets, safety, and future of the Three Hares are protected. You may believe that you stumbled upon this path on your own. I assure you, this is not the case."

Ethan glared into the eyes of their kidnapper, trying to understand what he was telling them.

"It seems you entered the test, embedded in the so-called 'treasure map,' sooner than we had intended. Still, it was only a matter of time before we tipped you off to its location, anyway."

"*You* put the map there in the attic? How did you do that? How did you even know we would find it? Why us?" After he lobbed out a barrage of questions, Ethan swallowed as he realized he was taunting this dangerous man, but he couldn't help it. He had a million more questions waiting in reserve.

"Ethan, dear boy, it is you we seek, but perhaps your friends may prove valuable as well. Unfortunately, as I mentioned, you were not intended to begin this quest until we deemed you ready."

"What are you talking about? Why me?" he prodded again.

The kidnapper broke his intensity with a slight smile at Ethan's relentless questions. "You will learn of the details shortly, as you will be introduced to the Elder. He will explain everything you wish to know. And he will ask you to do great and dangerous things."

A collective gasp came from the captives.

The man raised a finger and wagged it at Ethan. "I warn you that you are *not* prepared. I urge you to decline his request, no matter how hard he presses. He will not listen to my words of caution, despite the fact that I am the one who has been watching you, Ethan, since you were a baby. You are like a child of mine, one I have never been allowed to speak with."

Ethan was now officially creeped out by this guy. *He's been spying on me for my whole life?*

"It was my duty to watch over and protect you until you were ultimately brought to this very place. But I know, more than anyone, you are still just a boy. You are not yet prepared to follow your fate."

Ethan couldn't help but dwell on this whole Protector thing. He didn't want to anger this obviously unstable man, but he had to clarify. "You've been watching me my entire life?"

"I remember the night you were born, Ethan. I wish you no harm, which is why I beg you to decline what the Elder will ask of you."

Before Ethan could respond, the door abruptly swung open, and a tall, emotionless man with an overgrown beard said to the Protector, "Bring them before the Elder." He then turned and left the room.

The Protector bent slightly and looked into Ethan's troubled eyes. "Remember what I have told you. Now, follow me, all of you."

The three stood up from the couch and followed him into a long hall, which had obviously been created long ago. White plaster ceilings arched high overhead. In several areas, the plaster on the walls and ceilings was chipped away, revealing the old brickwork. Torches lined the walls, flickering their dancing shadows as they walked. At the end of the hall, wooden double doors were opened from the inside by two men.

Their kidnapper guided them through the doors and into a room, which once might have been quite grand, but now was tired and faded. The ceiling was supported by large wooden beams with intricate hand-carved designs. Paintings of unrecognizable people hung on the walls, covering centuries of fashion. A few people were in the room, but Ethan's eyes were drawn to a man sitting upon a large chair—almost like a throne—at the end of the long room.

The man looked worn and tired, just like the room, but he was not as old as Ethan had expected for someone called the Elder. In fact, he expected a wizard of some sort, but of course, he was not. With his round glasses, a thin gray mustache, and a thoughtful gaze, he exuded a professorial sense of wisdom. He had an air about him that made Ethan think: *When this guy speaks, people listen.*

The man's eyes, gray like steel, burned into Ethan. With a clear and articulate voice, he said, "I have waited many years for this moment, young man."

Ethan was startled by his directness. When the man spoke, Ethan felt as if all the other people disappeared. He felt alone, exposed, and at his mercy.

"It brings me great sorrow *and* great joy to see you walking this carpet long." The man tilted his head. "Do you know who I am?"

Ethan swallowed deep and, with a trembling voice, replied, "Well, I heard you were called the Elder. So, you are the head of the three rabbits?"

The old man laughed and stood up from his chair, extending his hand to Ethan. "I am Samuel Tinner, and, yes, I am the Elder of the Three Hares. You have already met your Protector, Arthur Russell, who kindly bagged and gagged you for me tonight."

Ethan, Jacob, and Liz turned around at the same time and looked at the Protector, who cracked his first full smile of the evening. Ethan wasn't finding any of this amusing in the least.

The Elder gestured with his hand in Arthur's direction but looked intently at Ethan when he said, "I am sure he has warned you against my wishes. Although he is a caring man, I assure you, you will want to hear what I have to say. Please, come with me." They began to walk down the long hall and through another wooden door into a shorter corridor.

As they climbed a set of stairs, Ethan finally recognized where they were. *The cave.* They had just come out of one of the locked doors they had seen before, just below the library.

The group moved to the center of the domed room toward the couches surrounding the mosaic of the Three

Hares underfoot, with the same image soaring overhead. Only hours before, Ethan and his friends had been sitting on these very couches. Only hours before, they had believed this place was abandoned. *Were these people hiding behind the locked doors when we were here?*

"I believe a nice comfortable place to sit would be appropriate, since I have a long story to share with you." said the Elder. Torches already burning, he and the three kids sat on the couches; the Protector and two others stood off to the side.

Ethan looked at his friends; their eyes were as wide as he knew his were. Anticipation filled the room.

The Elder cleared his throat, looking directly at Ethan, "The only way to begin is from the beginning," he said.

"In 1663, hundreds of years ago your tenth great-grandparents, Edgar Zephaniah Drake and Eleanor Drake, sailed from Amsterdam to New Amsterdam on *De Bonte Koe*." Smiling at the reference, he added, "That's *The Spotted Cow* in English, which I've always found humorous." He released a slight chuckle.

Out of the corner of his eye, Ethan could see Jacob look his way. Ethan shifted his head, and they locked eyes briefly before returning their gazes to the Elder.

"Their arrival, full of promise, unfortunately yielded conflict after conflict. They were surrounded by swindlers, thieves, and murderers. Within a year, when New Amsterdam was renamed to what you know as New York, your ancestors took to the road and resettled slightly west, here in Winslow Falls.

"It seemed that their ill fate had followed them, proving there was simply no hiding from this lawless land, far from home. They decided they must be vigilant, and take matters into their own hands. Edgar Drake, his best friend Alanson Simpson, and Eleanor's half-brother, Cornelius Jackson, banded together to become the Three Hares, protectors of Winslow Falls.

"They met in secret to discuss ways to compromise the most dangerous gangs in town. As time went on, the secret group grew a reputation. Many of the corrupted souls within Winslow Falls moved on to other cities to avoid the Three Hares and their form of justice."

Samuel Tinner exhaled loudly, and his expression turned serious. "On one fateful night, they plotted against the strongest remaining gang in town, the Red Fox Gang. Instead of redistributing their stolen cargo as planned, an unintentional fire broke out in the Red Fox's warehouse. The fire killed the wife of the leader of the Red Fox Gang.

"Although the Three Hares was a secret society, they were becoming quite well-known with a powerful reputation. At the height of their influence, Edgar and Eleanor were expecting their first child. Her pregnancy was no secret and was celebrated throughout the town. But, despite the undeniable progress of the Three Hares, Edgar feared for his family's safety.

"One night, Edgar and Eleanor drove to an undisclosed location to birth their first child. It was only then that they learned they would have twins. Boys."

Samuel's young audience was frozen like stone, hanging onto every word.

"Edgar's fear for the Red Fox Gang's taste for vengeance loomed heavily on him, so he decided to leave the newborn children under alternate care until the dust cleared. When Eleanor and Edgar returned to Winslow Falls, they learned there had been a slaughter. The Red Fox leader was on a blood rage. In a ferocious act of revenge, he had murdered Cornelius, Alanson, and their wives and children while Eleanor and Edgar were away. When the new parents finally returned, the Red Fox was waiting. That very night was the couple's last. They were not to witness another sunrise. They were not to see their newborn children again.

"After the Red Fox leader realized there was no baby with Edgar and Eleanor, he took it upon himself to find the birthplace of their child—for, at the time, it was unknown that *twins* had been born. Throughout the following months, he feverishly tracked the whereabouts of this child. Upon finding him, he cheered himself for having eliminated the entire bloodline of the Three Hares."

Liz jumped in with, "He killed the babies?" Her expression softened with sadness.

"However," Samuel said, raising a finger in the air, "he did not know of the surviving twin. The bloodline remained. That twin became the sole survivor of what is now known as the Three Hares Massacre, occurring on the fourth of May, 1670."

Ethan looked at his friends, who were completely absorbed in the story, as was he. The fact that they had been kidnapped against their will wasn't even on his mind right now. He would finally get some answers—he could feel it.

Samuel continued. "The surviving baby lived his childhood unaware of his dead parents, his twin, or the Three Hares. It was not until his thirteenth birthday that a cloaked figure showed up on his doorstep. He only introduced himself as the Protector."

Ethan, Jacob, and Liz all snapped their heads around to look at *their* Protector in disbelief. Arthur lifted his chin proudly.

"The Protector had been assigned by a small council to watch over the bloodline. His sole duty was to ensure the boy survived until he was old enough to rebuild the Three Hares."

Ethan squinted, trying to follow each detail. "So, the council was also part of the Three Hares?"

"The council was nothing more than a few townspeople, who were so inspired by the Three Hares that they could not allow their legacy to be exterminated.

"As time crept through the years, Winslow Falls did slip back into the hands of the wicked. The time was ripe for a hero; the town was ready for his return. As you might imagine, this young man, a boy rather, was shocked to have his original identity revealed to him. He was Edgar Zephaniah Drake the Second, named after his late father.

"It was this young man who resurrected the Three Hares into a formidable force. He grew the organization beyond just a few strategic members. It was he who had the vision of taking it to the next level, and it was he who built the Rabbit Hole, in which we are sitting at this very moment."

Liz whispered, "The Rabbit Hole."

A shiver ran down Ethan's spine as those words floated across her lips. Finally, they could now connect this grand place with an actual person.

"From the age of thirteen, Edgar Jr. worked in obscurity and built a truly magnificent shadow force to protect the weak and the poor from the vile and cruel. He worked in absolute secrecy. This would be the critical difference between father and son. Edgar had not retained the secrecy of the organization; therefore, this contributed to its downfall, not to mention the demise of Edgar, his wife, and one of the twins, along with other key players. Edgar Jr., on the other hand, considered secrecy the key element to the success of the organization. And it flourished under his new leadership. In fact, a hare lives above ground, and a rabbit burrows; hence, the change of name for this very special location.

"Ethan, let us leap forward to more current times. When your father Raymond was just a child, your grandfather Herbert was the leader of this great society. It was then that the Red Fox Gang returned in strength. Your grandfather gave his life to this cause. When your father was approached to take the lead, he was not yet prepared to take on this responsibility. Soon afterward, he had his first and only child. You.

"He was not willing to threaten your life with the risks that would fall upon his shoulders if he accepted the leadership position. He rejected the role, temporarily leaving it in my hands, until you were older, and he was prepared.

"One year ago, during the rallies of Maxwell Hofner, your father became ashamed that he had walked away from his responsibility to the Three Hares. He decided that he would not allow his child to live in a corrupt world, where few would fight for change. Because of Maxwell, he immersed himself in our world, at last becoming its rightful leader.

"Only weeks after he devoted himself to the Three Hares . . ." Samuel paused, releasing a sorrowful breath. "Well, it was a sad day indeed. Your father underestimated the extent and influence of the enemy. Red Fox killed your father on the side of that road, son. It was no accident."

Ethan shook his head at the devastating news, confirming his suspicions that indeed foul play was involved. He involuntarily shuddered at the cold-blooded wickedness as his thoughts raced back to the night he heard the news.

"On that fateful night, you, Ethan Zephaniah Drake, became the last of the bloodline of the original Three Hares. It is you who are destined to lead the organization. It is you who will empower it to rise from the ashes and fight against tyranny."

Ethan attempted to speak, but was unable to produce a noise. He swallowed and tried again. "Did this belong to Edgar Zephaniah Drake, the very first leader?" He opened his outstretched hand and revealed the golden pocket watch—the watch his grandmother had given him just days before.

The Elder glanced at the watch and slowly nodded, closing his eyes for a moment. "Actually, that watch was his son's, the surviving twin, Edgar Z. Drake the Second. There never was a third, by the way. Names changed, as they tend to do. Anyway, this watch has been passed down through the generations. It is a reminder of his secrecy and dedication to the cause.

"It is my duty to warn you, Ethan, that all who have carried this watch have died before their time. They died while leading the Three Hares, some sooner than others. But not one of them died of natural causes. Remember one thing about this responsibility: this role does not affect only you; it affects everyone around you."

"My friends . . ." Ethan started with a cracking voice as he quickly glanced at Jacob and Liz. "Will they be protected?"

Samuel clasped his hands together and looked to the expansive dome above as he paused for a moment. Then he brought his gaze downward, his eyes boring into Ethan's. "The fact is, Ethan, the closer people are to you, the greater danger they will be in. Consider it this way: you are the epicenter, and the shock waves roll outward. Those who wish to harm you may very well try to do so indirectly. This puts your closest friends and family in the gravest of danger. This is exactly why your father had avoided the responsibility for as long as possible."

Suddenly, Jacob shifted forward in his seat, leaning his elbows on his knees. "I want to join the Three Hares with Ethan."

The Elder smiled. "I have watched you boys grow up together for many years. And I have closely monitored your path through the puzzle map to find this very location. That said, your loyalty to each other is unparalleled. One reason I believe Ethan is ready for this significant and dangerous role is because of you, Jacob."

Jacob's face lit up.

"If Ethan chooses to join this mighty cause, you are absolutely welcome, but not obligated, to join the Three Hares."

Ethan gave Jacob a crooked smile. He didn't want to endanger anyone, but he had to admit: he couldn't imagine proceeding without his best friend by his side.

Ethan was terrified, and didn't know why he believed every word Samuel told him, but he then stood up from the couch and, in the most formal voice he could manage, said, "I am honored to join the Three Hares and represent my bloodline."

Jacob jumped up next to Ethan. "I, too, would be honored to join the Three Hares."

Liz, completely caught up in the moment, jumped to her feet. "I, too, wish to join the Three Hares."

Everyone looked at Liz. Caught off guard by her loyalty and enthusiasm, Ethan asked, "But you hardly know me, Liz. Why would you risk your life for someone you barely know?"

Her chin held high, Liz said to Ethan, "Me? You just announced that you would risk your life for *everyone* that you don't know, just because this man, who you just met tonight, told you a story? Well, dammit, I was inspired by that story, too, and I hope every word of it is true, because I *will* stand by you, the descendant of the Great Edgar Zephaniah Drake." She took a deep breath and then grinned. "Besides, this town is mind-numbingly boring, and I need something exciting to do."

Samuel Tinner stood to face the eager crew and broke his smile down to a stern look. "I am very proud of the three of you. It brings me great pleasure to induct you into the Three Hares. We will hold a formal ceremony with all of our members. And I will give you a chance to meet those who will stand by you through life . . . and death."

As the meeting concluded, Ethan turned to the Protector, Arthur Russel. "I know you had hoped I would decline this duty, but honestly, accepting the responsibility is the only decision I could make."

"I understand, young man. I am very proud of you." Arthur extended his arms, and Ethan went to him. The two embraced for the first time. "You are brave, young man, and I will always be here for you. Same goes for your friends."

Although Ethan had only just met Arthur, he suddenly felt a strong connection with him. This man had been with him his entire life; he was like a second father to Ethan, even if he was the one who lurked in the shadows.

## Chapter Ten

# Selective Sourcing

Each new city project required multiple quotes from contractors. Jim Stevenson, who had been the general manager at the Department of Transportation for eleven years, was the man who planned large projects and managed the bids. He had never been questioned as to his recommendations, though things were different now. Jim longed for the old days; he didn't care much for the mayor and his overbearing ways. Mayor Hofner insisted on making all decisions regarding transportation; he often overlooked key facts, almost intentionally.

And so there Jim sat, waiting for the mayor, for over thirty minutes now.

Finally, the mayor made his appearance. He sat down in the big, cushy leather chair, like a water buffalo buckling at the knees. He was not necessarily fat, but he was a large, imposing man—with a big head to boot.

Anxious to get in and out, Jim jumped to the subject at hand. "Mr. Hofner, we've received three official offers for the bridge construction project. Two firms from Winslow Falls, as requested. The third is from out of town."

The mayor seemed distracted by his own thoughts, only partially listening.

Jim waited, and when no response came, he cleared his throat and continued. "Since the out-of-town offer was actually higher, we have no need to discuss that offer . . . uh, unless you wish otherwise."

"No, that's fine, Jim. Proceed with the local firms," Maxwell said, still not making eye contact, instead looking at his hands, his fingernails.

*Time for a manicure? What's up with this guy? Geez,* Jim thought.

Jim flipped on the overhead projector and slapped a transparency on the glass. "Okay. Here is the detailed offer letter from EcoSteel. They're one of the last remaining steel companies to have survived the iron bust in town. They moved toward an environmentally green manufacturing process, which really boosted their success in the region. Reviews are excellent, and they have the best price of the three quotes. Their proposed project schedule is appropriate for this contract."

Maxwell grumbled something, now flipping through some papers on the table. Jim didn't know what was in those papers, but he was certain it had nothing to do with the bridge project.

Jim held back an eye-roll and continued. "They have also gained quite the following behind their bridge designs. One of their designers has won awards for his style. As you can see from the charts, EcoSteel gets a checkmark for most of the boxes on our specification list, and they are my official recommendation to you."

"What else do you have?" snarled the mayor, still pawing through his papers.

Jim's blood began to boil; he imagined climbing over the table and punching the mayor in the face, maybe choking him. His reasonable side prevailed, of course, and he chose the "keep myself employed" route. Flipping to the next slide, he said, "The second option is Daquan Construction. After some research, I learned they are only *technically* a local company. They outsource almost everything, including their labor. In fact, they don't even have a real office in town. Their business is only incorporated here.

"Their price is sixteen percent more than EcoSteel, but their project schedule is significantly quicker. You should know, though, that I'm not finding reviews about their work. This causes me to question what large projects they've done before. To be honest, I don't believe it's possible to build this bridge within their promised timeline."

The mayor finally looked up. "Well, we want this thing built fast. I don't want to waste time. Sign up Daquan Construction for the job and get them started immediately."

Jim coughed lightly into his fist and took a deep breath. *Here goes nothing.* "But, sir, perhaps I wasn't clear. I really don't believe Daquan is capable of achieving their schedule. They're also . . ."

Glaring at Jim, Maxwell raised his voice when he said, "I've heard what I needed to hear, Jim. Don't make me say it again. Sign up Daquan Construction and make a public announcement to the press that we have contracted with a local company to build the bridge."

"Yes, sir." Jim could barely get the words out, as he was left with a bitter aftertaste from the discussion. He packed up his transparencies and hurried out of the conference room.

\* \* \*

Once the door closed, the mayor picked up the phone and called Ezra. "I just signed off on Daquan Construction, as requested. But I must say, Jim Stevenson was quite concerned with the selection. He knows they outsource all their labor, and he has more than likely figured out that they are only a shell corporation."

"Keep his mouth shut and get him under control. He's your guy. His job is done. Make sure he knows it," Ezra barked.

"Don't worry. He won't link this back to you. I'll keep him buried in other work; besides, he'll have his hands full once this project kicks off."

Changing subjects, Ezra asked, "Have you cleared the land-ownership permits for Teumessian Industries? They need to begin their geological surveys right away."

"I'm working with the state government to reclassify the land usage. There are issues regarding the water runoff and Norfolk Creek. They're upset about some natural habitat of frogs or birds or some crap."

"Who's assigned to the case?"

"Brad Smith from the state's Environmental Protection Agency." His lips curled as he said the man's name; he despised Brad Smith.

"I will have someone *speak* to him," Ezra said. "It will be taken care of."

"Good. I'm tired of dealing with that self-righteous bum."

"Call me immediately if your pet dog, Jim, starts sniffing around," Ezra said as a last statement before hanging up.

"Adios, King Ezra," Maxwell sneered at the phone.

He grumbled his way back to his office. Somehow, Ezra had a way of making him feel "reduced," and that agitated him greatly.

## Chapter Eleven

# Grand Celebration

I n less than twenty-four hours, Ethan, Jacob, and Liz would be inducted into the secret society of the Three Hares. They gathered together in Ethan's attic so they could prepare for the event. Mentally prepare. They were nervous and excited and curious all at the same time. But Ethan had an additional reason for being nervous. Liz.

Ethan's mom was out for the day, so he would not have to endure the barrage of questions that would have ensued if his mom had been home. Still, it was the first time he'd invited a girl into the attic, and for some reason, the whole idea made him jumpy. His palms were sweaty. Each time he spoke, he had to build his courage and prepare the words in advance. Even then, the words tangled with one another.

"So, Liz, now that you have bravely joined this wild ride, I thought you might like to see where it all began."

"So this is the infamous 'war room,'" she declared with a smile. Her eyes darted around the attic, absorbing the environment.

Ethan and Jacob kneeled beside the floorboard that had the triangle branded upon it. They pulled the board up, withdrew the old leather satchel from its hidden chamber, and handed it to her to inspect, pointing out the torn lining beneath which the map had been concealed.

Ethan had already brought up an extra chair from his dad's office, anticipating her arrival. They sat together around the desk and laid out the old map. Ethan and Jacob yammered on about their many stories as they progressed through the clues. They made sure to emphasize how cleverly they had deciphered all the codes and riddles. Liz had already heard most of the stories, but Ethan wanted to review everything again, revel in it a little bit before the induction. Besides, she seemed to be really into it.

They let her examine the old watch again and told her of the few times when they'd believed they were being followed. Ethan explained how, from the attic window, he had spotted a shadowy figure by the barn—a story, he just realized, he had never shared with Jacob until now.

Jacob didn't seem to care; he had his own story to tell. He offered a turn-by-turn analysis of how he had lost a tail on his way home, on that same night that Ethan had seen the figure by the barn.

Ethan countered with a retelling of running into the suits at the library.

Liz seemed fascinated by it all—the stuff she knew *and* the stuff she was just now learning. She didn't ask questions; she just listened. When they talked about the "tails," Ethan noticed her expression changing a bit, like maybe she was concerned. And then another story would get her smiling. Occasionally her eyes would grow wide, and she would look off in the distance, like she was rolling their adventure 'round and 'round in her head. Like she was divided, uncertain, and undecided what to do with all of this.

Sometimes she would look at Ethan in a way that made him curious as to what she was thinking. *Is she wondering about me, who I am? The bloodline thing, or is it something more? And what's her story, anyway?*

He prodded a little bit. "I still can't believe you joined our group, Liz. Just a couple days ago, I had no idea who you were or where you came from."

She smiled at Ethan almost bashfully. "Just a girl trying to live my life," was all she said.

"How long have you been in Winslow Falls?" Ethan already knew the answer through Jacob, but he wanted to get her talking. He wanted to know more—much more—about her.

"Just a few months. My dad moves around a lot for work, so let's just say this isn't the first time I've had to settle in somewhere new. It's not like my mom helps any, either."

*Interesting.* Ethan gave her a curious look.

"She's just … I don't know. Just more interested in her social clubs and fitting in with those snotty, snobby people. I always end up as the outcast. Ever since my sister moved out, my mom leaves me home alone most of the time, just 'cause I don't look, act, or think like those stinking rich, spoiled brats."

Jacob laughed. "No risk of finding stinking rich kids here."

Liz and Ethan joined the laughter, which rolled out of control.

The conversation continued long into the afternoon, mostly circling around what was to come and how it would affect their lives. Of course, all they had were guesses; they were in uncharted waters, together. They prepared their cover stories, so the parents didn't get suspicious. For Ethan and Jacob, it was easy. Camping in the forest was their go-to solution. For Liz, she simply declared her parents wouldn't even notice.

As they parted for the evening, each of them radiated with anticipation for tomorrow's Grand Celebration. Tucked inside their healthy dose of enthusiasm was a core of fear—a fear of the unknown. *How do we know who Samuel and the Three Hares are, who he says they are* . . . Ethan couldn't shake the thought.

✳ ✳ ✳

Late afternoon the following day, they met at the old oak tree in preparation for their return trip to the cave.

The swearing-in was to be held at midnight, but they were invited to meet the other members of the Three Hares just prior. They were told to travel by bike and foot, as they had for their first visit; the road they'd traveled with Arthur was intended for only the most urgent of situations. They needed to ensure they weren't being followed and to let the forest be their cover.

Even though this was only their second time traveling to the cave through the trail system, the route was clear to them, even strangely nostalgic. The ride seemed immensely shorter; they had plenty to talk about, which helped to pass the time. It helped that they weren't searching for something, which had made minutes seem like hours. This time, they knew their destination.

Once they arrived at the cave entrance, they pressed on the pressure plates—the fox, the hare, and the swords—to unlock the door. A dozen people were scattered around the great hall. The place buzzed with various small-group conversations.

As they crept down the steps, still sizing up the situation, the room became ever quieter as the people gradually noticed their arrival. Soon the hall was so quiet that their footsteps echoed as they approached the seating area.

They were the main event, the guests of honor. A thought jumped across Ethan's mind. *Are we unsuspecting victims of a cult?* He pushed the thought away as quickly as it had appeared.

On the couches in the middle of the room sat the Elder, Samuel Tinner; the Protector, Arthur Russell; and another man and woman, both of whom were in their late thirties, and dressed in fine business clothes.

Samuel rose to his feet with arms extended upward in a V. "Welcome! I have looked forward to this day for some time, but not in my wildest dreams had I considered such a marvelous trio. How wonderful it is to see the three of you boldly, proudly, and majestically walk into this historic room."

The three new members offered their hellos.

"Please join us here. I would like to introduce you to a couple of dear friends and fellow Hares." Samuel motioned to the man and woman. "This is Jim Stevenson, general manager of the Department of Transportation, and this is Mrs. Alice Fischer, first lieutenant of the Winslow Police Department. They are both valued members of our society—our ears within the city's governmental system."

Ethan noticed that Liz suddenly looked a little uncomfortable, shifting her feet and looking to the ground. *Maybe she had problems with the law in the past.*

His thoughts were interrupted when Jim Stevenson stepped forward and enthusiastically extended his hand to each of them. "What a great pleasure to welcome you to the Three Hares, and Ethan Zephaniah Drake, it is truly an honor to meet you after all these years of anticipation."

"Thank you, sir." Their handshake became awkwardly endless, and Ethan felt his cheeks flush with embarrassment.

"Please, call me Jim." He actually bowed, as if he were a servant.

Alice Fischer then approached, which thankfully induced the release of Jim's hand from Ethan's. "And please, call me Alice," she said. "I'm so excited about the ceremony tonight. This is a major milestone for the long history of the Three Hares, and to be honest, the *most* anticipated event since I've been a member."

By this time, Arthur was in line to greet the guests of honor. "How are you guys doing? Ready for tonight?" he asked with a warm, proud, fatherly smile.

Samuel clapped lightly to get everyone's full attention. "Arthur, kindly take our guests around to meet everyone else before the ceremony." The Protector nodded. Samuel's smile then turned into an expression of concern.

"I would do so myself, of course, but Jim has brought some troubling news about the mayor, and I need to spend a few minutes with him, going through the details."

Arthur seemed genuinely pleased to have the honor of introducing everyone. "Shall we?" The new members grinned at each other, then followed the Protector.

\* \* \*

Samuel, Jim, and Alice remained at the couches, discussing the details of the bridge contract and the odd circumstances around Daquan Construction.

"I've been digging into this company," Jim said. "Each stone I turn over gives me more concern that this is yet another front for Ezra Reynard."

Alice asked, "Why would he be getting involved with the bridge contract, anyway? Isn't that a bit small-time for him?"

"I'm convinced there is more to this," Samuel said, "and we must figure out what that is. However, you two must be careful not to blow your covers. Your roles cannot be compromised. Perhaps this is a perfect assignment for our new members." He glanced across the room at the new recruits, who were mingling with other members near the library.

"Samuel, no. They're not trained for such an investigation. If something happens, we could be risking Ethan's future. Let either me or Jim do some more research," Alice said.

"Alice, we are in a shadow war—meaning, in order to thwart the progress of the wicked, we must stay behind the scenes, working secretly to achieve this goal. You know that. If either of you were exposed, the damage to our cause would be irreparable. We need your eyes and ears in the police department, Alice. We need your eyes and ears on the construction project and the mayor, Jim. Your roles are defined and should not be changed.

"Our new members have proven themselves to be eager, smart, and inventive. They can add to our efforts by doing research of their own—just like they figured out the map and found this cave. With Ethan at the helm, I have full confidence that the three will round out our efforts. And you two are in perfect positions to let us know if anyone becomes suspicious of our new recruits.

"Yes, the danger is always there, and everyone accepts that. But we cannot live in fear. We must continue to dig and dig and dig, until the trash in this town is incinerated, once and for all."

Samuel sat back, exhausted from his impassioned speech.

"I share Alice's concern," Jim said, "but you have proven your wisdom time and time again. We will follow your plan."

The men looked toward Alice, who nodded.

"Good. Now, with that business behind us, let us enjoy the evening." Samuel smiled broadly. "It will be a wonderful event. Much anticipated, indeed."

Ethan had noticed when Samuel left the meeting with Alice and Jim, he headed downstairs to one of the rooms. He now understood why.

At just a few minutes before midnight, the Elder appeared from behind the library, wearing a black cloak with crimson accents. It was time to begin the ceremony.

"Okay, guys," Arthur said. "Please follow me."

Reality began to set in. Ethan's pulse rose, and his palms began to sweat. *How did we get ourselves into this?*

The torches around the room flickered out, leaving only one burning vibrantly on each side of the ring, casting long shadows across the great hall. Arthur brought the recruits to the edge of the circle. "This is the sparring ring. Please wait here for a moment." He stepped away.

*Sparring ring?* Ethan was a little concerned with the description.

Jacob whispered to his friends, "Check them out." He did a quick head gesture at the other members. All members were now wearing a crimson robe as they approached the circle. Thoughts of cults and sacrifices flashed through Ethan's mind again.

"Okay, please put these on," Arthur whispered upon his return. "These are our ceremonial clothes. We only wear them for initiations like today and for memorial services for our fallen warriors."

The three looked at each other, faces heavy with concern, and then pulled the robes over their shoulders. Arthur ushered them into the inner circle of the ring, the three hares rounding the crimson floor.

Hands gripping an old, gnarled cane, Samuel now stood at the head of the sparring ring. The room was silent, and only the occasional crackle from the two remaining torches could be heard.

"Please kneel, young hares," began Samuel in a startlingly powerful voice, which resonated throughout the room like in an ancient cathedral.

They knelt, gazing up at the Elder.

"Today, we are initiating, not one, but three new members, which alone is remarkable. But furthermore, as we have long awaited, we will revive the bloodline of the Three Hares. Today, the final descendant of our founder, the great and honorable Edgar Zephaniah Drake, will join our war against evil, and, perhaps one day soon, will become a great leader, as his ancestral line has proven time and time again. I will now begin the official swearing-in. Please lower your heads and honor our new members."

All heads bowed.

"Evil is a part of nature and tempts one so feverishly from birth to death. Defending against such evil is an unwinnable feat. There is only our will to at least burden the wicked's progress. This burden we create allows light to shine through the cracks. With great people, there is great opportunity. It is we, the Three Hares, who approach this burdening as our cause. It is we who band together to fight from the shadows without celebration. It is we who band together to wage war against the unjust, the greedy, and the ill-willed. It is we who are the final warriors, protecting our world from falling victim to total darkness in an eclipse of its evil.

"Today we welcome our three new members, Jacob Carter, Elizabeth Walker, and Ethan Drake, as warriors of the Three Hares.

"Jacob Carter, do you understand the catastrophic consequences of fighting evil from the shadows, yet still bind yourself to the Three Hares eternally?" he asked as he approached Jacob and placed the tip of his cane on Jacob's chest, directly over his heart.

"Yes, I do," Jacob replied with a rattled voice.

"Elizabeth Walker, do you understand the catastrophic consequences of fighting evil from the shadows, yet still bind yourself to the Three Hares eternally?" As he had done with Jacob, Samuel placed the tip of his cane upon her chest, in the area of her heart.

"Yes, I do," Liz replied, her voice also shaky.

"Ethan Drake, do you understand the catastrophic consequences of fighting evil from the shadows, yet still bind yourself to the Three Hares eternally?" The cane ritual was once again performed. As the cane touched Ethan's chest, the torch behind Samuel crackled loudly.

"I do," Ethan replied as a shiver ran through his spine.

"I hereby deem and welcome Jacob Carter, Elizabeth Walker, and Ethan Drake as shadow warriors of the Three Hares. Arthur, please present our new warriors with their weapons."

Arthur handed each of them what looked to be a wooden sword, which was really quite beautiful. Ethan's fingers ran along the smooth grain of the natural hardwood. It was light, yet strong. Still, Ethan thought it wasn't much of a weapon. *Probably just part of the ceremony. Wait! Why do we need weapons?*

"This is your weapon, called a bokken. Your extension of your spirit. It comes from the earth, pure and straight. It is upon you to memorialize it by honoring its humble origins with greatness. You will master this tool, as its mastery may prove life over death."

Each of them gripped the handle, carefully looking at its handcrafted qualities.

Ethan suddenly felt a bond with the weapon. *Yes, a weapon.* It felt natural and balanced in his hand.

"We will begin your training tomorrow, but tonight, we will celebrate our growing family. We welcome you, all three," Samuel concluded with a bow.

The other members cheered and stepped within the circle to congratulate Ethan, Jacob, and Liz.

Later in the evening, Samuel pulled Ethan aside. "Are you enjoying yourself, young man?"

"Very much, sir. This is all very exciting for us." Ethan felt like he was glowing; unbridled adrenalin rushed through him.

"Excellent. There was a time that this room was completely filled with members, shoulder to shoulder, and what a sight that was to see. It was many years ago, of course. Now it is time to rebuild."

"Everyone has been very nice. I can't believe how interested they are in us, and how much they know about me and my family."

"Indeed. You are something special to these people. I know this is all new for you, but these people have been anticipating this night for a very long time now." He shifted to a more serious look. "I do need your assistance in the short term, Ethan."

Ethan didn't hesitate. "Of course."

"You and your friends have a task at hand, and I would like to meet with the three of you tomorrow to go through the details. Let's gather here at noon tomorrow, shall we?"

"I'll let the others know. We'll be here. And thank you for the nice ceremony. I still feel shivers from your words."

"It was entirely my pleasure, Ethan."

The evening's celebration continued for hours. The long, wooden table was filled with a mouth-watering selection of appetizers and finger food. Ultimately, that is where they all ended up, snacking and chatting and rejoicing into the early hours of the morning.

With dawn just around the corner, it was time for Ethan, Jacob, and Liz to head home. Arthur had installed some powerful lights on their bikes and mounted a black sheath to conceal their new weapons.

Just as the earliest light broke across the distant horizon, the three snuck into their beds without detection from their parents.

Ethan knew tomorrow was going to be a big day, and his curiosity ran wild. Although at first he was unable to sleep, exhaustion eventually overcame him. Memories of the evening's events flickered through his mind. His weapon, illuminated by the breaking dawn through the window, leaned against the wall near his bed. It would never leave his side.

Chapter Twelve

# Water under the Bridge

S ignificantly fewer members were around when they returned to the Rabbit Hole the following mid-afternoon. As they entered the great hall, Arthur strolled over to welcome them back. "Please have a seat." He motioned them to the couches. "I'll get Samuel, as he wishes to discuss some topics with you."

They sat, but Arthur remained, adding, "Before you leave today, I will personally give you an introductory course on wielding your bokken."

Jacob grinned. "Cool." He opened his eyes wide like a wild man at Ethan and Liz, who both had to stifle giggles at their friend's enthusiasm. Of course, they felt the same way.

"We can't wait," Ethan said. He was nervous that he would look like a fool in front of Liz, especially compared to his more athletic friend, Jacob.

Arthur disappeared behind the library for a few minutes and then returned. "He will be here soon. He's wrapping up his previous meeting right now."

They waited for a short while, admiring the room, and Liz was particularly enthralled by the painting encircling the domed ceiling. "It's just magnificent, isn't it?"

As they gazed at the artwork, they heard, "Welcome back, my young friends. I trust you've rested well?"

All three startled and shifted their positions to look in Samuel's direction. He was flanked by Jim Stevenson and Alice Fischer. They took a seat, and Samuel jumped right to the point.

"It has been brought to my attention that there is something suspicious going on with Mayor Hofner's planning for the bridge project. It seems there is a bit of a shell game being played, and we believe there are linkages to the leader of Red Fox: Ezra Reynard. If this is the case, we may have serious problems."

*Shell game? Ezra?* Ethan had no idea who that man was—or even what a shell game was. "Red Fox has always been involved in *major* schemes, and it consistently involves lining their pockets at the expense of Winslow Falls. Ezra is one of their most conniving leaders yet." Samuel shook his head, obviously frustrated with the situation. "We know he had a significant influence on getting the mayor elected, but how Ezra intends to use him and the motivation behind the bridge contract is unclear."

Ethan jumped in with, "What exactly are you asking us to do? Spy on the mayor for information?"

"Frankly, yes, that would be the first step. Also to find out as much as possible about Daquan Industries, the company recently awarded the bridge project contract. Jim has informed me that there are some . . . shall we say, suspicious activities he has discovered about this company. However, if he were to continue his investigation, his role within the mayor's office would be compromised. That is something we are not willing to risk. In their positions, he and Alice offer us invaluable insight into the internal workings of the government at hand." He nodded at Jim, who took the floor.

He explained what he'd uncovered thus far, offering some solid leads and starting places for them to take over the investigation. Questions and answers volleyed between the new members and Jim, as he familiarized them with the bridge project, timing, and other related history.

Samuel added, "In short, your task is to find out if the work the mayor is contracting is illegal and/or against the best interest of Winslow Falls. If it is, then we need some strong incriminating information that we can use to shut down the project before it causes irreparable damage."

Ethan looked at his two friends, and then back to Samuel and Jim. "Of course we'll help, and we'll begin as suggested: heading over to the bridge construction site for a personal visit. See if anything comes up that might be useful for us to know."

"No worries, sir. This is our kinda work," Jacob added with a silly grin.

Samuel raised his eyebrows. "I sincerely appreciate you three getting involved so quickly, but please take extra precautions for your safety. If you think someone is following you, asking strange questions, anything that makes you feel like something just isn't right—you must abort and regroup immediately. You are not yet trained to confront the evil you are chasing. Secrecy is your greatest ally, as it is ours."

Liz leaned forward and said, "We are great at secrets. We'll be careful and keep you informed of our progress."

"Excellent. Wonderful," Samuel said, his relief evident. "Now, speaking of training, we planned some time for you to begin your training with the bokken. Please report to the sparring ring, and Arthur will join you as soon as he is available." Samuel leaned in toward the three new members and whispered, "He may appear to be a warm and kind person, but I warn you, he is ferocious with that stick!" Then he leaned back and chuckled, his hands holding his belly.

The three teens rose and approached the ring, their initial task placed firmly upon their shoulders. Ethan felt the weight of it—not as a burden, but as something immensely important to the future. Their lives had taken a turn toward adulthood, and their chosen path was emblazed with potential. Potential for bravery and heroism . . . and failure.

After only a few minutes, Arthur ascended the stairs with his own well-worn bokken. "Okay, each of you stand upon one of the hares on the training floor and face center." He made his way to the middle of the ring. "Hold your bokken as I am, and be still, as silent and motionless as an alert hare."

The three did as requested: Hands one in front of the other on their bokkens, the sword tips pointing down toward the center of the ring. Bodies in a semi-crouched position, stock-still.

"First, you must master your breathing by controlling and slowing the rhythm. Follow my pace, and we shall breathe together. In . . . and out. In . . . and out." He repeated the words several more times. "Now maintain your breathing rhythm while I continue. Focus is directly related to calmness. The calmer you are, the more alert you can be." Arthur made a sudden move toward Jacob, who jumped back and let out a startled yelp.

Ethan and Liz laughed so hard, they nearly lost all control. Arthur's gaze encouraged them to suck it in.

Arthur continued. "Recompose yourselves, and resync your breathing. You will train so that each time you are 'disturbed,' you will return to composure more quickly than the last time. The more you train, you will find that the time it takes to settle back into a sense of calm will dwindle to—" He jolted toward Ethan, forcing him to jump back out of the circle. "Recompose yourself, Ethan," he barked. At that same moment, Arthur swung backward toward Liz, who moved her weapon in an upward direction, striking his bokken at a horizontal position. "Very good, Elizabeth." He cocked an eyebrow and smirked.

Liz stuck out her tongue at the boys, who both rolled their eyes at her.

Arthur patiently reclaimed the attention of his trainees. "I will now show you three symbolic positions that I want you to work on. And when I say 'work on,' I mean every day, every chance in every day, and when you are in a place you cannot work on them, I expect you to visualize your stick softly between your fingers, feeling the grain of the wood, sweeping swiftly toward each firm and final position." He demonstrated the three positions, then wrapped up the training session. "Keep practicing. We'll meet again tomorrow so I can see your progress."

Even after Arthur had left, the trainees stayed in the arena another half hour. They practiced their new sweeping moves and slowly became familiar with the weight of the stick and its balance point in their hands.

Of course, things got a little less professional during this time, as the boys couldn't resist sparring with each other, joking about being knights trying to win over the princess. Liz just stood back and watched, laughing hysterically at their craziness.

At the other end of the hall, Arthur and Samuel were conversing as another one of the boys' sparring sessions broke out. Samuel gestured with his head toward the arena, and the two men chuckled.

"Boys!" Samuel said.

Arthur added, "Our future, no less."

After a good night's sleep, the three of them met back by their trusty old oak tree, prior to heading off to the construction site of the bridge project. The ride was short, as it was just outside of town. Construction equipment and fences along Norfolk Creek were already in place.

From a hundred fifty yards out, tucked behind some bushes, they were able to see two people standing high above the river, pointing toward the other side, most likely discussing the future span of the bridge. The river was about fifteen feet below, flanked by a sheer cliff with a narrow gravel fringe at the water's edge.

"Let's get closer so we can hear them," whispered Ethan.

"No way, dude. There are construction fences all around. I don't think we can get much closer without being seen," Jacob said.

Liz started walking toward the drop-off and peered over the cliff, which was not nearly as high as where their targets were standing. "Look down there, below the cliff. There's a small edge we can sneak along so we get directly under them."

She started to climb down backward, gripping small bushes and rocks to steady herself on the way down. The boys didn't hesitate to follow.

Once at the bottom, they shuffled along the water's edge, keeping themselves pressed against the side of the cliff. Finally, they arrived at a spot directly beneath the men. Ethan put a finger to his lips, and they listened to the now clear discussion between the two men.

The first voice was mid-sentence: ". . . homeless people from Chester Hills are scheduled to come in for their initial training next week. They'll be set up as usual, with their free food and cots. We'll set up their camp across the river behind those trees to minimize nosy townspeople and reporters from getting too close.

"Great," said the second voice. "I have the materials planned for arrival as well. We're *borrowing* the steel from an abandoned factory. It's in pretty good condition, considering it has been exposed to the elements for several years. But, as the mayor said, we don't actually need the bridge to last very long. The people just assume it'll still be used once the factory is up and running, but once they have jobs, they would have no choice but to rebuild the bridge.

"Looks like things are lining up. Did you hear the mayor's speech last week?"

The first man chuckled. "What did he tell everyone this time?"

"He said that Teumessian Industries specializes in *nature's energy.*"

Both men laughed at this obviously fraudulent claim.

Ethan looked at the faces of his friends—they appeared as shocked as he was to hear what these men were saying.

"This town is as gullible as the last. They got no idea what's coming," the first man said. "They think it's gonna bring tons of jobs, but what the mayor conveniently forgot to mention was that after the mine is operational, it'll be nearly autonomous. Almost all the jobs will be removed again."

"I almost feel guilty," the other guy said. "Almost!" They both broke into laughter again.

At that moment, one of their phones rang. "Hello, Mayor." It was the voice of the first man. "We're both here. I'll put you on speaker."

The mayor's words were crisp and clear. "I'm concerned about how tight our security is, especially in guarding the homeless work camp. You guys need to keep your eyes open for anything suspicious. I know Jim is snooping around way too much. If you see him, watch him closely and keep him in the dark about the work camp."

At that moment, Jacob's foot slipped off the rock he had been standing on. The rock rolled down into the river, making a loud splash.

All three cringed and froze, hoping the splash had not been heard. There hopes were dashed when one of the men hollered, "What was that?"

The trio bolted down the gravel edge, heading toward their bikes.

\* \* \*

The men quickly moved to the edge of the cliff, looking down the steep grade toward the water, then snapped to the right, watching three kids sprinting away.

"What's going on!" yelled the mayor over the speakerphone.

"Sir, there were kids hanging around the edge of the river, just below us, under the cliff. Probably just playing where they shouldn't be."

"Did they hear our conversation?"

"I don't think they heard anything, sir."

"You know what? I didn't ask what you thought. I want to *know*. Grab those kids and squeeze it out of them."

"Yes, sir. We'll be in touch." The man hung up the phone and slipped it in his pocket. He turned to his buddy. "Let's go."

The two took off running, trying to catch up to the kids.

After only fifty yards of chase, the two men abandoned their pursuit. "Nobody's going to believe some dumb kids, anyway, even if they did hear something. Come on. Let's wrap up and get out of here."

\* \* \*

Once they'd hopped on their bikes, Ethan, Jacob, and Liz burst out from behind the bushes, racing down the dirt path on the river's edge. They left a long trail of dust blowing across the field.

Ethan felt like he'd never peddled so hard in his life. Adrenaline pumped through his veins. "Crap," he shouted. "We're terrible at this."

Jacob gasped out his apology. "I'm sorry, guys. I was so shocked . . . at what they said . . . I lost my footing."

After a few minutes, they slowed down and tucked into a pocket of trees where they stopped for a moment's rest.

"Did I hear them right? Are they using homeless people from a different town as slave labor?" In a moment of drama, Liz grabbed her hair and pulled on it as she looked at the guys with a horrified expression. "This is so awful."

Ethan nodded. "Yeah, and apparently the mayor has no interest in the *quality* of the bridge construction as long as it gets the factory up and running."

"Whatever this factory is," Jacob said, "we can't let them build it. Otherwise, it'll be the end of Winslow Falls."

Ethan held up his hands, trying to keep everyone, including himself, focused on what to do next—acting, instead of reacting. "Okay, we gotta get this information back to Jim and Samuel. This isn't looking good for Jim, that's for sure—he's already suspected of snooping."

"I agree, but it's way too late to go back to the Rabbit Hole now," Liz said. "We'll have to go first thing in the morning. Right?"

Ethan and Jacob said in unison, "Right."

After confirming the coast was clear, they headed back to their respective homes for the night.

Chapter Thirteen

# Containment Plan

The following morning, the three young hares charged out to the Rabbit Hole to share their information with Samuel. Jim had to be made aware of the potential danger he was in—though he probably suspected it somewhat anyway. They just didn't want him snared in some sort of trap set by the mayor and his deceitful minions.

On the way to the cave, the air was damp and cool—like a storm was on its way. The day had begun drearily; and their thoughts were worse.

They dropped their bikes at the front of the cave, and Ethan pounded in the code. He then flung open the door and called out, "Samuel!" They stormed into the Rabbit Hole, scanning the room for his location, hoping he was there.

And he was. Samuel had been facing the library shelves, apparently looking for a book. When he heard his name being shouted, he spun around to find the kids racing toward him. There were a few other members present, and they stepped out of the way, startled at this irregular turn in the day.

With only half the distance covered, Ethan had already started talking, projecting his voice forward. "We overheard some terrible things about the bridge project, but most important of all, we think Jim is already a suspect for leaking information." By this time, they had arrived at the bookshelf and had Samuel's undivided attention, not to mention that of the other members from a distance.

"Okay, catch your breath. Focus," Samuel said, indicating for them to sit. He peered through his glasses at his riled young members. "Start from the beginning."

Jacob jumped in. "Okay, we overheard two men at the bridge site talking about using homeless people from another town as slave workers, and they were laughing, and then the mayor called."

Liz took it from there. "He was on speakerphone. The mayor . . . he's in on all of it. He even mentioned Jim by name, said he was a *risk*. We have to warn Jim immediately! How can we reach him?" Her eyes bugged out as she stared at Samuel.

The Elder nodded and held up his hands. "One thing at a time. Please, let's stay calm. Jim should be at work by now, at the mayor's office. But I don't think it's wise for you to go in there. I'll place an untraceable call to his office, and hopefully, I'll get in touch with him." He stood and looked at each of them in turn. "You have done a fine job." Then he headed down the stairs behind the bookshelves.

The trio waited impatiently for his return, even though it had been just a few minutes. When Samuel walked back into the library, he was shaking his head. "I was unable to reach him by phone. You'll need to go down there, after all. We will continue to try to contact him by phone, but as much as I do not want this . . . well, you should depart immediately. Find a way to reach out to Jim."

Ethan and his friends had already turned toward the exit. "We're on it," he shouted over his shoulder. "Will get back to you as soon as possible!"

At the mayor's office, Maxwell Hofner and the head of Red Fox, Ezra Reynard, were holding a private meeting. The meeting was not a planned one. Ezra had barged into the mayor's office, not even giving the secretary a glance. As a result, the air was thick with tension. It was their only face-to-face meeting since the mayor had taken office.

Maxwell stood and rounded his desk to greet the rude Ezra. His displeasure at the intrusion, the lack of protocol was obvious in his demeanor. "Ezra, to what do I owe this *pleasure?*" he asked, his words laced with sarcasm and spite.

Ezra walked right past Maxwell without a word or even accepting the offered handshake. He continued behind his desk and sat in the oversized chair reserved for the mayor. "Maxwell, I'm hearing rumblings that things are getting out of hand here. Do you have news for me?"

Maxwell knew Ezra had received information about *something*—that much was clear. But what? He took a shot, hoping he was on target. "Yesterday, I was told there were some kids poking around the jobsite. My guys figure they were just playing around, didn't hear anything that was said. By the way, I was on speakerphone for part of the time." He shrugged and tilted his head side to side, lips tight. "Could be true; could be false. But there is a chance they'd overheard me talking about the, uh, workers coming in."

Ezra shook his head, acting terribly disappointed. "Interesting. I did not know of this, and I should have been told by—" He stopped himself and waved his hand in the air. "Anyway, you guys are really running a sloppy ship here. I'm losing confidence in your abilities, Mayor Hofner."

Maxwell chided himself for missing the mark, only making things worse. *Think, think . . . What does Ezra know?* He cleared his throat and attempted to gain control of the situation. This was his office, and he would not be toyed with, not even by the head of Red Fox. "Okay, Ezra. So, what *are* you doing here? Why have you graced this office with your presence?"

Ezra smiled, apparently unfazed by Maxwell's aggressive response. "Tell me about this Jim Stevenson person."

Maxwell changed his aggressive demeanor, not knowing how much information Ezra had—maybe more than he had himself. He approached the subject cautiously. "I'm concerned that he knows too much about Daquan Construction. He spent a great deal of time investigating them, trying to find recommendations, reasons they would be the best choice for contractor, but all he found were dead ends. Nothing. He expressed this to me. I simply made the decision and would not be questioned." He tugged on the lapels of his jacket and shrugged his shoulders.

"And what *exactly* does he know?" asked Ezra.

Maxwell ground his teeth at the sound of condescension in Ezra's voice.

"It's hard to tell. I know Jim well enough, and I know he'll keep digging into the details, no matter what I say. It's the way he is."

Ezra lifted slightly from the mayor's chair, leaned over the desk, and jabbed a finger at him. "Organize a meeting with him near the job site, on the far side of the river. Your meeting will be to discuss the workers' conditions, but ultimately, I need you to get him standing on the edge of the forest. Two of my guys will meet you there." He settled back in the chair again.

Maxwell narrowed his eyes. "What do you intend to do, Ezra?"

"If you had only stayed the course," Ezra said, adding a dramatic sigh, "I wouldn't have to do anything. Apparently that was too much to ask. You have no need to know my tactics, but I assure you, this will no longer be an issue."

"When should we do this? I can probably work something in by the end of the week."

Ezra abruptly stood from his chair, sweeping his hand across the desk, throwing papers everywhere. "TODAY, you idiot!"

Maxwell jumped back and held up his hands. "Okay, Okay. I'll get something organized right away."

Ezra took a deep breath, composed himself, and left the office without another word. Maxwell walked over the papers and other items on the floor, grabbed the side of his chair, and slowly lowered himself into it.

✽ ✽ ✽

The trio rode up to the front of the government building. Ethan said, "I'll go in alone to warn Jim. You guys wait here. I don't want to raise suspicion with all of us tromping through the halls."

The team agreed, and Ethan headed for the main lobby, steering his way toward the reception desk. This was his first time in the building, which was much larger than he had anticipated. High ceilings, marble floors and walls. Rather magnificent, really.

"Excuse me, ma'am," he said to the lady working behind the reception desk. "I have an appointment with Mr. Stevenson regarding a school project I'm doing."

She offered a friendly smile. "What is your name, young man?"

"Ethan Drake." He realized after it was too late that he should not have given his real name, but how else would Jim know who he was?

The lady turned back to her computer to search the visitor-request log, "I have no registered visitors for him this morning. Is he expecting you?"

Ethan had to think quickly. "We had planned to meet at lunch today, but he had to make other plans, so he suggested I stop by during the morning sometime."

"Okay, let me call him." She picked up the phone, and after a short discussion with Jim's department secretary, she turned back to Ethan. "Unfortunately, the mayor has just joined him in his office. If you would like to wait over there," she pointed to some wooden benches, "I'll let you know when he's available."

"Thank you, ma'am," he said, even as his pulse rose in fear of what that meeting may be about.

While Ethan waited, his mind ran wild with terrible thoughts about being too late to save Jim. The large clock on the wall of the waiting area could not have ticked slower. He felt like he'd been waiting for an eternity. In reality, it was less than twenty minutes before the receptionist finally called him over.

"Okay, Mr. Stevenson has agreed to see you. Please go down the hall, and take the elevator to the third floor." Leaning over the desk, she pointed in that direction. "His office is 327, left from the elevators. Just check in with the department secretary when you arrive."

"Thank you, ma'am," Ethan said, trying not to reveal how anxious he was. He quickly covered the ground to the elevator, impatiently waiting for the doors to open.

As soon as Ethan stepped out of the elevator, he nearly collided with the mayor, of all people. Their eyes locked for a brief moment—Ethan's looking as if he had just seen his lifelong nemesis, and the mayor's looking irritable. Without a word, they went their separate ways.

In room 327, Jim's secretary asked Ethan to sign in as a visitor and pointed him in the direction of Jim's office.

As Ethan approached his office, which was all glass, including the door, he could easily see Jim at his desk. Jim had not yet seen Ethan. A soft knock on the door to gain his attention, and Jim waved him in.

When the door shut, Jim started at him right away, "You shouldn't be here, Ethan. We can't be seen together, especially here, of all places."

"I know, I know, but I have news you gotta hear immediately. In fact, Samuel sent me to tell you. He's been trying to call you without success."

Jim sighed in appreciation of the situation. "The external phone lines to this floor have been dead all morning, and we have a service company here trying to fix them. What is it that you need to say? I need to get ready to head out to the construction site."

Ethan jumped forward. "Why are you going there?"

Jim looked out through his glass walls to see if anyone was around. "The mayor asked me to meet him at the bridge site. Wants to discuss the plans so far. Something about the working conditions on the far side of the river, where the tents are to be located."

"That's what I wanted to say," Ethan said, his voice pitching high. He paused to compose himself, then began again. "Yesterday, we overheard two guys talking at the construction site and then they received a call from the mayor, put it on speaker so they could both hear. Well, we heard too. They're suspicious you've caught on to something."

"Ethan, I appreciate you warning me, but the mayor isn't going to do anything to me. Yes, I'm sure he has suspicions; he's a suspicious guy, and he knows I don't let things go so easily. But he's not going to harm me. Yes, he yells a lot, but I have too high of a role in his organization. There's no way he'll do anything that will draw unwanted attention."

Ethan was still unsettled. "Yeah, but . . . well, I don't like this at all. I mean, Jim, these guys are really scary, and I'm including the mayor in that description."

Jim came around the desk and put an arm around Ethan. "It's okay. I'll watch out for myself; I promise. I'll also pay very close attention to what is said and how it's said. Maybe I can pick up on something that will help you guys with your investigation as well."

Ethan sighed, still not convinced, but he gave Jim the benefit of the doubt. "Okay, Jim, if you think it'll be fine."

"I do. Now, you should go before the mayor sees you here."

Ethan squirmed a little. "Um, he already saw me getting out of the elevator, but I don't think he knows who I am or why I am here. We just bumped into each other, but nothing was said."

"Hmmm, okay." Jim rubbed his forehead, which was crinkled with concern. "That's too close for comfort. It's best if you take the stairwell down the hall instead of the elevators. Less people."

"Good luck, Jim. Maybe I'll see you at the Rabbit Hole later?"

"I'll head over after work today so we can compare notes. Now go!" He opened the door and swished Ethan out.

"I don't like that at all," Liz said.

"Not good," Jacob agreed.

Ethan had just come out of the building and given them the rundown of his conversation with Jim.

"I know, but what are we going to do about it? He said he'd be okay." Even as he said this, Ethan felt like he wasn't doing enough to protect Jim. Jim hadn't heard the tone the mayor and his men had used when speaking about him, not to mention what they'd said about the workers, the community, the bridge—all of it. These were menacing men, with the mayor leading the way.

"Heck with that," Jacob said, now straddling his bike. "We need to get out there and spy on them from the forest."

Liz and Ethan looked intently at Jacob. The wild risk he'd just suggested took Ethan by surprise—and apparently Liz, too.

"Hello?" Jacob snapped his fingers. "Anyone home? Let's go."

"I think you're right," Ethan said, then looked to Liz. "You agree?"

Liz nodded. "Totally."

As Ethan walked to his bike, he saw Jacob smiling. Seemed like his friend was pretty pleased with himself, offering up the bold idea. Ethan didn't blame him. Truth was, Ethan wished he had thought of it himself.

They took off on their bikes, taking the long way to the opposite side of the river. They would be able to monitor things through the thick of the forest and avoid detection. Hopefully.

Ditching their bikes just before the forest by the main trail, they hiked through the trees, stopping just shy of the forest's edge facing the river. They couldn't get any closer without becoming too exposed. They could see a car waiting, but they were too far to make out who was inside.

All they could do was to wait, stay low, and keep their eyes peeled.

A second car pulled up alongside the first—it was Jim. He exited his vehicle and approached the first one, from which two men stepped out. A moment later, the mayor arrived in his personal Town Car and quickly joined the others.

Ethan looked at Liz and Jacob, whispering, "Here we go."

They were much too far away to hear voices, but they watched with eagle eyes.

"I don't like the looks of those two tall guys," Liz said.

The mayor abruptly pointed toward the forest, precisely in their direction. The three hares quickly ducked behind some trees.

"What's happening?" Liz hissed. "Did they see us? Are they coming?" She sounded a little panicked.

Jacob slowly moved behind a bush, which maintained good coverage and allowed him to see the suspects. "They're all walking directly toward us. Seriously."

Ethan shushed them. "Hold still and be quiet."

From his vantage point behind the bush, Jacob watched intently as Jim, the mayor, and the two unknown men approached the edge of the forest, still fifty yards away. One of the two men slowed until he was walking directly behind Jim. He pulled something from his pocket—a syringe!—and as quick as lightening, he jammed it directly into the side of Jim's neck. Jim fell to the ground in a quake of convulsions.

Jacob gasped as he stared in horror.

"What is it, Jacob?" Ethan's heart sped up, fearing the worst.

Jacob did not respond. He didn't move.

"Jacob!" Liz snapped out his name in a frantic whisper, trying to break him from his trance.

Jacob slowly looked back at the others, who could not see what was going on. Terror gripped his trembling voice as he whispered, "They injected Jim with a shot of something; came up behind him with a syringe. Jim's . . . he's on the ground. He stopped moving."

Liz's and Ethan's eyes went wide. Liz put a hand to her mouth.

Jacob gulped then turned back to the action. One of the goons had pulled out a rope from behind a tree. "Crap! They're tying Jim's hands behind his back now. Oh! They just put a pillowcase over his head." This was all said in the softest voice possible but still allowed his friends to hear him.

"The mayor. What's he doing?" Ethan whispered.

"He's casually going back to his car. What a jerk. I mean, like nothing happened! He's just left the two guys with Jim. Oh, man. Oh, man, this doesn't look good." He quickly glanced back at Liz and Ethan. "Nobody move, please."

The two goons had fully bound Jim's body with the rope. One of them grabbed him under the arms, the second by the legs. As the mayor zoomed away, leaving a trail of dust behind him, the two goons carried Jim's motionless body toward their own car. While balancing Jim's legs, the one guy was able to open the trunk, and then they proceeded to stuff Jim's limp body inside, head first.

Jacob gestured at his friends to meet behind a common tree, and they all scuffled in that direction. He updated them on what had just happened, and that the mayor was long gone.

"I've never seen anything like this before! It was . . . it was terrible." Jacob's head dropped for a moment. He felt like he was going to burst into tears but fought to restrain it.

"Where do you think they're going?" Liz asked, pointing to the car as it pulled away—the car that held Jim captive.

"To stage an accident." Ethan's voice was flat as he stared into the distance.

Jacob had no doubt where Ethan's thoughts were going—he was thinking about his father. It was all becoming clearer, what had likely happened. Jacob reached out a hand, placed it on Ethan's shoulder, and squeezed gently.

Liz, on the other hand, was borderline hysterical. "They can't do this! Are you saying they're going to murder him and cover it up?

Jacob looked over at his lifelong friend with sympathetic eyes while answering Liz. "They've done it before, Liz." Ethan nodded at these words. "And they have so many insiders. They know exactly which rugs they can sweep things under."

She started pacing in a small circle, fists clinched with fury. "What do we do? How do we stop them from killing him?"

Ethan broke his distant stare and looked back at his friends. "All we can do is wait until it's printed on the front page of tomorrow's news."

Jacob was unwilling to give up so easily. "No, Ethan. We need to contact Samuel and Alice immediately."

"Okay," Liz and Ethan said at the same time, though their tones were much different . . . Liz's upbeat, and Ethan's defeated.

They ran back through the forest to their bikes. It was late afternoon, and they found themselves peddling back to the Rabbit Hole for the second time in the same day. Unlike this morning, not a word was spoken, only thoughts dashing through their minds as fast as their wheels were turning on the bumpy trail.

They were searching again. This time, not for a cave, but for answers, solutions, clues, a path for rescuing Jim before his demise. The clock was ticking.

* * *

They blasted down the steps into the Rabbit Hole, startling Samuel, Alice, and Arthur, who were seated at the long table.

Samuel stood first. "My word!" he exclaimed as he rushed toward the youngsters. Alice and Arthur popped up in reaction.

Ethan dropped to his knees right there and then. Liz and Jacob sat on the steps, heads down.

"Ethan, tell me," Samuel insisted.

So he did. Ethan explained his encounter with the mayor in the morning and Jim's lack of concern about

Ethan's warning. He told about the goons, the syringe, what the getaway car looked like—with Jacob chiming in to complete any missing details.

As troubling as the story was, their audience maintained a calm, controlled appearance as they listened.

Liz pleaded to Alice, "Call in the police. Call everyone. We have to do something. This is a kidnapping. They're plotting cold-blooded murder. It's . . . it's *real.*"

Samuel held up a hand. "Let's all move to the long table. I have something to say." Once everyone was seated, he began. "We live in a world where we must fight evil at evil's doorstep. But in this world, evil's doorstep is immediately outside our own. I fear there is nothing we can do about Jim . . ." Ethan gasped and Liz began to sob. Samuel pursed his lips for a moment, then started again. ". . . unless new information becomes known. I cannot risk losing Alice in the process; she understands she must not interfere."

Liz pushed back from the table and started pacing. "But we have to do something. They'll kill him. They will. I know they will!"

"Perhaps, but it is the unfortunate fate of a shadow warrior. Besides, I know Jim well, and I have not yet given up on his perseverance."

"You think he'll escape?" Ethan asked as he pulled Liz back down to her chair next to his.

"Let's just say I will not be planning his memorial just yet." Samuel looked at each of them directly. "We must maintain calm, and although I appreciate that this is a new world for you, it is time for you to practice control. Now would be a perfect time, in fact—given your present built-up energy—to learn self-defense." He looked to Arthur.

"Our young friends need to burn off some of their intense emotions. Can you help them?"

Arthur smiled and bowed slightly. He turned to the young warriors. "Please grab your bokkens. It is time we learned the art of defense."

Liz pushed away from the table, again with a fierceness in the action. "We can't waste our time playing with some stick! We have to find him."

Samuel looked into Liz's fiery eyes. "You will need to trust me, Elizabeth Walker. This is exactly what you should do with your time right now."

She pursed her lips, arms crossed tight, and looked away.

Arthur led them to the arena, where he proceeded to drill them on defensive moves and breathing techniques. When the training session ended, they could hardly stand on their feet and their stomachs grumbled for food.

But their minds were clear, and their rage was focused.

## Chapter Fourteen

# From the Pines

He could barely move the next morning, every muscle in his body crying out in anguish. Ethan carefully adjusted his position on the bunk bed and rubbed his eyes. "Uggh," he groaned. On two other bunks in the room, Liz and Jacob were slowly awakening to the same agony. They'd all stayed at the Rabbit Hole last night.

"I slept like the dead," said Liz through a yawn.

"I feel worse than dead, more like liquefying from the inside out," Jacob added, moaning as he sat upright.

Ethan stood and stretched. "Okay, team. We've slept half the day away practically. Let's get moving." He clapped his hands a couple of times for motivation, though he hardly felt any himself. "So, to keep it straight, we were out fishing, and it got late, so we stayed at Fort Tomahawk." Jacob said, then rolled himself out of bed. "Liz?"

"All good here," was all she said.

When they finally assembled in the main hall, Arthur was nearly complete with his morning routine in the practice arena. His eyes were closed, and his body, despite his age, moved with precision, fluidity, and intent.

Ethan watched in awe. Arthur inspired him, made him want to learn everything he could from the man. Without removing his gaze from his mentor, he leaned closer to Liz and Jacob. "Look at him. It's just unbelievable. His control and movements are just . . . I don't know, artistic."

Jacob laughed. "It's so pretty, like a butterfly," he teased.

"Oh, shut it, Jacob," Liz countered. "You wouldn't know art if it smacked you between the legs."

Ethan and Jacob looked at each other with wide eyes, and then all three burst into laughter. Liz was a riot, and Ethan was really glad she had come into their lives.

Once Arthur wrapped up his morning routine, he came to the centralized couches and offered a morning session to his young protégées.

Both Liz and Jacob vibrantly declined, groaning about their muscles being too sore.

"I want to!" Ethan said without hesitation.

Arthur bowed to the young Drake, encouraging his eagerness. Ethan jumped up from the couch, and they walked over to the sparring ring together.

"Motion is simply energy and time. You will learn that to be a master with your bokken, you will need to understand how to apply the specific amount of energy at a precise location within an exact moment of time. If you can master this, you will be able to dominate opponents twice your size, and even multiple opponents at the same time."

Ethan licked his lips nervously. He wasn't so sure he'd ever be able to do all of that, but he was willing to try.

"Do not look at the arena as only a three-dimensional space. You must visualize your target's location traveling through that space. When you can precisely predict your target's future location, plan the exact moment when your opponent is thrusting toward you, and have the awareness to strike with your bokken at its maximum velocity, you will collide with an extraordinary, unearthly force."

Ethan listened intently. The room faded away, his concentration hanging onto every word, every syllable. His mentor's calm, rhythmic voice drew him in.

"We will begin in slow motion," Arthur continued. "Your goal for this lesson is to strike your bokken exactly six inches down from the top of my bokken." He marked the exact location with green chalk. "Close your eyes and visualize this location."

Ethan closed his eyes and allowed the image to burn into his mind.

Arthur offered a series of attack moves in slow motion. Ethan tried to meet the attack zone each time without success. After several attempts, Arthur began to talk through the moves, explaining the acceleration and deceleration of his stick while it was moving through various swings.

"The transitional period between the increasing velocity and decreasing velocity is the striking zone's *maximum* velocity," he said. "If this maximum velocity is in the exact opposite direction of your swing, when the sticks collide, they will have the maximum velocity of both weapons combined."

Arthur continued to go through the swings in slow motion, simply stating, "Now," each time his stick was at maximum velocity. Ethan continued to try to strike the stick at exactly that moment, but was clumsy, out of sync, and missing the intended location.

"You will practice every day. Your timing will become perfect along with your accuracy. This will not happen with you working alone. You need several sparring partners, with different patterns and styles, with whom you can practice." Both Arthur and Ethan quickly glanced over at Liz and Jacob.

Ethan said, "Thank you, Arthur. I'm really fascinated by this, and can't express how awesome it is to watch you move with your bokken."

"I have several pressing things to take care of this morning, but I wish all three of you good luck in your investigation today. It is imperative that we gain more intelligence behind the mayor's plot . . . before it is too late."

Ethan responded with some rekindled confidence from his sparring activity. "We will figure this out and destroy his plans!"

Arthur nodded, looking pleased, and headed down the stairs. Ethan returned to his friends, who complimented his efforts with Arthur and, of course, teased him about getting his butt kicked by an old man.

"While you were screwing around with your stick," Liz joked, "we've decided that we should head back to the area where Jim was taken."

Jacob added, "Maybe there are some clues left by the two goons. I'm thinking they had that rope hidden behind a tree, so there could be some other evidence lying around. Maybe something that would give us a hint as to where they're holding Jim."

Ethan was exhausted and sore, but he didn't hesitate. "Good idea. Let's head out."

The three grabbed their bikes and hammered through the trails, back toward the construction site.

As they approached the end of the trail where they'd ditched their bikes just yesterday, they saw several people snooping around that very area.

Ethan, who was leading the group, pulled off early and ducked behind some bushes. The others followed without question.

Ethan pointed from behind cover. "Look. They're searching exactly where we left our bikes yesterday. Do they know we were in the woods when Jim was taken?"

"This doesn't look good," Jacob said.

"How in the world do they know where we ditched our bikes? They must have followed us when we left yesterday," Liz said. "We should back out of here before they see us."

Without another word, they turned their bikes around. Unfortunately, as Ethan climbed back on his bike and started to peddle, a stick buried under the pine needles snapped.

One of the men down the trail whipped his head in their direction and shouted, "Hey, stop right there!" He started toward them.

There was no chance they were going to stop after what they'd seen yesterday with Jim—this was life or death. They pedaled furiously down the trail, bikes swinging left to right with each pump, as if a raging bull were chasing them.

After several minutes of this, they finally felt reasonably sure they had not been followed.

Jacob pulled into a clearing on the side of the trail. "There are some hills about a hundred yards back through these trees. Let's hide there and discuss a plan."

They dismounted their bikes and pushed them through the thick pine needles toward the hilly terrain.

"This should conceal us for a little while," Jacob said, as he pointed toward a safe area for them to sit out of sight.

They plopped on the ground, and Ethan said, "We gotta get back to the construction site, but these guys are obviously on to us."

"Maybe we should walk straight through to the site," Liz suggested. "You know, completely off trail. There's no way they're watching the *entire* forest."

Ethan nodded, adding, "It'll take much longer, but I think you're right. It's our only chance."

With no counterproposal, they left their bikes tucked behind the hills and headed out on foot.

Ethan pulled out his compass, conferred with his trail map, and guided the team through the dense forest. Once they arrived at the construction site, they immediately noticed that the construction company had already started clearing the ground where the bridge would begin, on the other side of the river. A construction trailer was now installed as well.

"Look." Ethan pointed across the river. "They have an office set up. Maybe there will be some information in there that we can dig into."

Jacob shook his head. "Uh . . . no. Not now, anyway. It's swarming with people. We'd never get in there unnoticed."

"Well, we need to come back at night. Tonight," Ethan said. "It's definitely a place we need to check out. Maybe we'll find new information about the project, clues about Jim . . . who knows? We gotta do it."

Liz nodded and looked around. "Okay, but for now, let's search around the edge of the woods like we planned."

They fanned out and poked around all the trees at the edge of the clearing, but they found nothing they could call a clue. After nearly an hour, their search drew them deeper into the forest.

"Guys, over here!" Jacob said suddenly.

"What is it?" Ethan and Liz said at nearly the same time.

"It looks like someone was digging here. Doesn't it?" He was standing in front of an area where the pine needles had been disturbed. He began clearing the pine needles away, uncovering the bare ground—where the dirt had obviously been dug then covered back up.

"That was a big hole," Ethan said, looking at the wide area in question.

The boys began pawing at the ground. Liz's attention stayed focused on the dark forest around them.

"Guys. Guys!" she said suddenly, but Ethan and Jacob did not stop digging, their concentration so focused on uncovering what lay beneath the dirt. She reached down and swatted at Ethan's shoulder.

"What!" Ethan shouted as he looked up. She was frozen, staring into the forest with big eyes and a worried expression.

Ethan followed her gaze. He then saw what was of such grave importance.

"Jacob, stop digging," Ethan said in a low stern voice.

Jacob stopped, followed his friends' gazes . . . and gasped.

The boys slowly made their way to stand on either side of Liz.

In the distance, a man with a black, hooded cloak stood beside a massive, white-spotted horse. The man's face was hidden by the shadow cast by his hood. He slowly approached, almost like a ghost in his silent movement.

"Who are you?" yelled Jacob.

The man walked a few more steps and then stopped just far enough away to maintain his concealed identity.

When Jacob began to repeat his question, the dark figure raised his finger to his lips and released a haunting, "Shhh."

The hooded man began to speak in a low, yet strikingly powerful voice. "You will not receive another warning, for this is your last. Leave what is below the pines beneath, or you, too, will find yourselves under its sheath."

His horse bellowed a loud snort. Without another word, the cloaked figure gracefully swung himself up onto the horse's back, turned the magnificent animal, and charged off into the shadows of the forest, kicking pine needles behind.

The three friends stood in a fog of total silence. They looked at each other, mouths partially unhinged.

Ethan broke the eery quiet. "We should go."

Wide-eyed, both Jacob and Liz agreed with a simple head nod. They headed back toward their hidden bikes.

Not a word was spoken as they gathered their bikes. They departed the forest as quickly as possible, knowing that *he* was out there . . . somewhere.

They went directly to Ethan's house and barreled into the attic.

Ethan said, "How did he sneak up on us like that?"

Liz shook her head in disbelief. "I was looking directly out into the forest when he just appeared from behind a tree. I don't even know if he was there the entire time or if he just rode in at that moment."

"Between last night's events and now this seriously creepy dude, we can't do this anymore," Jacob said, throwing his hands in the air. "I know they said this was going to be dangerous, but I think it's becoming more suicidal than anything."

While Liz paced the attic floor, Ethan pushed back at Jacob. "But we have to find Jim. We can't just leave him to die!"

Jacob scoffed at the comment. "Are you serious? Who do you think was buried under the pine needles?"

Ethan wasn't buying it. "It doesn't add up, Jacob. Why would they kidnap him alive, only to kill and bury him in the forest later?"

"Torture, Ethan," Jacob said, fire in his eyes. "They took him away to torture him. Then killed and buried him. That's why!"

Liz stopped her pacing and said softly, "You know, Jacob, I have to agree with Ethan. I don't think that was Jim under that dirt."

"You're both nuts!" he barked.

She tightened her lips. "If they kill Jim, who is an important member of the mayor's office, I think they'd have to stage an accident, or suicide, or something. But leaving him 'missing' doesn't make sense to me."

"If not Jim, then who was buried there?" Jacob asked.

Ethan looked up to the ceiling, collecting his thoughts, "We have to go back," he finally said.

"Are you kidding? Or insane?" Jacob said, his eyes bugging out. "The only thing *that* will get us *is killed*!"

"I'll go with you," Liz said to Ethan.

Jacob's head snapped in her direction, his expression one of utter disbelief. "What? Well, I'm staying here. That way, all three of us don't die tonight!"

"Fine," Ethan said, intentionally not making eye contact.

For the rest of the afternoon, they did not mention another trip to the construction site again. Ethan's mom came up to the attic to chide them about not letting the parents know where they had been, but she calmed down when Ethan apologized and explained they'd just fallen asleep at their campsite and gotten a late start that day. Jacob then realized he needed to call his parents, too, and did so, to a barrage of *you-should-haves*. Oddly, Liz didn't feel the need to reach out to her parents. Neither Ethan nor Jacob pursued that weirdness; their thoughts were encumbered enough as it was.

As the evening approached, Ethan suggested they prepare for their night ride into the forest. He and Liz discussed retreat points, which they would use if they got separated or chased; call signs to alert each other of danger; and some basic hand signals so they could silently communicate. Maybe they had watched entirely too many spy movies, but they were comforted to have at least a few plans for protection.

Jacob sat off to the side, arms crossed, scowling.

It was well after midnight, and Liz and Ethan headed downstairs to get their bikes. Ethan wasn't completely comfortable with what they were about to do—essentially walking up to evil's door—but he also felt strongly that this was their calling. He was seriously pissed at Jacob for wimping out on them.

He offered a simple and short, "Later," as they left Jacob smoldering in his own anger there in the attic.

By the time Ethan and Liz started wheeling down the neighborhood street, Jacob had run out of the house. "Wait! I'm coming, you idiots!"

Barely looking over his shoulder, Ethan flatly replied, "Better catch up." Liz howled with laughter.

And he did catch up. Off they went, side by side, into the crisp summer night.

Once they drew closer to the trail, their pace eased, though their senses were on high alert. They could smell the damp ground. They could see the subtle movements of leaves rustling in the breeze. They could hear the chirps of crickets in the distance.

They were acutely aware of their surroundings, scanning for signs of trouble. Finally, they reached the small grouping of hills where they had parked earlier. They left their bikes, just as before.

They gathered close to each other, and Ethan said, "Okay. From here on out, we're in total silence. No lights, so take it slow. It's really dark, but our eyes will adjust."

Liz and Jacob gave a thumbs-up. Ethan responded the same way.

Carefully watching every step and squinting through the darkness, they eventually made it to the area of disturbed pine needles and dirt.

Ethan signaled by raising his hand in a fist as high as his head and then pointing toward the site. They approached cautiously.

Ethan offered his thumbs-up again and then settled down to his knees to unearth the body, or whatever was buried there. Liz and Jacob stood lookout, covering each other's blind spots.

Determined, Ethan dug through the loose soil, eventually grabbing a piece of fabric, a shirt perhaps. "Psst," he whistled to the others.

He tugged on the fabric and it didn't give much, so he continued to clear out more dirt. After doing that for a few minutes, he pulled again on the fabric, hard. The object gave way, tossing Ethan to his butt as each of them let out a gasp.

A human arm protruded from the soil. Ethan picked himself up and moved in closer to investigate. He whispered, "I don't think it's Jim. That's not what he was wearing yesterday."

He moved up higher, where the head would most likely be, and quickly pawed at the earth. Perhaps he would recognize the buried corpse.

After only a few minutes, he found himself sweeping dirt off of a dead man's face. Something he could never imagine doing a couple weeks ago. He looked up to his partners, shaking his head. "I don't know who it is," he said somberly.

Jacob nudged at Ethan. "We need to rebury him and tell Alice about it tomorrow. Let's get outta here."

Liz continued to act as lookout. Ethan and Jacob knelt on the ground and began to pile the dirt back where it had been. They nestled the arm back into the hole, covered it and the face with dirt, and then sifted the pine needles over the whole area.

Ethan motioned for everyone to gather next to a nearby tree.

"Okay, that's not Jim, but now we have another victim," he said.

Liz held up her hand. "Uh, maybe we can discuss that later. I think we should get our butts across the river, so we can check out the construction trailer and then get the heck out of here."

Ethan wasn't so sure about that plan. They were messing with some pretty heavy stuff—like a dead body and another missing person. "That's totally exposed from here to there. Besides, there are floodlights beaming all over the place."

"That would really be pushing our luck," Jacob said.

Liz rolled her eyes and let out a big sigh. "Fine. I'll go alone, then. I've always wanted to do something like this. You boys are too emotional. Bye-bye." She waggled her fingers at them, turned on her heels, and started walking.

The boys stared at each other. Ethan could almost read Jacob's mind. *Is she for real?*

"Okay, wait. Liz, wait. Jacob and I will keep watch from the edge of the forest here. We'll do the call sign, like an owl screech, if someone's coming. If anything goes out of control, we'll go to rendezvous position B, where our bikes are located."

Jacob looked back and forth between Liz and Ethan. "Do you guys *wanna* get caught?"

Neither responded. Jacob shook his head, and then swatted in their direction, as if shooing them away. "Go on, go on. I'm in."

Ethan nodded at Liz. "Go."

Liz stayed low until the forest's edge, where she got down on her hands and knees and crawled through the brush to the riverbank. Fading out of sight for a moment, she reappeared, hopping from stone to stone across Norfolk Creek. She made quick work of it.

Ethan looked at Jacob, eyebrows raised. "Miss Walker got skills."

"Totally."

Liz scaled the rocky edge of the river and then army-crawled across thirty yards of open terrain, staying away from the floodlight beams. Once she reached the last shadowed area, she looked around, bounced to her feet, and ran in a hunched position directly to the trailer door. After a quick unsuccessful tug on the door handle, she pulled something out of her pocket. In a flash, she'd jimmied the door open and was inside.

Jacob let loose a low whistle. "Crap, how'd she do that?"

Ethan only offered a flabbergasted "huh."

Several minutes later, Liz slipped out of the trailer, making sure the door was locked, and retraced her steps across the field, creek, and finally back to where Ethan and Jacob were keeping watch.

Ethan ran up to her. "You're crazy, Liz. How did you do that?"

"Did you pick that lock?" Jacob asked.

Liz smiled and fluttered her eyelashes. "Boys, you have much to learn." She giggled.

"Whatever. Did you find anything?" Jacob asked.

Immediately, her expression changed to serious. "No, not about Jim, but I did find a lot of interesting stuff about the project. Let's get out of here first. I'll tell you more once we're safe."

Neither boy argued with that. Soon, they were back at the edge of town, safe from any onlookers, where she shared her findings.

"We have to get this information to Samuel first thing in the morning," Ethan said.

They agreed to meet at the old oak tree again in the morning, and then they would head off to the Rabbit Hole.

\* \* \*

The air turned humid, and the winds had begun to pick up, which made their ride to the Rabbit Hole quite unpleasant. The skies were darkening, black in the distance—a storm was coming. They desperately tried to get to the cave before it arrived in force.

The final minutes of their ride was interrupted by blasting wind, and sputtering rain, but they were able to take shelter in the Rabbit Hole before the brunt of the storm came through.

When they entered the cave, Arthur was going through his morning routine in the sparring ring. Samuel was sipping a coffee at the long table, reading a book.

They promptly headed over to Samuel. Arthur noticed their hurried arrival and joined them.

"Is Alice here?" Jacob asked, not waiting for a response before adding, "We found a body in the forest near the construction site, but it wasn't Jim's."

Ethan gave his friend a quizzical look, thinking, *Okay, that was blunt*. He noticed Liz was looking at Jacob the same way.

Liz's gaze stayed on Jacob as she started with, "So we were scoping out the location where Jim was taken, looking for clues." Her eyes then slowly panned over to Samuel and Arthur. "And we came across some scuffed-up pine needles, so we decided to investigate by digging. When we were poking around, this cloaked man on a horse rode up to us and warned us away. A *very* creepy dude. "

Samuel and Arthur simultaneously sat bolt upright with wide eyes.

This caught Ethan's attention; it was the first time he had ever seen either of them react so emotionally to something. He pointed back and forth between the elders. "You know who the creepy guy is?"

Samuel let out a gust of breath, as if he'd been holding it a long time. "Consider yourselves very fortunate, my young friends." He shook his head, wiped his brow. "You have just come face to face with the Red Fox's elite assassin."

Jacob gulped loudly. "Assassin?"

"It is a rare day, indeed," Samuel said, "that one sees this dark, mysterious being and lives to tell about it. In fact, it has been so long, he has become more legend than man. Present company excluded." He nodded in Arthur's direction.

Arthur placed his palms down upon the table, and looked gravely into Samuel's eyes. "We need to end this, Samuel. This has become entirely too dangerous for them."

"We went back," Ethan interrupted, hoping to quell the worries, "under the cover of night, as cautiously as possible, to investigate further. We dug up the body."

"I have to admit, Arthur is right," Samuel said. "The three of you are in way over your heads. I have no choice but to pull the plug on this. At least until the dust settles."

"But it wasn't Jim," Liz jumped in. "Unfortunately, we didn't recognize the man, but from the paperwork I'd found in the construction office, I think he might be from the state's Environmental Protection Agency. There were all kinds of documents about the EPA's attempts to stop the forward progress of the strip mine."

"Mine? What, you broke into their construction office?" Arthur asked, shocked.

"She did," Jacob said with pride in his voice. "It was awesome!"

Liz grinned. "I found lots of stuff about the project there. Like, I confirmed they're bringing in homeless people from other towns to build the bridge. No payments, just food and a place to sleep until the job is done. I also learned this is not some green-energy factory they are building. Teumessian Industries is actually going to rip out a huge part of the forest and build a massive strip mine for coal. Just on the other side of the river from town."

Samuel sighed at the new information. "I knew there was something bigger than that bridge. Red Fox will make a fortune off this project, while bleeding the local people and natural resources dry."

"This will be the end of Winslow Falls as we know it," Arthur said in the saddest voice Ethan had ever heard.

Ethan had to stop this gloom-and-doom attitude. "See? You need as much help as you can get. We did find out some good information. You can't take us off this case. We've come so far."

Liz and Jacob nodded in agreement.

Samuel paused and looked deeply into Ethan's eyes. Under his breath, he asked, "Are you there inside?"

Ethan shook his head in confusion, "What? Of course I'm here. Why would you ask that?"

"Never mind, Ethan. I'm just an old man seeing things. Never mind." Choking on the last few words, he wiped a single tear from his eye.

An uncomfortable silence hung in the air. Then . . .

*Bang, bang, bang* echoed through the hall.

They all pushed back from the table and looked toward the main entrance door. It blasted open with the wind and rain behind it, nearly tearing from its iron hinges. Two bodies, one carrying another, collapsed across the threshold onto the floor. Howling wind blew through the Rabbit Hole.

*Who are these soaking wet and muddy intruders?* Ethan wondered as they rushed toward the fallen men.

It didn't take him long to figure it out.

One was Eric, a member of the Three Hares, whom Ethan recognized from the welcoming ceremony. Eric was dragging the nearly lifeless body of Jim Stevenson.

Chapter Fifteen

# Deep Inside the Den

East of the city, the mayor's limo pulled up in front of 1970 Water Street. Set back from the street was a massive Victorian Gothic-style palace infamously known to be the mysterious headquarters of the Red Fox Secret Society. The house had been built at the pinnacle of the society's success in the mid-1800s, when they'd dominated the trade business covering the entire region.

Few nonmembers had made it past the lobby or any of its adjoining meeting rooms.

At two in the afternoon, the mayor walked unaccompanied along the path through the ornate gardens. He proceeded up the broad stone stairs to the main entrance. He was greeted at the front door by an armed guard, who welcomed him into the home. Well, sort of welcomed him. The guard's face was expressionless, his back ramrod straight.

"Mayor Hofner, please wait over here." He guided the mayor to a bench inside the front lobby. "Mr. Reynard will be with you momentarily."

Unsettled and rubbing his hands together, the mayor said, "Thank you."

The lobby was dark with its wood paneling, narrow windows, and high ceilings. After several minutes of waiting, Maxwell's anxiety swelled. He wondered about the reason for this meeting, whether his safety was at risk.

A second guard entered the room, as stiff as the first. "Follow me, Mayor Hofner. He will see you now."

Maxwell rose to his feet. His nerves were rattled; he hoped he appeared calm on the outside. He was led down a long hallway and then up a marble staircase to the second floor. They entered a dimly lit office with a massive wooden desk located in front of the windows overlooking the central courtyard.

Ezra Reynard was sitting at the desk, silhouetted by the light coming in from the window behind him. There were no other chairs in the room.

Maxwell had spent his life making sure he was in control—of everything and everyone he came across. In the presence of Ezra Reynard, however, he felt like an intimidated school child.

Ezra remained seated and offered no welcome. "You are failing me," he said in a low, deep voice.

Maxwell started to wring his hands, then caught himself. "We're taking care of everything. It will work—"

His words were cut short as Ezra stood, slamming both hands on the desk. "It will not work. You're losing control of this situation, and you're oblivious to the threats upon your doorstep."

At that moment, Maxwell sensed they were not alone in the room. He snuck a quick glance over his shoulder. Standing motionless in a dark corner behind him was a man in a hooded, black cloak. "Who's that?" Maxwell asked, nodding toward the hooded man.

Ezra calmly turned away from his desk and looked out the window. "He is only a shadow; do not mind him."

"What is this new threat you speak of?" His stomach turned over.

Ezra inhaled deeply and tightened his lips. "Those three children you mentioned by the river . . . they are not just any three children. We believe they are a part of the resurgence of the Three Hares."

Maxwell's face melted in confusion. "The Three Hares?"

"In 1663, a group of three self-righteous immigrants decided they were going to force everyone to follow the rules designed for poverty control. At that time, there were many gangs within Winslow Falls, and this group, the Three Hares, started driving them off, one after another.

"In doing so, the Red Fox Gang grew stronger as the competition was driven away—until an epic confrontation occurred. The Three Hares had murdered women and children, sending Red Fox into a fury of revenge. For many years, the Three Hares would rebuild, then be dismantled time and time again by Red Fox. It has been a long time since they've had any real strength."

Maxwell didn't know what to do with his hands and was nearly pacing. "Are you saying this group is back?"

Turning to face Maxwell, Ezra firmly placed his fingertips upon his desk and leaned forward. "I'm saying that these kids are the rebirth of the Three Hares. And I believe one of them . . ." he paused as if to swallow some of his rage, ". . . Ethan Drake is a direct descendant of one of the founders."

The mayor shook his head in disbelief. "Are they trying to stop our project?"

"Yesterday, we confronted these children while they were snooping around the construction site. My friend here," nodding to the hooded figure in the corner, "issued a stern warning. It brings me great displeasure that, despite the fear we have instilled within them, they proceeded back to the construction site late last night. They broke into the construction shed, finding who-knows-what.. And they unearthed the body of Mr. Smith."

Maxwell considered this information for a moment. "There was a boy who was in my office building the other day—"

"Mr. Hofner, this is where my patience runs thin. You were face to face with Ethan Drake, and you had absolutely no clue that he was there to warn Mr. Stevenson of our plot against him." Ezra clenched his jaws in anger. "You are an incompetent fool!" he spat.

Maxwell felt himself cowering slightly from the scolding. "What are you going to do?"

Ezra began a slow grin. "I'm going to kill Ethan Drake." His grin turned into a wide smile. "Which will, in turn, kill any dreams of the Three Hares rebuilding. Once and for all, the bloodline will be exterminated."

"You can't just be killing children, Ezra."

"This child's murder pales in comparison to the blood that would spill across Winslow Falls if the Three Hares group grows and begins a revolutionary war. I promise you, this is the most civilized and humane thing we can do." His smile gone, Ezra pulled out his chair and sat down once again. "Leave now. I have much work to do."

The guard entered the room and escorted the mayor out of the office before he had a chance to respond.

*\*\*

As the door closed, the hooded man approached Ezra's desk.

Ezra did not look up from the papers on his desk but shook his head in frustration and rage. "This ends now!"

*\*\*

It was now late afternoon in the Rabbit Hole. Alice was explaining that the police had received a missing-persons report for Brad Smith of the EPA.

She sat at the long table with Liz and Samuel—the boys were in the sparring ring, half practicing and half clowning around. Sifting through some papers in front of her, she held up a photo. "This is the guy who caused all the red tape for Teumessian Industries. Now he turns up missing?"

Liz swallowed hard. "Uh, that's the guy we found buried at the edge of the forest."

"This has gone way too far," Samuel said, "but I fear we are not strong enough to fight them. We need to find a way to disrupt their plans indirectly." He looked over at

Ethan and Jacob sparring in the ring. "We just aren't ready for a direct confrontation."

Alice nodded. "At least Jim came home to us last night."

At that moment, Arthur and Jim emerged from behind the library, slowly walking up the steps. They headed to the couches in the center of the room. Samuel, Alice, and Liz promptly stood up and rushed over to meet them. From the sparring ring, Ethan and Jacob halted their training to do the same.

Samuel's face seemed to melt with sadness as he got a good look at Jim. "Oh, Jim, I had nearly lost hope."

Jim's lower lip began to quiver as he embraced Samuel. "Me, too, old friend. Me, too." A tear streaked across his bruised cheek.

Ethan looked on, a trickle of terror rolling along his spine. A grown, confident, strong man brought to tears. *What did they do to him?*

Jim began to tell the story in a frail, wavering voice. "So, this is how it went down. I was in the fields meeting the mayor. This was shortly after Ethan had come to my office to warn me of the threat against me." He looked into Ethan's eyes apologetically. "The next thing I knew, I woke up in a dingy, dark room, chained to a radiator.

"I sat there for half the day without food or water before anyone came in. Finally, one of the two men who had met with me at the forest's edge entered the room."

The Rabbit Hole was dead silent as Jim explained his disappearance.

"He stood over me, looking down at me on the floor. He asked questions about what I knew about the project. I only gave him a little information, hoping he would believe that was the extent of it. But he knew there was more."

Jim paused to catch his breath. "That's when he became physically aggressive. He bent down and grabbed my arm, twisting me facedown, and drove his knee into my back. He asked more questions. I could only plead ignorance and maintained that I had limited knowledge of any grand plot. Then his questions turned from the project to the Three Hares."

Samuel exhaled loudly, dipping his head down. "They know you're associated with us?"

"Yes, Samuel, and that's not all. They asked about Ethan." Jim's swollen eyes peered back to Ethan.

A collective gasp. Everyone's eyes were on Ethan, who didn't know where to look. His eyes bounced from one person to the next.

"How much do they know?" Samuel asked.

Jim's eyes were bloodshot and washed over by a heavy sadness. "They know he's the descendent of the bloodline. They know he's the spark to ignite the rebirth of the Three Hares."

Ethan was in complete shock. "I'm not the spark, Jim. Why would they believe that?"

"My boy," Samuel began, "what you see all around you are only cooling embers. Merely remnants, after centuries of raging fires. These fires would come and go in cycles, but this last cycle has nearly been the end of us.

"You are more than just a young man who joined our ranks. You are a symbol of hope. If history tells us anything about your bloodline, you will be the catalyst of our next raging fire. It is a great misfortune that our enemies have learned of this so soon. They will do anything to extinguish that hope."

Ethan's jaw dropped. "So we are no longer hidden in the shadows?"

"I fear not," Samuel said, then looked back at Jim. "You have not yet told us why they let you go."

"They didn't let me go. After seemingly hours of physical abuse, I faked that I had passed out from the pain. In reality, I wasn't far from it. I noticed he had a knife in his belt, so when he bent down to pull me back to the corner, I jumped at him, knocking him into the radiator. His head bashed into the heavy metal pipes, and he fell limp to the floor. I grabbed the knife, cut off my restraints, and I tied him down so I could make an escape without him giving chase.

"My condition deteriorated quickly, and I really don't remember much from then on. I do have flashes of dragging myself through the dark forest in the rain and mud, but then everything went black. It was only just this afternoon that I returned to consciousness. I was dry and warm, and everything that had happened almost felt like a vivid nightmare. Until I move, that is."

Samuel looked over at Eric who had joined the group. "Your friend Eric found you lying facedown on the trail, not too far from here."

Jim looked up at Eric, then closed his eyes, nodding in appreciation as another tear streaked down.

"Jim, you must get your rest. Your story was important for us to hear, but you need sleep," Alice said, her eyes weepy.

Arthur nodded in agreement. He gently moved Jim around so that he lay on the couch. "Okay, everyone, find somewhere else to talk," he said.

Eric leaned over and momentarily rested his hand on Jim's shoulder. "Sleep well, my friend."

Arthur moved alongside Ethan, Jacob, and Liz, placing his hand on Jacob's back. "It's time, young warriors."

"Time?" Jacob asked.

Arthur made his eyes go wide, attempting to look scary, but his grin gave him away. "Now we learn how to attack. Grab your weapons!"

Energized, the four of them moved to the sparring ring with a taste of vengeance on their lips.

"Today I will show you four cornerstone attack moves. They will complete the core set of moves. Everything we learn after this will mostly be variants or combination moves. It is imperative that you master these basics."

Arthur proceeded to the edge of the ring, where a practice dummy stood. Ethan, Jacob, and Liz moved to the side so they could watch the lesson.

"The first attack is a disarming move," Arthur said as he made a blazing-fast spin, concluding with a crash into the dummy's arm. He showed three other attack moves and then asked the young warriors to find their places on the practice ring.

For each attack, he taught them the reciprocal defense position.

Ethan had been practicing a great deal, and what had first seemed to be disconnected movements now had become part of a much bigger picture. He began to see patterns and was able to read a person's movement. He could identify openings and defensive positions. With practice, his physical body would catch up with these visions. His confidence was growing, but would he be ready in time?

Chapter Sixteen

# Deadly Duel

Within the dark chambers of the Red Fox's palace, Ezra sat in front of his grand fireplace. A roaring fire cast dancing shadows across the room as it burned with intensity. Lazily swirling his cognac, he thought back to simpler days.

His loyal assassin entered the otherwise empty room and said, "I will strike tonight."

Ezra, still gazing directly into the torrent of flames, slid his finger back and forth across the rim of his glass. "I will be pleased to hear of your success."

"I'll report back when the deed is done."

He looked over his shoulder into his private assassin's eyes. "Very well."

The assassin closed his eyes, bowed, and exited the room.

Ezra spent the remaining hours of the evening contemplating how these nuisances could actually become his greatest legacy. He will be the presiding leader of Red Fox when the Three Hares are finally exterminated, after centuries of attempts by the organization. This realization brightened his mood, and he looked over toward an old painting on the wall. He said aloud into the empty room, "Is this how our mayor sees me?" The painting immaculately captured a red fox dragging a dead hare across the ground, his teeth buried deep into its throat. *If only the mayor were so ferocious himself*, he thought.

With a conniving grin, he refilled his cognac glass and settled back into his plush leather chair, comfortably watching his blazing fire, daydreaming of the day when his master plan is finally realized.

Ethan, Jacob, and Liz headed back into the forest on a quest to find more information about the coal strip mine. Each time they left the cave, their caution levels were further heightened. But tonight, after the recollections of Jim, these levels were higher than ever. The air seemed thick with danger.

They pedaled slowly, heads on a swivel, and moved as stealthily as possible. Multiple times along the ride, one or another raised a hand, halting further progress until they'd assessed their surroundings. Every sound, movement, or simply a bad feeling was a time for extra caution.

After a long, tedious trip, they finally tucked their bikes away behind some large boulders and then walked through the thick pine needles into the forest. They relied on their compass, and targeted a general direction that should lead them about one mile behind the location of the new bridge.

Jacob lifted his hand, halting the team. He leaned toward the other two, trying to keep his voice down, "What exactly are we looking for? How do we know when we have gone too far? I don't want to walk all night into the next town."

Liz rolled her eyes. "Keep moving. We'll know when we have gone too far."

After a few minutes, they heard a stick snap just ahead of them. They dropped low and slid behind the closest trees, waiting for a follow-up noise. It never came.

Ethan raised his hand in front of him for the others to see, signaling for them to proceed. As soon as they emerged from their trees, a loud rushing noise broke the still night. They hit the ground, taking cover, as three deer bounded off to the west.

Their hearts were pounding with fear, but as Arthur had taught them, they composed themselves quickly with breathing techniques. They pushed forward into the darkness.

Liz raised her hand next and motioned toward a bright-orange painted band around a healthy pine tree.

Jacob approached the tree, pointing at the stripe. "This is probably a tree they'll be cutting down for the strip mine."

They continued their journey, and even in the darkness, the bright-orange color broke through time and time again. As far as they could see, every tree was marked for death. Obviously, an enormous amount of land would be consumed by this project.

The forest was dead quiet. Out of nowhere, echoing through the trees, they heard Ethan's name being called out in a raspy whisper.

Eyeballs went wide as the friends froze in their tracks.

Ethan whispered, "Stay together."

Bokkens were drawn. They stood together, prepared.

"Ethan!" echoed again, bouncing between the trees.

They looked feverishly around the darkness for the source, but it was impossible to detect the voice's location.

The next time, his name was no longer whispered, but rather delivered in a crescendoing battle cry. "ETHAN!"

A cloaked man on a horse—apparently the same man from the other night—hammered between the trees and directly toward them.

The massive steed encroached on them at great speed. The hooded man blasted directly into their position, leaving them scattered across the ground.

Twenty yards past, he slowed and made a turn to come back at them.

Liz stood next to Ethan but could not find her stick. Jacob had jumped in the opposite direction and was separated from his friends as he tumbled down a small hillside.

The horse reared back and charged at Ethan and Liz. As the hooded man approached, he leaned off to the side and grabbed Ethan under his arm and around the neck.

Ethan swung his stick in defense of the attack, which did nothing more than bounce off the toned, flexing chest of the horse. The bokken dropped from his grip. In a headlock, he dangled from the cloaked invader's arm and was carried away, deep into the forest. He could hear Liz and Jacob shouting, but their voices grew fainter with each beat of the horse's hooves. There had been no time for them to do anything more; Ethan knew this. He just hoped they were able to follow. He had never been tortured before, and he did not want it to begin today.

After a few painful minutes, the horseman dropped Ethan onto a rocky area near the edge of a stream. He quickly dismounted and moved toward Ethan with haste.

Ethan shuffled backward on his butt until his retreat was blocked by a large stone. He was exposed, vulnerable, and unprepared.

"I am here to end your life, young man, but I will not murder a defenseless child." The hooded man pulled a pair of short swords from his belt and tossed one at Ethan's feet.

When the man tauntingly lunged at him, Ethan quickly grabbed the weapon and sprung to his feet.

The hooded man made several light advances, and Ethan was pleased that he was able to defend against them.

"You have learned a few things, young man. It is a pity you will learn no more." The force of the man's swings became more violent, more powerful, and more unpredictable.

Ethan knew he was outmatched. He could barely bring his weapon forward to defend against the onslaught of ferocious thrusts.

The man made a spinning advance, which hooked the cross-guard of Ethan's sword, throwing it into the nearby stream. He followed up with a backhand, crushing the side of Ethan's face, nearly knocking him unconscious. The hooded man then towered over the boy. "Goodnight, young man, and goodnight to the Three Hares forever."

He raised the short sword, preparing for a finishing plunge.

Ethan knew his life was over. *Better than torture.*

At that moment, a blurred figure blasted into the hooded man's ribs, knocking him ten feet into the stream.

Ethan was unable to focus as a splashing struggle at the stream's edge ensued. Once he regained his will, he propped himself up from the ground. His vision sharpened, and he could see his rescuer was Arthur Russell, the Protector. Ethan wondered if he always followed them when they went on their missions.

The assassin and Arthur squared off, encircling each other as Arthur said, "Oh, I have been waiting to meet you again, old foe."

"I did not come for *you* tonight, but I will certainly take your life with pleasure."

Both men were armed with only bare knuckles. They wrestled each other at the water's edge, striking with fists when possible. Each of them had the upper hand from time to time. In the art of pugilism, they were both masters.

Ethan knew, if he could regain his stability, he could assist Arthur. His first attempt to stand left his head spinning, and he tumbled back to the ground.

Arthur reached for his bokken, which had been knocked free during his initial attack. To Ethan's surprise, he paused just long enough for the assassin to grab his short sword. *A code of honor perhaps?*

Their battle continued, sword to bokken, and with amazing ability, Arthur was able to wield the warm, natural feel of wood against the cold, forged steel.

Their movements were both eloquent and ferocious, delicate and powerful. Bounding from rock to rock for better footing, searching for enhanced positioning, each man was poised and prepared to bleed the life from the other.

At that moment, the assassin was able to destabilize the rock Arthur was positioned on. Inch by inch, move by move, he began to overcome Arthur. One strategic act after another, and then, at one inspired moment, it happened.

With one fluid motion, the assassin unarmed Arthur and slid the short sword with perfect precision directly into Arthur's chest.

Piercing the center of his heart.

It seemed like the world had frozen in that fatal moment. If not for the babble of the stream, Ethan would have believed it. He sat there, screaming inside his head, watching as the assassin laid Arthur across a large stone and retracted the sword from the Protector's limp body.

The assassin took to one knee next to Arthur. He placed his hand across the fatal wound on his chest.

Ethan's rage grew within him, and his adrenalin drove him to his feet. He regained his strength and courage . . . and charged the predator of the night. It was an act of bloodthirsty revenge for the murder of his protector, his mentor, his friend.

Upon collision, the cloaked villain effortlessly stood in a twisting motion, throwing Ethan well beyond his position.

As Ethan lay in the dirt in burning pain, he looked upon his nemesis.

The assassin spoke. "I came here tonight to kill you, young man. Your death would have been the end of the Three Hares—and the most significant event in our history. Your death would have been remembered and retold for years to come."

He looked back at the limp body sprawled across the rock. "But tonight a great warrior has fallen, and his story should dominate this moment in time; he should be remembered for his bravery, his ferocity, and his honor. His memory should not be linked to a failure to protect you and certainly not be minimized to a footnote of your falling. For this, you shall go now . . . but prepare. For I shall have your death soon."

The cloaked assassin turned his back to Ethan, mounted his steed, and rode off into the darkness, just as he had come.

Liz's voice rang out. "Ethan!"

"Ethan, where are you?" Jacob shouted.

Ethan attempted to respond, but his chest burned and only a muffled, painful breath was released. He reached to his side and swung a stick against a tree, making a loud cracking noise as he grimaced in pain.

His friends soon found him as he lay there next to the babbling stream.

He pointed to the body of Arthur, awkwardly splayed over the rock, cooling in the night air. His blood stained the ground black under the moonlight, an occasional trickle dropping into the water.

"Oh no," Jacob said.

Liz repeated the refrain. "Oh no. Oh no. Oh no." Finally, she burst into tears as she ran to Ethan's side, grabbing his hand. "Are you okay?"

Jacob looked back and forth between Ethan and Arthur, obviously in shock. He knelt beside Ethan, opposite Liz, and gazed off at the distant moon. "We need to get him back to the Rabbit Hole right away," he said to Liz.

She looked back at Arthur, tears staining her face. "What about him?"

"Bringing him back tonight, or tomorrow, won't change anything for him. Slowing our return by taking Arthur, too, may have terrible consequences I don't even want to think about. Or instigate."

Liz sniffled, nodding. She suggested building a simple sled from sticks, in order to pull Ethan back to the cave. He was in no condition to walk.

Together they built a sled, heaved Ethan onto it, and began to trudge their way back to their bikes, where they would attach the sled to Jacob's bike, leaving Ethan's to be retrieved at another time.

It was a long trip home for everyone, but particularly so for Ethan. He was in bad shape with a wound on his head, a pain in his heart, and boiling with rage.

Chapter Seventeen

# Above the Crowns

H ope. That was what Arthur had stood for. Yesterday's events dominated the thoughts of the members of the Three Hares. The legend of Arthur Russell was cast, and a memorial of his life's dedication to the cause of hope was planned for late afternoon. Samuel would lead the service.

Just days ago, the Three Hares had welcomed three new members. Soon, on the very same sparring ring, a warrior's life would be remembered. So much had changed so quickly.

Jacob and Liz were exhausted, physically and mentally, and quickly fell asleep in their bunks at the Rabbit Hole. Ethan, on the other hand, felt no exhaustion—only surging energy. His wounds hurt, yes, but they were silenced by a renewed inspiration, drive, obsessions even. The pain made him sharp and focused. He had lain awake, remembering every detail, every motion, and every drop of blood. He could still smell the air deep within the forest.

Sometime in the wee hours of the morning, he slipped out of the sleeping chambers and ascended to the sparring ring. The great hall was dark, and the only light was from the flame of a candle he'd brought with him. He placed it on the ground at the edge of the ring.

His hands grasped the warm, smooth wood of his bokken, each grain familiar, and his senses heightened.

At first, he slowly moved through the different positions. His mind was pained about his inability to fight back and disrupt the assassin. He had been inadequate and weak.

He closed his eyes, remembering Arthur's instructions, his explanations about maximal power at the point of impact. He began sparring with his phantom Protector. With precision, he placed the tip of his stick at the exact moment the Protector shouted, "Now!" He could almost see the green chalk burst into dust at each strike. Young man and phantom danced through the ring together for hours.

He didn't notice his friends at the edge of the sparring ring until Jacob said, "Ethan."

"Huh? Yeah?" he responded through heavy breaths as he was abruptly shaken back to reality.

Liz grabbed her bokken and entered the ring in her "ready" stance.

Ethan looked her in the eye, gave her a slight grimace, and tapped his stick on the ground, inviting her into his sparring practice.

At first they didn't speak—moving from one combination to another, connecting in a nonverbal way.

After several minutes, she cautiously asked, "Are you okay?"

He slammed his bokken into hers, nearly knocking it from her hands. "Liz." He clenched his jaw. "I'll talk when I wanna talk. Right now, I want to hit something."

She offered him a spinning combination move, and he defended it with a loud, cracking noise as the sticks clashed. "Okay, then. First we spar, and then we talk." She adjusted her grasp on the bokken.

He returned with an aggressive move and, again, nearly whacked her stick from her hands. "Fine," he growled.

Jacob stood at the edge of the ring. "Come on, guys. Let's cool it for now. It's time for breakfast."

Liz looked at Ethan, who nodded. He suddenly realized he was starving.

The meal was a quiet one, everyone withdrawn in their own thoughts.

Slurping through his cereal, Jacob broke the silence. "So, tonight will be sad, huh? I don't know if I'm really ready for it."

Pushing her bowl away from her, Liz said, "It's not about *you* being ready."

"I know, but I can't believe this happened. I dreamt all night the craziest things. I was dreaming that he was going to come back tonight. Then I was dreaming that I saved him. And then I was dreaming the assassin showed up here tonight for the ceremony."

Ethan remained silent. He stood up from the table, put his dishes on the counter, and headed back to the sparring ring.

*  *  *

Samuel had been watching from a distance, allowing the boy to grieve for his protector and friend through the bokken exercises. He understood the passion in his movements. Samuel was preparing his speech for tonight's memorial—a speech which ripped his own heart in two.

There was commotion at the front door, and Samuel startled, swinging his head in that direction, feeling edgy. He released a heavy breath when he realized it was some of the members who had gone to retrieve Arthur's body. They held him reverently, the body wrapped in a heavy white blanket. A simple wooden casket with the Three Hares symbol burned into the top awaited. His body would now be cleaned and prepared for his permanent slumber.

*  *  *

Ethan and Jim stood together as the ceremony began. All members of the Three Hares gathered around the training ring as Samuel placed his hand upon the casket. A single torch burned just beyond his shoulder as he shared stories of the great warrior.

"This morning, I saw a young man battling his demons within this very ring, in grief over our fallen hero. What I saw was not the young man who had joined us only days before." He bowed his head in Ethan's direction. "What I saw was Arthur when he was a young man. I realized that *this* was Arthur's legacy. His final act was nothing more, nothing less, than passing the torch to the next generation of Warrior Hares."

Ethan was looking around the room, feeling uncomfortable. Not only was he the cause of Arthur's death, but now he was taking the spotlight away from Arthur at his funeral. He could not have felt more strongly that he was a fraud.

"Arthur was a modest man, and I never once heard him tell of his most heroic night. If I had not witnessed it myself, perhaps it would have simply slipped through the pages of history, forever lost.

"We were at war with Red Fox on many fronts that year. In this one particular case, they were converting the local orphanage into a textile factory. The orphans were literally being dragged into the streets to fend for themselves. Arthur, orphaned as a child himself, showed up at the front door, alone, with his bokken." Samuel turned and picked up Arthur's worn, yet beautifully crafted bokken, which had been leaning against the casket. He ran his fingers down the grain of the wood. "*This* bokken," he added.

"I followed him that night, to ensure his safety, although I ended up being the one who needed protection. The Red Fox guards started coming at him, one after another. They were no match for Arthur's speed and power. He sliced through our enemy, slowly moving deeper into the orphanage. As I followed him, quickening my pace to be of assistance, I was overcome by three guards. Arthur had to lose his position in order to double back and rescue me. After only a few moments, together, we had regained control of the room."

Samuel swung Arthur's stick through a few positions.

"At that moment, a dark figure appeared in a hooded cloak."

Ethan, Jacob, and Liz looked at each other with surprised expressions.

"Arthur, still quite young, went toe to toe with the Red Fox's elite assassin. He waved me back so he could fight, as he always said, 'with honor.' The two of them danced through the night in a way that I could never accurately describe. Nor shake from my vivid memory.

"Arthur methodically broke down the fiercest enemy, one move after another, until the elite assassin took cover and escaped from a window into the shadows of the night."

The members began to mumble among each other in awe—Arthur had faced the legendary Red Fox assassin and won.

"I have known Arthur for many years, but because of that fateful night, I felt I knew him in a way that no one else had. For this reason, against much controversy, I assigned him to be the Protector of Ethan Drake." Samuel looked at Ethan. "An assignment which Arthur carried throughout his remaining years with the pride of a father."

Ethan was speechless. The entire room looked in his direction.

Samuel concluded the ceremony by handing Arthur's battle-tested bokken to Ethan. The torch had been passed.

*** 

Down the stairs and in a back room, Ethan sat alone, looking at Arthur's bokken. He ran his fingers down the grain, felt the repaired nicks and divots it had endured in its many years of service. *I am not worthy to be this weapon's rightful owner.* Ethan could not get past the guilt, the grief.

Liz joined Ethan in the small, candle-lit room. As they had agreed that morning in the ring, it was time for Ethan to vent. Too much had happened, and nobody should carry that burden alone.

They spoke for hours of Ethan's insecurities and fears of being the future leader. He explained how his father had drifted further from his thoughts, and his new life had nearly overtaken his old.

His emotions coursed through his veins and ultimately broke him into a slimy mess of snot and tears, buried in Liz's embrace. *A man doesn't cry*, he thought. But he trusted her with this secret.

He had to admit: he may not have made it through the night without Liz's quiet counsel. She stayed by his side and ensured the conversations stayed light, cracking the occasional joke to break down any awkward moments.

That night, Ethan had shared a very significant piece of himself with Liz—the *real* Ethan. He was expected to be the great leader of the Three Hares, but he knew better than anyone else, that he was also just a boy.

*** 

The next day, Ethan was back in the sparring ring—with his own bokken. Arthur's bokken was simply too sacred, and besides, Ethan still did not feel deserving of ownership.

Sometimes he practiced with his friends, and when they tired, he would train by himself. He spent most of the day slicing the still air, building increasingly complex, compound moves.

Practicing with the bokken had turned from training to obsession. The only time he left the Rabbit Hole was to tell his mom that he was going camping with Jacob. Jacob used the camping excuse with his own parents. Liz . . . well, she didn't seem too concerned. Ethan hoped she wouldn't get into trouble, and he still didn't understand her family dynamics. Maybe one day she would open up. For now, he had more important things to worry about.

The following days continued in this same cycle, battling phantoms or any willing partner of flesh. It didn't really matter much.

He must train.

* * *

Both Liz and Jacob had become concerned for Ethan's well-being and mental state.

One afternoon, they joined Samuel at the long table. Jacob, not really knowing how to start, just blurted out, "This can't be healthy." He nodded back to the ring, where Ethan was practicing.

Samuel placed his book on the table and looked at the two young members. "Healthy? Well, I am not sure that is really what's happening here. What I mean is that Ethan is evolving. He's going through a transformation into the person he will become. For most people, this takes years, but for your friend, he is in a position where it must take place in a very short period of time."

"Yeah, but he's driving himself crazy. He's not talking to anyone. He rarely goes outside in the fresh air anymore. He loves the fresh air," Liz said, pouting.

"Well, he's certainly driving *you guys* crazy." Samuel chuckled. "I know you both love him dearly, which is why we are having this conversation. But what is 'healthy' for him is to channel his emotions into something constructive and empowering. He is doing this very well. Now, I do agree, he should get outside more. Fresh air would certainly help him become more aligned with nature, and I have been considering something over the past couple days. I have a safe place for him to continue his training, but I warn you: you must not follow him. He will return when he is ready, and not before. Do you understand and promise to give him the time he needs?"

Liz shifted uneasily in her chair. "How long will he be gone?"

"Perhaps days or maybe a few weeks. It all depends on him."

They unhappily agreed with Samuel and promised to give Ethan the space he needed.

Shortly after two in the morning, Samuel slipped into the sleeping chambers and found Ethan lying awake with Arthur's bokken in hand.

Samuel placed a finger across his own lips. "Shhh, follow me," he whispered.

Ethan climbed out of bed, and they quietly exited the room. They proceeded down the hallway to the last door, which was the storage room. Inside the small room, Samuel pressed hard upon a stone block. From behind a storage shelf, the wall slid open, revealing a passageway. He lit a candle with the torch on the wall, and they entered the dark tunnel—damp with a low, arched ceiling and narrow walls.

They continued through the tunnel for quite some time, until it abruptly ended in front of some stone stairs. Samuel said, "Up here."

The steep staircase was as dark as the tunnel had been. Finally, they reached a room with a cot and a small fireplace, a fire already crackling within. At the back of the room was a door with a small window. "Through here," Samuel said, and they headed out the door, and under the stars.

As Ethan stepped out, he realized where he was, but he asked anyway. "Is this at the top of the cliffs?"

"Yes, from here, you can see the lights of the town, way off in the distance." Samuel pointed out over the crowns of the trees across the vast forest.

Ethan noticed that the ground before him was marked like the ring in the cave. "A sparring ring?"

"It is."

A smile crept across Ethan's face, lit by the nearly full moon. As his eyes adjusted, he could see he was surrounded by various sparring targets and dummies. "This is beautiful."

"It is."

"Is this where Arthur trained?"

"Actually, no. This training location has been reserved only for the descendants of Edgar Zephaniah Drake," Samuel said. "I had the food stocks restored and some of your things brought up, including your bokken. You're welcome to stay as long as you need. Of course, you may come down whenever you wish and return here afterward. I suspect, however, that what you need most is time alone to reflect and focus. There is a rope in your room, which leads down to the kitchen. If you wish to have more food, you may pull the rope, and someone will bring you food and leave it outside your door."

"Wow, Samuel, this is really amazing."

"It is all yours, young man. Arthur would be honored if you gave his bokken a test drive up here."

"This is exactly what I need. Jacob and Liz . . . well, I know they just care so much, and I really am grateful for that, but I don't think they understand what I'm going through right now."

"I know, Ethan, but in the end, only you could possibly ever know what you are going through." Samuel placed his hands upon Ethan's shoulders and squeezed; then he turned to make his way back to the Rabbit Hole.

Ethan stood on top of the cliff in the night's still air, illuminated by the moon. Alone.

## Chapter Eighteen

# Reflection

Illuminating the cabin, the sun's rays broke the horizon, shining directly through the door upon Ethan's face. Birds were chirping, the air was fresh, and Ethan's achy bones seemed somehow insignificant. It was peaceful, with no expectation of visitors. He anticipated absolutely nothing.

Ethan swung his legs over the edge of the cot and began poking around the secluded cabin, now that there was ample light. The fireplace was actually carved into the natural stone wall and included a removable cooking grate. Above it was an intricately carved hare sitting upon his haunches, alone and alert. *The last hare*, he thought. The cot itself was a simple wood construction: a thin mattress across wooden planks.

Next to the bed was a small desk with some writing materials, and a single chair. Near the door leading back down to the Rabbit Hole was a small pantry, which held a variety of food and some dishes. A small sink without a mirror completed the luxuries of this mountaintop cabin with a view.

Ethan opened the creaking wooden door and walked outside. In all directions, he could see nothing but trees stretching across the earth until they curved away. The morning air was cool, and a low fog hung over the trees, creating a gentle, thin blanket. He grabbed his bokken and let it rest over his shoulder as he walked around the mountaintop, as if he were on patrol of his outpost.

"Squawk," yelped a large crow perched in a partially dead tree at the end of the terrace. Ethan looked at it with curiosity; the crow looked back at him in much the same way. He smiled at his uninvited guest and gave him a hearty "Good morning, feathered friend," before proceeding on his tour.

Several practice dummies were made from straw with red target markings, and others were solid wood dummies. They had obviously been battered in training over the years. He had not thought to ask when this place had first been built. Ethan paused a moment, placing his hand upon the worn wood, considering which of his ancestors had stood in this very spot, in isolation, blasting their emotions upon this defenseless chunk of wood.

The sun was warm and gentle upon his face. He felt a peacefulness, something he hadn't felt in a long time. He walked the perimeter of the stone platform, admiring all the training equipment. A few trees grew from the edges of the training area, providing a partial canopy. The low branches had been trimmed away so as not to obscure the view.

From the side of the deck, a small trail wrapped around the cabin. The front of the cabin was made from wood, and the back half was carved directly into the stone mountaintop. He walked along the narrow trail, which gradually climbed up and over the back of the cabin, directly onto its summit. A large tree grew there at the top, and a rope ladder hung from a branch. Ethan was normally not afraid of heights, but he felt uneasy with how quickly the mountain's edge dropped away.

He put his concerns aside, leaned his bokken against the tree trunk, and climbed the rope ladder into the tree. At the top of the crown was a small wooden platform. Upon it was a bench, from which he felt like he could see the entire world. Forest, rivers, and distant mountains. Farmlands and villages. A full 360-degree wonderland. Ethan's breath literally escaped him. It was spectacular.

As the sun rose, the morning warmed and the fog burned away, Ethan remained sitting on the bench up on top of the world. At first, his thoughts were entirely about the view, recognizing features from past adventures and admiring the lush beauty around him. Then other thoughts began to creep in.

Just yesterday he had been ashamed that his emotions about Arthur outweighed those of his father, but this morning, it was his father who first came to mind. Memories of his childhood with his father—camping in the forest, fishing in their old canoe—spilled through his mind. A time when this was *their* wilderness.

His view of the world from the top of that lonesome tree faded away as he receded into his internal thoughts.

Ethan's carefree memories were now battling with the new information he had about his father. The man had rejected the leading role of the Three Hares, so that he would not put his family at risk. But in doing so, the enemy had grown in his absence, while the Three Hares had atrophied and begun to wither away. What was Ethan to think of his dad? A coward? A hero? It was all a matter of perspective.

Ethan spent nearly the entire morning contemplating his father and his father's choices. It came down to a simple answer, which allowed him to move on and accept his father for who he was. He decided that it was simply complicated. Life was complicated. His father had made complicated decisions regarding complicated situations. They were neither right nor wrong, and his dad was nothing more or less than human.

"We can't find Ethan!" Jacob said as he and Liz ran into the library, where Samuel was reading a book. "Have you seen him?"

The old man placed his book on the end table, then motioned for them to grab a seat.

Liz, sitting on the edge of the chair, asked, "Did you take him to that place you mentioned?"

"Last night, Ethan and I took a journey, and he is now quietly finding himself."

Liz sighed in partial relief—she was happy he was safe, but wished he had said goodbye first.

Jacob's lips were drawn into a tight line as he looked at the floor. She guessed he was feeling the same way.

"I know you two care about him very much, but it's time you forget about him until his return. You will only drive each other mad thinking about him day and night. Besides, we have no idea how long he will take to complete his transformation."

Jacob shook his head in frustration. "Let's go, Liz. At least we can go get his bike, and besides, I gotta check in at home to let our parents know that we will be out for our long 'survival' trip."

After some oatmeal and juice, Ethan was anxious to get to the ring.

His first "victim" was one of the wooden practice dummies. He stood in a striking position and then made one or two swinging movements before proceeding to the next.

And so began the transformation.

As the day proceeded, Ethan became more and more intense in his training. He felt as if Arthur were there with him, guiding him through the various positions.

Cracking the wood structures as his ancestors once had done, he visualized his ancestors dancing through the training platform, smashing the obstacles. He was not alone. He was surrounded by greatness.

He worked his body and his mind until both were exhausted and the day was turning toward night. After some nourishment, he climbed back to the top of the tree and watched the setting sun. His muscles ached, and his hands were raw from the bokken. But he felt stronger and more confident than he ever had.

As the sun slipped behind the earth's veil, he climbed back down the ladder in the light of dusk and headed back to the cabin to enjoy the crackling fire in the fireplace. He noticed a stack of books under his bed and flipped through his choices. He settled on a book about martial arts, which he read late into the evening.

The next morning, he found an old, handmade book tucked behind the desk. The binding was leather, and inside were many pages of handwritten notes and some fantastic sketches. He sat at the desk and flipped through the pages. He was surprised to discover that the book had been written by those sitting in the very same location.

It dated back to the late 1600s and had been added to through the centuries. Now he knew this place had been around since the very beginning of the Three Hares. This book shared the concerns and insights of his ancestors while they, too, struggled to find themselves.

With the book in hand, he walked out onto the terrace, where his trusty old crow squawked at him. "Good morning, Berta," he said. It was the first name that came to his mind.

He took the book up to the heights of the tree and started a routine with morning contemplation and reading the words of his ancestors. Afterward, the training sessions would begin again.

He brought the martial-arts book out and attempted to replicate some of the moves he found within it. Throughout the day, he experimented with hybrid combination moves. His evening was much the same as the last, watching the sunset and then relaxing by the fire with a book. That evening, he'd found a book about meditation.

He quickly settled into a routine, and spent a vast amount of time thinking about the Three Hares, Red Fox, Liz, Jacob, and Samuel. His responsibility was slowly taking form; the actions he needed to take were sharpening in his mind.

Each morning, he was greeted by Berta on that same half-dead tree. Each night, he educated himself and then applied that knowledge the following day. By the third night, his hands were bloody from the bokken, as the wood had worn his skin raw. It was painful, but the pain across his palms only reminded him that he was alive and that the weapon within his hands was a means to an end.

With the blood from his palms, he would rub the bokken from top to bottom. The wood eventually darkened with a red tint. Each night, his wounds would scab over, and each day he would break them down again.

Over the ensuing days, he finished reading the words of his ancestors and began writing his own.

Ethan's routine continued for twelve days and twelve nights. He was centered, clear minded, and knew exactly what must be done. At the end of those twelve nights, Ethan had matured the equivalent of twelve years. He was fit, agile, and a force he previously would not have recognized.

He had been reborn . . . as a warrior.

On that thirteenth day, the sun came up as it had on all other days. But today, Berta was not sitting upon the half-dead tree. He had hoped to say goodbye to his feathered pal, but it was not to be.

He grabbed his now dark-red, worn bokken and descended the stone stairs back to the Rabbit Hole. His hair was dirty and gnarled; he smelled salty from his sweat.

Liz and Jacob were on the couches, and Samuel was in the library. As he ascended the steps into the Great Hall, it was Liz who saw him first. She hesitated, perhaps thinking he was an intruder, but then she shot to her feet and ran toward him.

"Ethan!"

Jacob's head snapped up at hearing his friend's name. In no time, he was on Liz's heels, heading toward his best friend.

Liz nearly knocked him over as she gave him a huge hug, hardly slowing before the impact. Jacob pushed his way in and gave the best man-hug he could muster, firmly patting his buddy on the shoulders.

Though Ethan's heart was warm from the welcome, he maintained a stoic disposition. There were things they had to do—and no time to waste.

His tone void of emotion, he said, "We must build."

Liz and Jacob stepped back, wary of the strange greeting from their friend. They looked at each other with raised eyebrows, and then slowly turned to face their friend again.

"Right, okay," Liz said. "So, where have you been? Samuel told us you were training by yourself in a secluded place."

"I've been training, and learning, and growing," Ethan said as some of the warmth came back into his voice. He felt rusty in his people skills.

Jacob jumped in. "We missed you, dude. It hasn't been the same without you."

"I missed you guys, too, but it was important to have that time alone."

Liz did a mocking swipe of her forehead. "Shew. Now you sound more like yourself."

"Come on." Jacob nodded toward the couches. "Sit. We want to hear everything."

Ethan told them about his training environment and his routine. Samuel watched from the library, catching Ethan's eye. They nodded to one another in silent understanding.

Jacob pointed to Ethan's bokken. "What happened to your stick? That looks awesome."

A smile glided across Ethan's face. "We spent many hours together." He showed his friends the palms of his hands.

Liz gasped. "Oh no, what did you do to yourself?"

Before Ethan could answer, Samuel joined them. He patted Ethan on the back and said to Liz, "He has merged his mental self, his physical self, and his environment into one."

Ethan stood up and embraced Samuel. "That was unbelievable. I can't explain it, but I am so . . . so . . . clear now."

"Some things cannot be explained, only experienced."

Samuel joined them in the circle of couches as Ethan described the sunsets, mists covering the forest at dawn, and the birds chirping in the morning. He was gushing with experiences he wished his friends could have witnessed. He never mentioned his feathered friend Berta—that was a memory just for him, not to be shared.

Ethan turned to Samuel. "There is something I wish to say to the Three Hares."

"I am sure you do. I will organize a gathering."

"There is a place within the group of hills outside the cave—a small clearing. Can you have everyone join us at sunrise tomorrow morning? Tell them I have something to share."

"Gladly," Samuel said, clasping his hands together.

* * *

The following morning, as Samuel had promised, the entire membership of the Three Hares had gathered between the hills just outside the Rabbit Hole. Samuel offered no introduction and simply stood to the side, nodding at Ethan for him to take the lead.

Ethan jumped up on a large log lying across the front of the clearing, as if it were a stage. He had never stood in front of such an audience before and had certainly not given a speech outside of the occasional classroom presentation. The audience was quiet, still, and attentive. His heart rate increased.

"Good morn . . . Good morning, Hares," he began, already stumbling on his words. "Thank you for joining me on such short notice. I feel I owe you an explanation."

Without waiting for responses, he continued. "As you know, my family can be traced back to the beginning of the Three Hares. For nearly three hundred fifty years, through thick and thin, alongside fellow members, they have proudly and honorably fought against evil. Some of your families have been loyal members for many generations." Ethan nodded in the direction of a few people he now knew had such histories—he'd read about them in the mountaintop journal.

"Although I'm new to the Three Hares, I do have this bloodline, which has great significance within this honorable circle. My first weeks of joining you were confusing and intimidating. How could I possibly be important amongst so many wise and dedicated members? My blood felt no different than the next person.

"Fourteen days ago, our wise Elder, Samuel Tinner, suggested I head above the tree crowns to 'find myself,' which I have done."

Ethan lowered his head, paused for a moment, and then regained his view of the audience. "It is not me, Ethan Drake, a young boy with few experiences, who is capable of leading the Three Hares; it is the Legend running through my veins and the shoes which I still must fill that you seek. In two weeks of solitude, I have acknowledged this fact and, furthermore, am willing to accept this challenge."

Ethan looked around the group illuminated in the morning sun. "If you wish for me to attempt to fill these shoes, I will honorably stand here now and dedicate my life to the cause, to leading the resurgence of the Three Hares."

Samuel began to clap, and the crowd quickly joined in.

With a humble smile, overwhelmed by the unanimous support, he continued, "After only two weeks, as to be expected, everything is more or less the same here. But now... now I see things in a new light, through new eyes. It is time for change. We will begin to strategically recruit new members and build the Three Hares back up to the days of its former glory. We will actively train, organize, and take Winslow Falls back from the wicked."

More applause filled the forest.

"Samuel Tinner will by my official Wise Man, sharing input and feedback upon each and every decision. I also will appoint," he looked at Liz and Jacob, "Elizabeth Walker and Jacob Carter as my generals, as well as strategists."

Whispers now within the crowd.

"Perhaps their inexperience is of concern to you, but it has dawned on me that our future is what we are protecting, not our past. It is the youth of today who shall guide our direction forward. I assure you, with everyone's support, we will take this town back from the crooked leaders of today and place it in the hands of our bright and vibrant future."

Ethan looked at Liz and Jacob, nodding for them to join him on the log. As they hesitantly climbed up and stood next to Ethan, the crowd began cheering for their new leadership.

The rest of the day was a celebration. The Rabbit Hole was buzzing with excitement and the potential of things to come. There was no doubt—the tinder box had been ignited.

## Chapter Nineteen

# Fresh Blood

The new leaders of the Three Hares took it upon themselves to slowly rebuild the organization. It was significant to Ethan that it was the youth of today who should finally have a say in their city's future.

Ethan strategized with Jacob and Liz about whom they would recruit. New members would have to be willing, clever, and above all else, passionate about a better future. Jacob offered his older brother, Mike, and possibly his girlfriend, too. Liz explained that her older sister was long gone, and she didn't know anyone else to suggest. They made a plan to meet later at the old oak tree. Ethan had a candidate in mind, but he needed to do some groundwork first.

\* \* \*

After they went their separate ways, Ethan continued along the town's outskirts, instead of going directly home.

Pulling up in front of a rundown farmhouse, he dropped his bike to the ground, approached the front screen door, and knocked.

"Get the door, Frank!" yelled a woman's voice from the back of the house.

The sound of boots against hardwood, and then a large, muscular young man came to the door. His shirt was covered in stains, and his jeans torn and grimy. "What the heck you doing here? I told you to never come around," he growled.

"I have a proposal for you and your brother. Get him, and meet me outside." Ethan stepped away from the door without waiting for a response.

"Travis, get out here," Frank barked as the filthy screen door squeaked open.

Ethan waited around the corner by the edge of the garage. When he saw them walk up, he had to force himself not to smirk.

They weren't just twins by birth; they were twins in their filth as well. Travis looked as scraggly as Frank, but just as strong.

Frank said, "You shouldn't be coming around here no more, man. Say what you have to say and get outta here." Travis nodded, still the quieter one.

"Listen, I know what happened last year was totally screwed, but I've learned something about my father's accident."

"We don't care nothing about him." Frank jabbed a fat finger in Ethan's direction. "*Our dad* was dragged through the *mud,* thanks to everything that happened. So, *you* can jump on your little bike and get lost."

Ethan was unfazed. "The car wreck was a frame job, and I know who did it."

Travis lurched forward. "You can spring him from jail?"

"Maybe, but only if we play our cards right."

Travis looked to his brother with hopeful eyes. Frank stood there with his arms crossed. "Why should we trust you? You're part of the reason they sent him away."

"I know, and I'm trying to fix that. Can you meet me by the old oak tree tomorrow at noon?"

Frank spat on the ground, just missing Ethan's sneakers. "We'll think about it."

"Okay, see you there." Ethan grabbed his bike and shouted over his shoulder, "Tomorrow. Noon. The old oak tree." Then he sped away on his bike, churning up some dirt clouds along the way.

The next morning, Ethan met up with Liz, Jacob, and Jacob's brother, Mike, who had brought his girlfriend along as well. "Great to see all of you," Ethan said. He high-fived Mike, whom he had known all his life, and then extended his hand to Mike's girlfriend. "I'm Ethan."

"I'm Ann. Great to meet you."

Mike clapped his hands together and said, "So, what's up?"

Ethan knew Mike was a huge proponent of "government by the people, for the people" and often participated in rallies against big government, particularly now that he was in college. He could only hope that Ann had a similar inspiration.

He glanced over his shoulder, hoping to see the twins coming up the trail. No sign of them. "Let's wait a few minutes before we get started. I'm hoping to have two more joining us."

After about ten minutes of small talk, there was still no sign of the twins. Ethan decided to not wait any longer. "So, the reason I've asked everyone to meet here today—"

Liz interrupted, "Is *that* what you were waiting for?" She pointed down the trail, where two oversized beasts were riding small bikes that strained under their weight.

Ethan snickered but tried to hide it behind his hand. "Nothing like first impressions," he mumbled.

"Is that the Baxter twins?" Jacob spat out. "Why did you invite *them*?"

"Yes, those are the twins, and there's one very good reason I invited them: they hate the mayor. We're gonna need them."

"The mayor? What's this all about?" Mike asked, straightening up on the bench.

Jacob put a hand on Mike's shoulder. "Bro, he'll explain in a minute."

The squeak of the bikes got louder as the Baxter twins approached. Finally, they made it to the tree, panting like dogs. Big dogs. "This better be good, Ethan," Frank said.

"Oh, it is." Ethan walked the group through the story of the mayor, the strip-mine project, and the predicted downfall of Winslow Falls. He explained how the propaganda machine had twisted the realities of the town and how the future would never be the same—unless someone stopped the wheels of the runaway train. "And I suggest that *we* are that 'someone.' We can make the difference. Who is with me?"

Mike smacked his thigh. "Heck yeah. What do you have in mind?"

Ethan grinned. "Glad you asked."

After preliminary ideas were discussed and commitments made, the group parted ways, though they were united in the idea of stopping the corruption and protecting the future—for themselves and their families. For *all* families of Winslow Falls.

Not a word of the Three Hares was mentioned, not yet.

✳ ✳ ✳

The Red Fox's elite assassin joined Ezra in his office at the palace. "You called for me, Ezra?"

"This is all unraveling, and for the first time, I am immensely disappointed in your work. Your 'honor' keeps getting in the way of our progress, and this boy is still running around encouraging the rebirth of the Three Hares."

"I'll take care of him, but finishing off Arthur Russell was a major accomplishment, he was—"

"AN OLD MAN!" Ezra barked. "You were in a position to end the Three Hares forever, and you chose to kill off some weak old man? Then you had the nerve to say that you had too much 'honor' to kill the boy as well!"

"Ezra, this was not some 'old man,' as you put it. He was training the boy and the others."

"If you kill the boy, then he has no one to train, you imbecile!"

The assassin slammed his hand down on the desk. "I'm not one of your goons, Ezra!" he snapped back. "If you think you and your lackeys can do this by yourselves, then do it."

Ezra let out a laugh. "Calm down. You always get so emotional about things."

The assassin exhaled loudly and started to leave the room.

Ezra softened his tone. "Fine. Kill the boy. There will be a handsome bonus in it for you."

The assassin paused at the doorframe and looked back toward Ezra, giving him an opening to continue.

"You will kill him in his sleep tomorrow night. I understand that he will be in his house. Finish this."

He shook his head. "You don't understand, Ezra. Will you *ever* understand? I won't kill him in his sleep, unarmed. He is just a boy. He will fight his way to the end, and *that* is final."

"I'm very disappointed. I shall send my 'goons' then. How hard can it be, really? Any fool can do this, and I'm starting to wonder why I even keep you around."

The assassin banged the wall next to the door and left the room without another word.

Ezra picked up the phone and dialed the mayor. After a few rings, he heard, "Ezra, what can I do for you?"

"I want to know when the bridge will be completed, and the site cleared for Teumessian Industries."

"Well, we've been making good progress. Buses will bring in the workers tomorrow, followed by a couple days of training, but we should be able to get the first steps going next week. I also have your logging company coming in over the next several days to start clearing the site."

"Excellent. Keep an eye out for those kids, in the meantime. They're still snooping around; I just know it. Although, that will be cleared up by tomorrow night."

The mayor paused, cleared his throat. "Right. No problem, Ezra. My guys are on high alert and keeping the communication flow tight."

The mayor and Ezra wrapped up their discussion as quickly as it began.

## Chapter Twenty

# Smear Campaign

Early morning, the team reassembled by the old oak tree. This time, the Baxter brothers were the first to arrive, as they were proud to share what new information they'd already uncovered.

Ethan nodded toward the twins. "Whatcha got for us?"

Frank and Travis jumped off the picnic table, radiating smiles on their faces. "We have . . . well, we got some great dirt," Frank said.

The unlikely speaker of the two, Travis, could hardly contain himself. He blurted out, "Okay, so the mayor claims he's from Springfield, but that's not true at all. He's from Vulpes Valley. What's funny is nobody cared about his unproven history." He held up a finger. "*But*, if they knew what happened in Vulpes Valley, no way would he have been elected!"

Liz swung her head around. "The suspense is killing me. What happened there?"

Frank looked over his shoulder, like he was making sure nobody could hear their conversation. "He had a partnership with a local black market ring, which sold stolen crap . . . paintings and stuff. He was actually caught by the Feds, but he disappeared before they could send him to the Big House. He changed his name, got a bad face lift and a terrible toupee, but it's gotta be the same guy."

Jacob shook his head in disbelief. "How do you know for sure it's the same guy?"

"Look." Travis held up an old newspaper clipping from the *Vulpes Valley Herald.* "Look at the sign in the background. It's the same construction company, Daquan Construction."

Frank continued, oozing with excitement, "And if you look really hard at his picture, it *has* to be the same guy. Look at his eyes. How he stands. It's that same stupid look."

The group huddled around the picture, inspecting all the details. "I think you're onto something here," Ethan said, admittedly feeling surprised at the twins' discovery. "Great job, guys. Has anyone else found anything?"

"Ann and I dug through all his speeches used during the campaign," Mike said. "He said a few things that sounded really fishy, so we did some fact- checking. Turns out, his opponent, the previous mayor, Steve Richardson, had been blamed for tons of stuff—all untrue—and the people believed every word of it."

Ethan nodded. "Yeah, my parents were really pissed during the debates about how the smearing campaign destroyed Mayor Richardson's chances. Do you have proof?"

"Yup," Ann said. Her smile looked almost devious. "At the debates, he said that, while Richardson was mayor, the total unemployment numbers increased by fifteen thousand people. That's not even possible. Here's some old data from the city. The only way that could've happened is if he counted all of the elderly, who were no longer able to work. Truth is, Richardson actually stabilized the unemployment rates."

The group continued to plow through additional findings that had been discovered in the last eighteen hours. It was astounding to Ethan how much more ground they had covered with just a few more eager people on the team. *We have chosen well*, Ethan thought, smiling.

"You know," he said, "I do believe we have enough proof to impeach the mayor."

They got down to business, gathering around the picnic table to delegate assignments. Ethan could feel the energy; he was proud to be a part of it.

"Our next step is to prepare posters—anonymous posters—and spread them all across the city, tonight," he said. "We gotta push the mayor on his heels before we release information about the strip mine and the homeless labor camp."

Liz pulled some blank paper and colored markers from her backpack. "We'll draft some designs and take them to a print shop to make thousands of copies."

"If we're gonna be anonymous . . . I mean, won't the print shop people know who we are?"

Mike held up a hand. "Ann and I got that covered. We'll print them ourselves at the college. It should only take a few hours, which leaves us plenty of time to post them all over town tonight."

Jacob snapped his fingers and winked. "Good idea. Alright, let's get started."

Ideas spilled across the blank pages. Bold lettering, vibrant colors, and place markers for photographs. After several hours, they went through the many options and selected the two most impactful posters, both of which held a current picture of the mayor beside the news clipping from the *Vulpes Valley Herald*. The first poster included in bright red text: *Our future is rotten. Throw out the trash.* The second poster had huge black lettering above the photos: *He does not represent us!* And below the images was: *He is not on OUR side.*

Time to roll.

Mayor Hofner and Ezra met at the construction site to inspect the progress. "Let's head over to the tents. I have something to show you," Maxwell said.

Ezra looked skeptical as always but followed him across the field to the edge of the forest. Two large tents had recently been constructed. Mumbling voices came from within the tents.

"Here they are," Maxwell said as he opened the first tent's door. Sitting inside was a ragged group of a few dozen homeless people. The tent was lined with old cots and tattered blankets.

"Bah, that stinks," said Ezra, backing away from the door and placing his arm over his mouth and nose. "Can't you get these guys showers?"

"Well, there's no city water here yet, and the tanks we have are needed for the bridge's substructure. If you want, we can bring in more tanks, but that's gonna cost more."

"Ah, leave it. They're working outdoors anyway. But I'm absolutely not going into any of the tents again."

"Right. The other tent over there is the mess hall, where we'll feed the crew. It'll double as a training room to give these guys the basic education on how to work with concrete, how to weld, and so on."

At that moment, one of the homeless men came out of the tent, lumbering right up to Ezra and grabbing his lapel. "Please, I don't belong here. I wanna go back to Ridgeview," he pleaded.

Ezra shoved him away and brushed at the invisible germs left behind by the homeless man's hand. "Back into the tent. If you want government support, you need to join the workers' program."

"But . . . that's what I'm trying to say. I don't belong here," he said as desperation tore across his face.

One of Ezra's guards approached the man from behind, grabbed him by the arm, and pulled him back into the tent.

Ezra said, "Let's get outta here. What was he talking about, anyway?"

The mayor chuckled as they walked to their cars. "Yeah, we were a little short on workers, so we 'escaped' a few from Ridgeview State hospital. Don't worry; we have their meds."

Ezra's disgusted look gave way to a huge smile. "Well, look at you, Maxwell. Very creative. Very good. Just keep your eye on things."

They shook hands and parted ways.

❋ ❋ ❋

With Ann in the passenger seat, Mike barreled down the road at the edge of the field, right up to the old oak tree. He stuck his hand out the window, giving a proud thumbs-up. "Mission accomplished," he said.

They quickly exited the car, Ann holding up copies of the posters. "There's more in the back seat," she said.

"This is really great." Ethan said, thoroughly impressed with the final product. "We'll wait until dark and then wallpaper the town."

"What'll we do till then?" Frank asked.

Ethan looked over at Liz and Jacob, and they all grinned.

"What *will* we do?" Ethan raised an eyebrow at Frank. "Well, now I have a surprise for all of you." He walked to the edge of the forest and rustled behind a bush. When he rose, he held a handful of the infamous "sticks"—not actually bokkens but darn close.

"I was thinking that it would be a good idea for all of us to have at least some basic defensive skills," he said, holding one stick in the air. "This is a bokken. I propose we use this time to familiarize ourselves with a few defensive moves. They could save your lives or the lives of those close to you."

"Bokken? What?" Frank's brow furrowed, and he looked to his brother, who shrugged.

Mike added, "Uh, you serious?"

Ethan nodded to Liz and Jacob. "Can you two demonstrate your skills to our new members?"

"Demonstrate . . . your *skills*? Jacob, you have no skills," Mike said. "Since when have you learned something interesting?"

"You don't know everything," Jacob said as he and Liz grabbed their own bokkens. He waggled his eyebrows. "Watch and learn. Ready, Miss Walker?"

"Ready."

Under the canopy of the oak tree, they took their positions and began to spar. They started simple, slowly adding complexities and combinations, until they looked like two swashbucklers battling on a pirate ship.

Ethan watched their audience. It was clear they were completely captivated and in awe. Just as he knew they would be.

Eventually, he held up his hand and said, "Thank you for that fine performance." He winked at his generals and then turned to the others. "Now, please pick a stick, make a circle around me, and stand with your feet positioned like mine."

The new recruits circled around him. The Baxter brothers started bashing each other with their sticks. Ethan allowed them to make fools of themselves until they stopped on their own when Travis got cracked in the knee by his brother, releasing a loud yelp. "Ouch!"

"May we proceed?" Ethan asked.

As Travis rolled on the ground, holding his knee, Frank said, "Yup."

Travis hobbled back to his feet, and the new recruits set their feet. Ethan walked them through the different defensive positions, as Arthur had shown him what seemed like a lifetime ago.

They all did a few moves, and then Frank broke the training focus with a question. "Why haven't we seen *you* swing your stick around? Don't you know how?" he teased Ethan.

Liz and Jacob started laughing out loud. "Shut it, Frank," Liz said. "Pay attention."

Until nightfall, the team played around with their training, told stories, and bonded before the big event. Ethan awed them with his prowess, emphasizing how essential it was that they bring their makeshift bokkens everywhere they went.

Mike said, "Huh. Learn something new every day." Then he punched Jacob hard in the arm. Jacob didn't flinch. He just grinned.

After agreeing on splitting into small teams for their poster rally, they broke off into the night.

Chapter Twenty-One

# Rabbit's Intuition

Recognizing the extraordinary dangers that lay ahead, the new day was only for Ethan, Liz, and Jacob. They named it "Operation Insurgence," and it was the greatest risk any of them had ever taken.

"This is our first target," Ethan said. His finger pressed down on the map of the forest, which was stretched out on the picnic table.

"That's where the homeless camp is, right?" Jacob asked.

"Exactly. We need photographs of the workers, but it's critical that we can see the bridge project in the background," Ethan said.

"I brought my dad's camera, as requested." Liz said, raising the camera in the air. "I learned how to use it during some of our nature hikes—not that we do that much anymore. Anyway, I should be able to get some good shots from a distance with this telephoto lens."

"Cool. So, you'll be positioned here." Ethan pointed at a spot at the edge of the tree line.

"Got it."

"Jacob, you'll run distraction, if needed, from here." He pointed at another spot on the map. "You'll sneak around to the other side of the river, downstream, and duck under the cliff's edge behind the bushes."

Jacob gave a mock salute. "Ready and able. I brought the bottle rockets and lighter."

Ethan grinned and continued. "I'll be the eyes. I'm going to be positioned here." His finger snapped down upon a small hill on the map. "From this position, I'll have a sweeping view behind you, Liz, to ensure no one can sneak up on you. I'll also have a clear view of you, Jacob, so I can signal the need for distraction. I'll cover our exit point so we don't find ourselves boxed in."

The team nodded, acknowledging their roles.

"Liz, any photos with the mayor in them would be excellent. But anyone, anyone at all, could be equally important. We may just not know it yet. Best to take the shots, even if you're not sure if they would matter. We only have one run at this; let's make it count." Ethan said.

Liz flipped her hair. "Of course."

Jacob bobbed his head up and down. "Let's do this."

The team grabbed their gear, mounted their bikes, and headed off to the camp. They were focused, and the ride was silent with the exception of the crunching gravel beneath their wheels. They'd strategized fallback locations, call signals, and rescue options in worst-case situations. Today would be intense, but they were prepared.

As they arrived at Checkpoint A, they wished each other luck. Jacob took off first, and then Ethan headed out. Liz stayed back for a few minutes until Ethan signaled that her destination was clear.

Ethan continued down the trail on foot, staying low to the bushes. He circled up around the bluff and struggled through a thick section of underbrush prior to reaching his viewing point. When he arrived at his lookout position, he lay down on the rocky edge, pulled out his binoculars, and scanned the area.

On his left, he could see Jacob stalking through the river's edge, fairly far away from any possible observers. On his right, he could see the tents, the forest's edge, and a decent view through the thin pines. Everything was clear. He looked back toward Liz, who was holding position, looking in his direction. Ethan brushed his hand across his chest, and Liz proceeded to her destination.

Liz had already proven herself to the boys that she was quite covert, but the risks were much higher today—broad daylight and lots of people. She proceeded with extreme caution to her position, where she signaled back to Ethan that she was ready.

Ethan confirm that Jacob had reached his destination and gave him the "hold position" signal. Then he gave Liz the order to proceed.

Liz pulled the camera from her bag and scanned the area through her telephoto lens for photo opportunities. Then she remembered Ethan's instructions—take as many as possible. She had plenty of film in her bag. She started clicking away.

The camp was crowded—people milling about, trucks pulling in and out, even some armed personnel at the opening to one of the tents. When the door to the one tent opened, Liz recognized the homeless folks as they poured out, looking small, tired, unfulfilled. Her blood boiled at the sight. She clicked and clicked as the workers were led to the other tent, which she assumed was like a mess hall. *At least they're getting fed.*

Liz took pictures of the guards and the construction site in the background. In some shots, she was able to get the *Daquan Construction* sign in frame as a few homeless people walked in front of it.

She also kept her eye on Ethan as he periodically gave "all clear" signals to her and Jacob, letting them know there was no sign of danger just yet.

A short while later, Ethan flagged Liz, alerting her to the approach of the mayor's limo. She raised the camera to her eyes again. *Click, click, click.*

The mayor was noticeably furious, most likely regarding the posters that had been plastered all over town in the middle of the night. He was yelling at everyone, his arms flying everywhere with his hissy fit. Liz giggled. This was golden stuff. *Click, click, click.*

During one monumental moment, a homeless man came up to him to ask for something. The mayor shoved him to the ground and kicked him two or three times in the ribs. *Click!*

"That should do it," Liz said, pleased with what she had captured on film.

She gave the signal to Ethan that she was good to go.

\* \* \*

Ethan looked toward Jacob to signal that they should now fall back. Instead of seeing Jacob, he saw an armed guard heading in that direction. Jacob was out of visual contact and unable to receive warning. Ethan desperately scanned the area for his friend and then checked on Liz's retreat route, which remained clear.

When he swung back to Jacob's area, Ethan breathed a sigh of relief—the guard had returned to the bridge project. Suddenly, Jacob's head popped up from some bushes, like a gopher. He gave Ethan a frazzled thumbs-up, and Ethan replied with the "fall back" signal.

They each made it back to the checkpoint unscathed. Liz glowed with enthusiasm, ready to share her photographic work with her fellow conspirators.

"That went really well," she said as she presented three rolls of film.

"Jacob almost got nabbed," Ethan said. Jacob nodded, breathing rapidly.

Liz quickly snapped her attention to Jacob. "Oh no! What happened?"

Jacob was amped up from the close call, "Some guard started coming much farther down the riverbank than I expected, so I buried my nose in the bushes."

"We got lucky this morning," Ethan said. "Everyone did a great job."

"Let's get outta here," Jacob said.

No one argued against the suggestion.

**\* \* \***

Later that afternoon, the mayor and Ezra met, yet again, at the bridge construction site. Maxwell was steaming; Ezra was forty-five minutes late. "Where have you been!" he barked at Ezra as he exited the car.

"First of all, if you ever address me in that tone of voice again, I will have your tongue, you feeble-minded puppet." Ezra's voice and expression were icy. Frightening, really.

Maxwell's anger shifted to shock, and he began to backpedal. He flailed his arms as he said, "Did you see all the posters around town?"

"That's the second thing, Maxwell. You're losing control. How in the world did they connect you to Vulpes Valley?"

"I've no idea. I've covered my tracks perfectly."

Ezra chuckled at that. "Well, no, actually, you did not. Anyway, I know it has something to do with those kids; the leader, Ethan Drake . . . well, he's going to be gone after tonight. And you know what I mean by 'gone.'" He slid his finger across his throat. The mayor blanched. "Meanwhile, I surely hope you are not already too far exposed. The minute I learned of the posters, I sent my people to remove them immediately. By now, the city should be clear of them."

"Ezra, they had the nerve to put one right on the front door of my office. The door was under guarded surveillance. You think they have an insider?"

The Red Fox leader scowled. "Maybe. All we can do now is stay alert. However, I've never seen anyone so inept as you at doing what should have been such a simple job.

You even hired people who were secretly against you! How could you have turned out to be such a fool?" Ezra turned his back on Maxwell and headed to his car.

Maxwell's hands trembled, as he called out, "So, what do I do now?"

Ezra climbed into his car, "Do your job as I've instructed, and I'll do mine . . . cleaning up your mess." The door slammed shut.

Ann returned from her college photography lab, where she developed Liz's film in secrecy. The team swarmed together to look through the pictures and share the war stories of "Operation Insurgence."

Now to plan their next steps.

Ethan stood in front of the team. "We've made excellent progress with gathering photographic evidence today, as you can see." He winked at Liz, then looked over at the twins and Mike. "How did 'Operation Broadcast' go?"

Frank cleared his throat and said, "We broke into the TV station early this morning and installed the transmitter."

"That's fantastic," Jacob said.

Mike tilted his head and pursed his lips. "Unfortunately, we couldn't test it. If we turn it on for a test run, it'll likely alert their techs. So, basically, when we officially send out the video clip, it'll be the first time we turn that thing on."

Liz added, "Well, we definitely don't want to ruin our chances of hitting all the local channels by testing it. Right, Ethan?"

"I agree," he said, holding his chin in his hand, thinking about the situation. He could see no way around it. They just had to believe it would work on first try.

"After doing a little research," Ann said, "I think tomorrow at eight in the evening will get the most viewers, which gives us all day tomorrow to prepare the final video."

Travis, clearly giddy with excitement, said, "We're gonna change this town. I can feel it. And help my dad."

Frank looked at his brother with pride in his eyes and tousled his hair. "You're absolutely right, brother." Then he looked at the rest of the group. "Hey, I walked through the city earlier today . . . you know, to admire our handiwork. All the posters we put up were already taken down."

Jacob waved him off. "Shoot. Are we really surprised? But you gotta know those posters made an impact. I'm sure once the mayor saw them, especially the one on the front door of his office building, he sent an army out to get rid of them."

Liz rolled her eyes. "At taxpayers' expense, I'm sure."

Ethan had to laugh, just thinking about the mayor's reaction. "To him, it must have seemed like a ghost had followed him from Vulpes Valley." He pumped his eyebrows at his dedicated team and added, "And there are more ghosts in the wings."

That night, Ethan woke abruptly from a strange and eerie dream—a fox was chasing him into the forest. After his heartbeat slowed some, he realized he shouldn't be so surprised that his mind had gone wild, given everything they were involved with. He lay back on his pillow and closed his eyes, trying to drift off to sleep again.

A tapping sound from outside his window thwarted that idea immediately.

Ethan scooted out of bed, stood to one side of the window, and slowly shifted the curtains so he could take a peek. He saw nothing out of the ordinary. The tapping had ceased by that point, and the calm night was intensely quiet. As he headed back to his bed, the tapping sound returned. He whipped around and back to the window. The tapping sound continued, and he was able to get a general feel for the direction from which it came. Over by the driveway. Still, he saw nothing, and the tapping stopped. He waited as his pulse increased.

Sure enough, the tapping sound returned. "Where the heck is that sound coming from?" He was tired, agitated, and . . . then he saw it. A small object on his mother's car. A cat? He rubbed his eyes. *A cat doesn't tap. I'm losing my mind.*

His eyes focused once again on the object. And his heart nearly flew into his throat.

It was a rabbit. Without a doubt, a rabbit! The animal was periodically thumping his hind leg on the hood of the car.

Sleepily, Ethan smiled and returned to his bed. *Just a rabbit. Nothing to worry about.*

As he started to wiggle under the covers, his brain slapped him, and he sat bolt upright. *A rabbit!*

At that moment, he could hear the floorboards squeaking outside his door.

Ethan grabbed his bokken, which had been leaning beside his bed, and ducked into a dark corner.

The doorknob on his bedroom door began to turn. Ever so slowly, his door inched open.

Ethan held his position, focusing on his breathing, and preparing a plan. Was it his mother? An intruder? Jacob perhaps? He dared not call out.

As the door widened, two figures came into the room, as silent as ghosts. Both men, Ethan guessed. They headed over to his bed and looked at one another in confusion. As one of them shifted his body, Ethan saw the dagger reflecting off the moonlight coming through the window. The mission of these men became clear to him. He was the target of an assassination.

Ethan slowly sucked in a breath and waited for the perfect moment—that moment about which Arthur had trained him endlessly. When the intruders turned their backs to him, apparently ready to exit the room, he surged from the shadows, his bokken in hand.

The first strike was clean across the knuckles of the dagger-wielding hand. It dropped to the floor in a loud clang, accompanied by a yelp from pain.

The second man quickly turned and charged at Ethan.

With all his might, Ethan swatted him to the side, directly into the wall.

The first man had recovered, and the second man was nearly there. The dagger was nowhere to be found, and for that Ethan was grateful. Now it was just a matter of controlling the movement, predicting . . . all those things. What were all those things? For a moment, he lost all confidence, his mind reeling, not remembering, his training lost. He was just a boy. He was nothing.

He fell to his knees, bokken useless in his hands.

Then he remembered something. Just one thing, but it was definitely something. *The rabbit.*

Was it Arthur, reminding him to stay on task, stay alert, stay strong?

Suddenly, Ethan was sure of it.

He lifted from his knees and swung with an elegant ferocity that he had forgotten. He now had the intruders cornered in his room, landing punishing blow after punishing blow.

Hunched and howling, they scrambled for the bedroom door and ran like the hounds of hell were after them.

*Don't let me catch you, you losers.* Ethan grinned like a maniac and took chase. He followed them down the stairs and into the front yard, wielding his bokken like the majestic weapon it was.

The cowards who had come to harm him cursed and howled and ran off into the night.

Ethan fell to his knees, exhausted yet exhilarated at the same time. He raised his eyes to the sky and said a "thank you" to Arthur.

"Ethan!"

As if the evening hadn't been crazy enough, Liz and Jacob were speeding toward him on their bikes.

"What are you guys doing here? How? Why?" He couldn't collect his thoughts to accurately express his mindset just then, so he opted for a simple: "Uh, it's the middle of the night."

Jacob hopped off his bike, letting it fall to the ground. Liz did the same. They were both in their pajamas, and for some reason, that made Ethan smile. He looked down at his own pajamas.

Liz said, "What's so funny? You look crazy. Why are you out here?"

Words once again failed Ethan. He said nothing, staring at his friends in their pajamas.

"Dude, it was so weird. I had a dream—it was so real—that you were going to die. I shot outside to head over here and saw Liz getting on her bike. She had the same freaking dream, man!"

Liz nodded, trying to catch her breath. "I did. The exact same one."

When Ethan still didn't respond, Jacob snapped his fingers in front of his friend's face. "Hello? Why are you out here? It's true, isn't it? Someone tried to kill you! Holy crap!" Jacob spun around in a circle, his arms splayed.

Ethan finally caught back up to the moment, and found his voice. It was surprisingly calm. "Yes. I was attacked by two guys. In my bedroom. Okay, well, first I was sleeping, and I heard this thumping noise, and when I peeked out the window, I saw a rabbit on the hood of my mom's car, tapping away with its hind leg." He walked over to the car. No rabbit. No sign that a rabbit had been sitting on the hood; the dust that was typically on his mother's car was undisturbed.

"I don't understand. He was right here." He ran his finger along the hood, creating a line in the dust.

Jacob twisted his lips and looked at Liz, who looked at him with wide eyes. He said, "Forget about the imaginary rabbit. The point is, someone did try to kill you."

Ethan said, "Yes."

"But the rabbit put you on alert," Liz whispered. "Ethan, something's happening here. I don't know what it is, and I can't explain it, but something's watching over you."

Ethan said, "Arthur."

At that moment, Ethan's mom burst through the door. "What in the world is happening? All this banging around in the middle of the night!"

Ethan let his bokken fall behind the car, out of view. She had never seen it, and now was not the time to explain what it was.

Jacob stepped forward. "I'm sorry, Mrs. Drake. Really, I am. This was all just part of a little game we were playing, a mystery we made up, and so . . . uh, Liz and I came to surprise Ethan when he was asleep. And, well, we didn't expect him to, uh, freak out."

Ethan rolled his eyes. Jacob was pushing it, but honestly, it was the best explanation for the moment.

"Ugh, you guys and your mysteries and treasures. No more. Not after bedtime, you hear me?"

The group replied in unison, "Yes, ma'am."

She stomped back into the house.

Ethan high-fived Jacob. "Quick on your feet. Thanks, dude."

Liz huffed out a breath and ran her fingers through her hair. "This is just so weird. I know weird, and this is weirder than weird."

Ethan looked back at the car. "It is rather strange," he said in a monotone voice.

"You were probably just seeing things, dude," Jacob said.

Liz glared at Jacob. "He said, 'Arthur.' Did you hear that? I heard that." She flashed her eyes at Ethan. "You said that, right? You think it was Arthur. That rabbit represented Arthur. Right? The Three Hares?"

No one responded, so she added another, "Right?"

Ethan said, "Let's all get back to our beds. We'll talk about this more tomorrow. I promise."

Reluctantly, Jacob and Liz hopped on their bikes and rode away. Ethan stared at the hood of his mom's car for a long time.

His conclusion: *This is all just a dream.*

## Chapter Twenty-Two

# Counterstrike

All his muscles ached. The sun had risen, and so had Ethan, who was surprised that he had been able to sleep at all. The events of the night were a haze, still dream-like in quality.

*It was all just a dream,* he reminded himself.

He rolled out of bed and pulled on the same clothes he'd worn the previous day. Though there was nothing particularly special about this morning—the sun was beaming and the birds were chirping—he felt something was off.

When he saw the dagger on the floor, near the wall, he knew why.

*It wasn't a dream. Someone had tried to kill me. There was a rabbit on the hood, warning me. My friends had come to help me.*

He grabbed his backpack and threw the dagger inside of it. He ran out of the house, avoiding any encounter with his mother, who would surely remember last night's disturbance and have quite a few thoughts about it.

He traveled alone, directly to the Rabbit Hole, in hope of finding Samuel. Sure enough, the Elder was reading the morning paper at the table, sipping on his coffee.

"Ah, Ethan, I am glad you're here."

He plopped down at the table. "Hi, Samuel."

"You guys made the front page." Samuel flipped the paper in his direction. "Your poster, directly on the mayor's front door, was captured by the media before Maxwell was able to take it down."

Ethan wasn't sure how Samuel knew that the posters had come from his crew, but it was not of importance at this moment. The rabbit on his mom's car, the would-be killers in his room—those were the things he wanted to discuss.

"Not to be disrespectful, Samuel, but I need to talk about something else right now. Something huge happened last night. *Huge*."

The Elder sat back in his chair and folded his hands in front of him. "Go on."

The words fell from Ethan's mouth, rapidly and without a break in momentum. He wrapped it up by asking, "What do you think about that, Samuel? The rabbit. How could a rabbit warn me of such things, be sitting on my mom's car, and then leave no trace that it had been there? I wasn't imagining it. I know I wasn't. It had been there."

Samuel's gaze had been intense when he listened to the young warrior's story. Now, he smiled. "I knew it."

Confused, Ethan threw his hands in the air. "Knew what?"

"Well, Ethan, our minds are rather puzzling things. What you saw, which warned you, could simply be explained as *instinct*." He shrugged, as if downplaying Ethan's story.

"It was not just instinct, Samuel. I actually *saw* the rabbit just before the intruders came to *assassinate* me."

"Please, let me explain what I mean. Instincts come in many forms, and what I have learned from instincts is that one should always follow their lead. From deep down inside of you, there is something that sees things much clearer than our cognitive selves can comprehend. Most people simply ignore these innermost sensations. Toss them to the side and move on with their lives. But those of us who can recognize them for the vital sensations they are, will have limitless advantages in life. I think that your time on top of the cliff has done a tremendous job toward connecting you to your inner self, as well as your bloodline. And that has saved your life, as well as many other lives in the future."

Ethan shifted in his seat. "I think that, too. I do. In fact . . ." He paused, not sure if he wanted to express what was on his mind. The real deal.

"Go on, son."

"Okay. I think the rabbit was actually Arthur. I think it was a spiritual connection that I have with the Three Hares. I think my Protector still lives, maybe in another way, but he's still protecting me."

Samuel bowed his head. "I see. I think you are . . . you could be right." Quickly shifting gears, Samuel pushed forward, "Well, I'm anxious to hear about your progress. It seems that you've really gotten under the mayor's skin."

Ethan broke away from his deep thoughts and lightened up to tell of their conquests. "Yeah, we put those posters up, in the thick of the night, all over town. Our new recruits have made a major difference in our efforts. In fact, they got their hands on a transponder that we will use to interrupt all live TV feeds into the city *this evening*. We'll broadcast a video of the homeless labor camps across the river and organize a rally. It's going to be *epic*."

"This is all great news, and finding the information on the mayor's past will make a huge difference. But I must caution you on something, so it does not come as a surprise. No matter how hard it is to believe, many people who have supported Mayor Hofner from the beginning, desperately wishing his promises will be fulfilled, will not see or hear your message about him."

"Well, we know we can't get the message out in front of everyone, but the video should really help."

"That's not what I mean, Ethan. The thing is, people tend to be blinded by what they *believe* they know, which prevents them from accepting that they are wrong. They don't want to acknowledge that they've been . . . essentially tricked."

"But we have evidence and pictures of this guy with the slave camps. How can they ignore that?"

"Well, to be honest, I don't understand it myself fully. But you should be prepared, because denial will happen. Meanwhile, keep your focus clear and build upon those who are willing to see things in a new light. Do not be deterred. Your strength comes from your supporters, not your deniers. That is all I can say at this point."

Ethan was disappointed in the whole conversation. He'd come to Samuel for support, for answers, and he felt like he'd received a pittance. He pushed back from the table, suddenly weary. "I'll keep that in mind. Thanks for your time."

"My pleasure, young man. Anytime."

"Okay, so, I'm gonna head back and get together with our team. We have a big day of polishing up our final video so we can broadcast it tonight."

"I look forward to your results. Stay safe. You know by now that these guys will stop at nothing."

"Now *that* is something I understand." He grabbed his pack and headed for the door.

The full team rallied once again at the old oak tree.

Ann jumped right in. "We already came up with some video ideas and made some cuts we can choose from. We have everything from overly dramatic to simple."

"It needs to be honest, straightforward, and startling," Ethan said.

"And short," Liz added. "We don't want our feed to be cut off before the entire message is out."

"Maybe we can run it in a loop, that way it keeps re-running until they find our transponder," Jacob suggested.

Ethan winked at that. "Excellent idea."

Ann had brought along a laptop from the university's computer science department. Ethan had never seen such a device before.

The team worked through several versions she had prepared. After a short while, they had something which really hammered on the message. They were careful not to overdo it, which may inadvertently cause people to not believe the message. Ethan thought of Samuel's warnings.

The video also suggested a protest rally at the construction site for the bridge. They hoped the people would come out and see for themselves.

Ethan said, "We're ready. It's perfect."

*Time to flip the switch.*

\* \* \*

The team broke into Winslow Falls High School's computer lab and waited until precisely 8:00 p.m. All their fingers were crossed, hoping the transponder connection would work as planned. As the clock ticked to the whole hour, Ann clicked on the mouse button, activating the live feed that would interrupt all broadcasting in town.

The team stared at the small TV, but nothing happened. Just as Ann started to fumble around with her program, the TV went to snow momentarily, and then their video began to play. Under her breath, she mumbled, "I forgot about the lag time." No one acknowledged her words. All eyes were focused on the TV as the feed started with the horrendously annoying sound they had added to grab everyone's attention. Ethan proudly noticed Mike smirking at his contribution of the idea.

Their vision became a reality.

\* \* \*

Ezra and his elite assassin were discussing the failed attempt on Ethan's life when the phone rang.

Ezra exhaled in frustration for the interruption. "What?" he barked into the phone.

It was Maxwell. "Turn on your TV. I thought you were going to end this crap!"

"What are you crying about now?" He motioned to the guard to turn on the TV.

Maxwell was frantic. "Just turn it on. It's on every channel!"

Ezra's TV flickered on, showing photograph upon photograph of their workers' camp. Intense music dramatized the scenes, along with words written at the bottom of the screen, describing everything they had been working on.

Ezra simply hung up the phone. He and the assassin stared at the feed. After a few moments, Ezra picked up the phone and dialed the security office downstairs. "Kill the TV station's feed. NOW!"

The film was filled with information about the mayor, including his acceptance speech and pictures of his former self at Vulpes Valley, standing in front of signs for Daquan Construction. The film described Maxwell's past, his facial reconstruction, and his crimes. Not to mention the photograph of the mayor kicking a homeless guy on the ground.

He and the assassin watched in horror as their entire plan became exposed in front of the entire city. After the feed looped a few more times, Ezra licked his lips and tried to contain the pandemonium, if only in his own head. "Really, so far, this only reveals the mayor's activities and this one specific project. We're not directly linked, which is good. But these kids are going to pay for this."

"My offer still stands. I'll take care of Ethan, but I will do it in accordance with my methods, not yours," the assassin said.

"Fine. Do it your way, but finish this kid once and for all. End the Three Hares. If I have one more initiative interfered with, I'm going to start an all-out war against this freakin' city!"

"I will take care of this." The assassin left the room.

This could not have been a more exciting evening for Ethan and his team. They gazed at the TV, which repeated their video transmission an uncountable number of times for at least an hour. At just about 9:00 p.m., the broadcast terminated. The usual programming did not return. There was only static.

Ethan laughed and said, "They cut the hard lines! Great job, everyone, I've never seen anything like that before!"

"Well, dang. Tomorrow's gonna be a big day," Frank said. "You three are not gonna be there? Seriously?" He was addressing Ethan, Liz, and Jacob.

"It's best that we lie low. I have a bad feeling that they suspect our involvement for some reason." Ethan said as he glanced over at Jacob and Liz. "I think it's better to be at a safe distance. If there is any fallout, I don't want to be within an arm's reach of these guys. Besides, if the normal TV broadcast is up and running again, we will be able to watch the whole thing unfold through the media's eyes. After all, that's more important than actual events."

"Such a cynic," Liz teased, knowing full well that he was right.

Ethan offered his best eye roll.

Mike rustled Ethan's hair as if he were a kid brother, which, really, he kinda was. "Well, I really hope people show up," Mike said. "We need some serious media attention. I think this is going to play out as something for the history books."

The team's enthusiasm was on high. Still, Ethan's mind was running through *all* possible outcomes for tomorrow. There were too many variables, and he was unsure exactly how he would be able to protect the team. The mayor and Red Fox were not known for being predictable, that was for sure.

Liz's key slid into the lock of the front door, making only the slightest sound as the deadbolt disengaged. She slipped into her darkened house, intent on not waking her parents. It was well after midnight and had been a long day; she was exhausted. As she carefully closed the door behind her, the lamp beside the couch flipped on, causing her to depart from the ground, releasing a loud shriek.

"Dad . . . what are you doing up so late?" she asked as her father glared back at her.

"Where have you been, Elizabeth?"

"With my friends. I'm tired, and I'm going to bed."

Mr. Walker stood and pointed to the couch. "Sit down, young lady."

Liz exhaled loudly and dropped her head, shaking it slightly from side to side. She flopped on the couch. "What?"

"Were you and your *friends* behind this stunt tonight? The video of the mayor?" he asked. His voice was intense, burning with rage.

"Ugh, Dad. Leave it alone. I'm exhausted."

"I noticed that my camera was missing. Did you take those pictures?"

"No, I didn't take the pictures. Where would you get such a stupid idea?" She knew that he knew it was a lie, but she didn't care.

"Your *friends* are going to ruin everything, and I forbid you from *helping* them with these ridiculous stunts." He shook his head as if he had been betrayed. "We're new in town, and I will not allow you to tarnish our family name by helping these idiots destroy the mayor. Put your family first . . . for once in your life."

"Drop it, Dad. You have no idea what I go through for this stupid *family*. Why can't we just be normal, like everyone else?"

"Normal? Is that what you want? You don't have a clue what it would be like to be normal. *Normal*, what a terrible way to live."

"Whatever. I'm going to bed."

Liz stormed out of the room before he could respond.

## Chapter Twenty-Three

# Crumbling Down

Before the looming rally, the mayor was summoned to an abandoned warehouse at the old trainyard. Ezra and his guards were standing there, waiting for his arrival. "Were you followed?" Ezra asked as the mayor approached on foot.

Maxwell clenched his teeth "No. I'm not an idiot."

"Under the circumstances, I'm seriously doubting your competencies," Ezra said as he shook his head in disbelief of last night's media disaster. "You've become a liability to my organization, Maxwell, and my clearer mind tells me to finish you off right now."

"I can still fix this, Ezra, just give me some time to get things back on track."

"What could I possibly gain by allowing you to live? It is quite clear what I have to lose!"

Maxwell, all but on his knees, begged for his life. "I can salvage this. Maybe this project is lost, but these people are wrapped around my finger. You know that's true. You'll see how this comes out, for the better. We must not lose hope."

"The only thing more foolish than you is the voting public!" Ezra said sharply.

"Yes, I'll use that to our advantage, of course! I always have. They won't even blink an eye at this event. Everything is going to—"

"You will have one more chance, Maxwell," Ezra interjected as he shifted his view to one of his goons. "Please prepare a burial site in the pines, one which would fit Mayor Hofner. You know, just in case things don't go well for him today."

"I'll fix this Ezra, I promise."

Ezra offered an evil smirk, "Fare thee well, Maxwell." He fluttered his hand, indicating the mayor should return to his car.

Maxwell uneasily turned his back to the goons, not knowing if his next breath would be his last.

\* \* \*

The crowds began to grow at the bridge complex. Among the angry mob was Mike, Ann, and the Baxter twins. They weren't going to miss the event of the century. Although the number of protesters continued to grow, there was nothing more than insignificant chirping in small groups. No leaders for the cause had emerged so far.

The media circled the still-growing crowd like starved buzzards.

Finally, a black sedan with tinted windows pulled up to the edge of the crowd. TV cameras zoomed in as the door of the sedan opened.

Out stepped the former mayor, dressed to the nines.

"What's he doing here?" Mike asked.

Frank responded with some pride in his tone, "That's the leader we're looking for, but I didn't think I would see Mayor Steve Richardson's face again after all that campaign mudslinging."

"This is great publicity. The media has all their cameras on him. We finally have a focus point for the protest," Ann said.

Surprisingly, pockets of protestors started booing his arrival. The team was stunned.

"What's with the booing?" Frank asked.

"I don't know. Maybe they think he's behind the video. I just don't . . . I don't get it," Mike said.

"But the truth is right in front of them. The camps are right there, on the other side of the river," Travis said.

And so the charade continued. Mayor Hofner arrived just seconds later, on the other side of the river, equipped with a bullhorn. He accused the shamed former mayor for inciting the "blatant mistruths" that had encouraged today's strife. He revealed the innards of the tents—now nothing more than storage for building materials. A sleight of hand that sent shock waves through Ethan's team.

Travis lowered his head, gazing at the trampled ground between his feet. "This didn't go well at all."

\*\*\*

At the Rabbit Hole, Ethan, Liz, and Jacob watched the news coverage in shock. "How could this be?" Jacob asked. "How could they doubt what they saw flashing across their TV screens last night? They could do their own research and confirm it all. Wouldn't it be worth a few minutes of their time?"

Samuel walked up to the three, "My friends, I wish to introduce you to the power of propaganda." He nodded in Ethan's direction. "I warned you of this."

Liz fidgeted in her chair. "Warned of what?" She had not been clued in on Ethan's discussion with Samuel, nor had Jacob. "Whatever. We showed everyone the truth. I thought seeing is believing."

Ethan sat silently, twisting his lower lip between his fingers. Samuel *had* warned him. He realized there was much still for him to learn. But he wasn't giving up hope. Perseverance trumped weakness. Every time.

He waited, eyes glued to the screen.

The angry mob on TV became distracted by a thunderous noise overhead. Two black helicopters hovered above the throng of people, one with a sniper sitting at an open door. On the other side of the creek, three black vehicles left a long trail of dust blowing across the fields.

The reporter said, *"We have two unmarked helicopters now hovering above the mayor's position. Three unmarked black vehicles are approaching as well. It is unclear what they are doing here, and who they are, but they seem to be targeting Mayor Hofner."*

"There you go," Ethan said, sending a sideways glance in Samuel's direction. Ethan had a renewed sense of what "instinct" really meant.

"*This is unbelievable,*" the reporter said. "*The mayor is running away, into the cover of the forest.*"

"He's gonna get away! Again!" Liz shouted.

"I don't think so," Ethan said.

The cameras now panned across the edge of the forest. "*We have just identified half a dozen or more men, in full tactical gear, rushing at the mayor, blocking his . . . escape.*" The reporter was obviously flabbergasted at what was happening. "*Wait. Now the mayor is heading for the river. My goodness, what a scene!*"

The cameras continued to roll. The men in tactical gear fanned out, and the lead man gave direct chase. He reached the mayor in no time, tackling him to the ground, tumbling in a cloud of dust.

The video showed the mayor being dragged toward the three black vehicles. The reporter, after several minutes of silence, began to speak. "*I have just received word that the mayor has just been apprehended by the Federal Bureau of Investigation. His apprehension is because of an alleged identity associated to Vulpes Valley, where he had been mayor under a different name.*"

Ethan stood. "We got him."

Later that evening, they joined the other members of their little team at the old oak tree, excitement buzzing through the air.

Ethan chose to take advantage of the moment, to explain the significance of their efforts. "Within a short few days, we have been able to topple our corrupt mayor from office. We, regular teenage citizens, have accomplished a greater feat than most people achieve in their entire lives. I'm so proud."

He looked at Liz and Jacob, who both nodded.

"I have a story to share with you."

It was then that he revealed to the new members of his team the story of the Three Hares.

The Three Hares secret society soon had four new recruits.

Chapter Twenty-Four

# The Letter

Breaking the mayor was one of the most talked-about events in Winslow Falls. Ethan returned to the Rabbit Hole the following day, and the members of the Three Hares applauded his accomplishments. He insisted it was the team's effort which overcame the mayor, but they knew and believed in the influence of their great young leader. His ego was stroked; he was proud of his progress, and the immediate future of his city was better because of him.

Searching for some solitude, he notified Liz and Jacob that he would once again spend a little time in the cabin on the cliffs. He needed some "alone time" for reflection.

He climbed the cold, damp stone stairs to his retreat perched high above the Rabbit Hole and entered the reverent space. To his surprise, he found an envelope on his pillow. Ethan quickly looked around the room, grabbed the letter, and proceeded outside to the training platform, but no one was to be found.

He looked at the envelope. In an old-fashioned handwritten script were the words "Ethan Zephaniah Drake." He followed the trail around the back of the cabin and climbed to the viewing deck. After he scanned the surroundings, he sat down, broke the wax seal, and opened the letter.

*Ethan Zephaniah Drake,*

*It is with great honor that I may write to you. I have been watching your progress with fascination. Although Arthur was a fierce foe, it is you who I am destined to battle.*

*In honor, I wish to meet you alone on the same fateful ground where Arthur breathed his last breath, tomorrow evening as dusk turns to night, with your weapon of choice, the bokken. I intend to finalize our warring clans for eternity.*

*Bring yourself, and your soul, but no one else can know.*

*Sincerely,*
*Your Fate*

As he read the letter, a chill ran down his spine. Ethan knew this was the man who'd defeated his mentor, Arthur. How could he stand a chance against the elite assassin? He could not bring himself to the reality that tomorrow night may very well be his last night on earth.

Ethan returned to the cabin where he pulled out the journal left behind by his ancestors and read through their ghostly entries. He found encouragement in their words, but they, in no way, prepared him for tomorrow night.

After hours of reading in the glow of the flickering fire, he fell asleep with the book splayed across his chest. The fire turned to smoldering embers.

Throughout the night, variations of this forthcoming battle played through his dreams. In the dim moonlight on the bank of the stream, where the color of Arthur's blood stained the earth, he could foresee his very own final resting place. A simple wooden box, with the Three Hares image branded on it, was being prepared.

Upon awakening, he felt the intense morning sun beaming upon his face. Dust particles sparkled in gold.

He was prepared to meet his fate. His golden deed had been fulfilled.

Ethan headed back down to the Rabbit Hole; he'd decided against telling Jacob and Liz. Instead, he left them a note, attaching the letter from the assassin:

*I have something I need to take care of, need to do alone. I'll be back soon. If for some reason you do not hear from me after tomorrow night, read the letter in the envelope, and you will understand. But please, not before then.*

Ethan left the Rabbit Hole and headed off into the forest.

He spent most of the day walking through the forest, contemplating his situation while centering himself with nature. He carried his red-stained bokken, occasionally swinging it through positions, bashing unsuspecting and defenseless branches hanging low across the trail.

What was to come? Could be an ambush. Could be an honest duel. Or anything in between.

Dusk came before he'd really expected it. In a moment of regret, he was saddened that he hadn't had time to say goodbye to his mother, that he hadn't spent his last moments around family and friends. Rather, he'd walked through the forest alone. It was too late to correct this, he knew.

It was time to proceed to the blood-stained rock.

He walked, not feeling fear so much as an overwhelming sadness. Suddenly, a sound caught his attention, and he stood on guard, bokken poised to attack.

Before him stood a large, white rabbit, just ten feet away. They looked at each other for several moments before the rabbit hopped off into the forest.

"Arthur." He said it out loud and with a prideful smile. Ethan was no longer alone.

His trip to the battlefield was immersed in fresh thoughts. Thoughts about instincts. He needed to tap into his instincts. The most primal instinct is self-preservation . . . that's what he needed.

When he arrived, the hooded assassin was already waiting, apparently alone and seemingly relaxed. His white-spotted horse was tied up to a nearby tree, casually drinking from the stream.

"Hello, young man."

After a moment's pause, Ethan simply said, "Hi." Through all his planning and scenarios, none had included a friendly discussion.

"I understand that you only know me as the man who murdered your mentor," the assassin said, "but I wish you had an appreciation for the significance of our meeting tonight."

Ethan swallowed down his thick saliva. "You want to kill me to stop the Three Hares. Well, trust me, even if you kill me, the Three Hares will continue to grow and thrive. Your efforts tonight will only motivate them to strike back even harder."

"I do not believe this to be realistic, but perhaps," he replied as they approached each other. "What I wish to share is this: my duty as the elite assassin of Red Fox is to destroy the descendants of the Drake family lineage. And tonight, I will go down in history for eradicating your blood from this earth forever. However, for that, I have mixed emotions."

*Well, I didn't expect that last comment.* Still, Ethan was infused with the responsibility of protecting his family lineage, which in reality, was himself. He would not go down easily. "I promise you that I will battle you until dawn if I must, but I will not give you the satisfaction of taking away the bloodline of the Three Hares."

The assassin smiled and stepped into fighting position. "I do enjoy the color of your bokken. Is it blood?"

"It's *my* blood, as the wood grains have become me and I have become them," Ethan said as he established his position.

"Well, then I shall coat my bokken with your blood as well." The assassin took an initial jab at Ethan, who easily swatted it away.

Their sparring began gently—in fact, delicately—as they danced around the forest floor under the cold, blue moonlight.

"It is really quite a shame," the assassin said while swinging through different combinations. "You have made such progress in your training at an astonishing rate. I nearly feel badly for killing you before you have reached your full potential. A grand warrior you might have been."

Their encounters intensified; the cracking of their bokkens grew louder and more frequent, echoing through the immediate forest. Ethan, by this point, had essentially tuned out the assassin's ramblings and focused on his bokken. *Speed, position, time,* he repeated in his head.

"Unfortunately, if I had waited much longer, I would not stand a chance in beating you, and it would be my blood spilled tonight," the assassin said between the cracking sounds.

Eventually, the assassin's dialogue ceased as the battle grew in intensity. Ethan had entirely played defense thus far, but started to drop some light counterattacks whenever openings appeared. There was no doubt—the assassin was phenomenal. Trained, talented, and innovative. Ethan could hardly keep up.

Ethan began to think of the white rabbit on the trail just before arriving at this spot. Somehow, he was able to maintain his presence in battle while his mind drifted. He began to feel sharp, his focus intensified, and he could see trails behind the slicing bokken. His training from Arthur rushed through his mind as the sticks cracked louder and more frequently. They became less rhythmic and more ferocious.

The assassin had shifted into full battle mode, and Ethan responded in kind.

Ethan began to push. He shifted from the irregular counterattack into forging an occasional full offensive.

The fight for life was on.

\* \* \*

Hiding in the forest, at some distance were, Liz, Jacob, and Samuel. Liz had read the letter, against Ethan's wishes, and shared it with Jacob and the Elder. Samuel informed her that their interference could jeopardize his concentration, so they stayed in the background, ready to move in if their young leader became incapacitated.

However, this was not the case. Ethan moved through the night like a poet's pen surging across the page, with an unstoppable, emotional fury. From an outside observer, two men battled by that stream. But it was so much more than that. Liz, Jacob, and Samuel were well aware of what was happening—Ethan was channeling his great ancestors through his blood-stained bokken. And probably Arthur, too.

\* \* \*

Thoughts of his father crept into Ethan's mind, and an anger surfaced. He bashed upon the assassin's stick. He could "hear" the accelerations and decelerations of his opponent's weapon, and at one exact moment, he unleashed a swing at maximal speed, descending down upon his enemy's forthcoming bokken. Smashing them together yielded a booming, shattering sound as the assassin's bokken split into many shards, flying in all directions.

The assassin released a gasp of surprise. Ethan followed through in a swinging motion, swiping his feet from under him. The assassin landed on the ground in a crash. Ethan's continuous combination moves, still unfinished, circled back around at a ferocious speed, stopping just short of obliterating the assassin's throat.

Ethan held the bokken there, still as a stone.

The stream gurgled in the dark not far away. The breeze stopped, allowing the leaves to find a temporary resting place. Steam pushed from his and the assassin's noses and mouths. One quick move would end the assassin and his threats forever.

"A man of honor," Ethan finally said aloud, pondering the words. "My fury tells me to destroy you, yet I have not done so."

The assassin stared up at him, waiting.

Ethan said through gritted teeth, "You will tell Red Fox that you have defeated me. You will tell him of your glorious victory tonight. Lead him to believe that the Three Hares have met their demise. You will become *my* spy deep inside his organization. You speak of honor, assassin. Do you wish to redeem your honor amongst humanity? Will you redeem your honor with the nature that surrounds us? Give me your word that you will join our forces as a spy. Otherwise, you will die here tonight, alone, with no honor. Only a speck of dirt littering this forest floor."

Ethan slowly removed the tip of his bokken from the assassin's throat. Just a little bit.

The assassin looked up into the eyes of not a boy, but a battle-proven warrior. In a raspy voice, he replied, "I will serve you, Ethan, noble warrior. My services are at your command."

Ethan reached his hand down to his foe, helping him to his feet. "Tell of your great victory, and I will retreat into the shadows and build my army. You shall hear from me again."

Ethan turned and slipped back into the cold, dark night.

Tonight, Ethan became an untold legend.

\* \* \*

Liz, Jacob, and Samuel had witnessed everything, barely believing what they'd seen. Liz watched Ethan glide off the battlefield, victorious. It was as if he were ten feet tall and chiseled from granite.

After a short while, they broke from their concealed positions and began to walk back to the cave.

Behind them, from the darkness came a voice, "I thought I asked you not to read the letter until tomorrow."

Liz and Jacob jumped in surprise, and as Ethan came closer, Liz swatted his shoulder for startling her.

"You two really need to practice your sneaking around," Ethan said as a smile crossed his face.

"What? Samuel didn't see you, either," Jacob said.

"Actually, he winked at me just a few minutes ago when you guys started to walk away."

"I'm gonna get you guys back!" Liz said in a huff.

The four of them walked home together. Not a word was spoken of the assassin's defeat. There was nothing that could be said to enhance the events of this pivotal night. Ethan noticed how fresh the air tasted as he inhaled deeply.

Chapter Twenty-Five

# The White Rabbit

Insisting that last night's event remain a secret, Ethan wanted to wait until the information would be useful. Besides, tonight was a special evening. Under the stars in the clearing between the hills, their new members would be sworn into the Three Hares. Ethan decided it was appropriate for them to bond with nature in their ceremonies—hiding in a hole was the wrong message.

Samuel led the ceremony, as he had done when Ethan, Jacob, and Liz had joined only weeks earlier. He finished by saying, "I have been with the Three Hares since my adolescence, and in recent years, I have watched it slowly slide into ruin. However, the future is bright. I have long awaited for a resurgence, and it is happening now.

"Although I have sworn not to tell you of some very special events, I will say that I have recently witnessed something which I have never seen in all my years. It is something I have only heard as it was passed down as legend amongst the Three Hares. It is the legend of the White Rabbit. It is the spirit of the Great Edgar Zephaniah Drake the Second, who has periodically selected an ancestor of phenomenal insight, will, and humanity, to reform himself within. I wish to inform you tonight that, based upon these recent events, without a doubt, Ethan Zephaniah Drake is indeed the White Rabbit."

*Edgar . . . I thought that was Arthur.* Ethan bowed his head and grinned at the enormity of this information.

The crowd immediately became silent.

This was the first time Ethan had heard of the White Rabbit, but it certainly answered many questions about his visions, and "instincts." He even recalled the strangely awkward moment when Samuel had looked him in the eye and asked if "he was there."

Ethan moved to the front of the crowd where Samuel stood. "A few words?" Samuel asked.

With warm smiles from his fellow members, he decided to attempt some kind of brave, unprepared speech.

"Um. Well, first I wish to welcome Frank, Travis, Mike, and Ann. They are tremendous people who will be great assets to the Three Hares and our community."

There was a hearty round of applause, all eyes focused on Ethan, the White Rabbit.

He closed his eyes and took a deep breath. "I do not know how I came to be standing in front of you tonight. Honestly, the events of the past weeks are simply unbelievable. My two best friends have stood by me the entire time, giving me courage. Liz and Jacob, sincerely, thank you." As he looked at his friends, emotions swept across him in a wave as his throat constricted.

"Some time ago, I placed myself into confinement, to train, to learn, and to simply have some peace and quiet." The audience offered a gentle laugh. "While I was there, I read some writings from the great leaders of our past. These writings went all the way back to Edgar the Second.

"After the events of last night, combined with the information from those memoirs, I have decided something. I have decided that we will no longer be living in a Rabbit Hole. I have decided that we will no longer *hide* from the Red Fox. I have decided that we will no longer claw our way through survival." His voice increased in pitch and intensity as he spoke. "We will blaze our own path. We will destroy our enemy. We will take the offensive and chase down our former hunters. I have decided that we will realize a dream of Edgar the Second. We, together, will create the army of the Three Hares."

The audience erupted into a roar of applause.

Ethan's eyes meet with Samuel's. The Elder was smiling. He bowed to Ethan and then turned and walked away.

Anxious to catch up with Samuel, Ethan brought the speech to a close. "Tonight, we will celebrate our new recruits, and tonight, we will celebrate our future."

Amidst the applause and rejoicing, Ethan rushed into the forest, in the direction Samuel had gone. There were no signs of him.

Ethan turned in circles, unable to fathom that he could not find the old man. He had walked away only moments ago.

Dejected, Ethan turned back . . . and ran straight into Liz. She surrounded him with open arms and buried her head in his neck. They stayed like that for several minutes.

"He's gone," Ethan said.

"I know. He didn't know how to tell you, so instead of leaving you with words that you would analyze and interpret, he thought leaving with a bow and a smile would be the most appropriate."

"Crazy old man," Ethan joked, but a tear crept across his cheek. Samuel was the wisest man he'd ever known.

Chapter Twenty-Six

# The Council

The assassin was in turmoil as he waited inside a quiet chamber deep within the palace of the Red Fox. His meeting with Ezra was quickly approaching, and the most consequential decision of his life was upon him.

Should he uphold his promise to the White Rabbit, Ethan Drake? Should he lie to Ezra about the battle and spy for the Three Hares, his lifelong sworn enemy?

Or, his second option: Tell Ezra of his defeat. He would suffer the consequences of his failure and break the promise he'd traded for his own life to Ethan.

His code of honor was at a crossroads. There was no way forward without his honor being tarnished. Would his ancestors simply have allowed their lives to be taken?

Pondering the options, weighing the pros and the cons, it was clear that he was, quite simply, in a mess.

A loud knocking rapped upon the door. A guard poked his head in. "Ezra will see you now."

Still without a decision, the assassin took a deep breath and headed down the long hall of the dark palace toward Ezra's office.

Ezra stood at the window, silhouetted by the sun. "And?" he simply said.

Intending to delay the point of impact, the assassin said, "It was an epic battle. The boy has progressed beyond anyone's expectations."

Perhaps smelling the delay in the air, Ezra barked, "Is he dead?"

The assassin's reaction was one of instinct. He said, "Yes," although he was unsure what he had just done. His fate was now sealed. Lying to Ezra was a death wish, but upholding the promise he had made to Ethan meant he was already on borrowed time. He was now owned by his enemy.

"Very good." Ezra turned back into the room with a grin. "We have some plans to discuss."

The assassin's attention was limited, still running through the lies in his head. It was imperative he kept his story together.

"I received word this morning about Maxwell," Ezra said. "The FBI came down hard on him, prying for information."

The assassin, very curious about the situation, asked, "Are they fishing for a bigger scheme? Our scheme?"

"Indeed. But we have some friends at the jail who have given Maxwell an *incentive* to not talk," he said as a conniving grin crept across his face. "There are some loyal men locked up there, where he will be staying for the rest of his years. And those men would take great pleasure in making Maxwell's life most miserable."

The assassin snorted at the thought. He was standing directly in the dragon's lair. No longer in a sworn allegiance, he was a spy, a traitor. This could only end very badly.

"We lost the contract with Teumessian Industries." Ezra shook his head, "They want to distance themselves from the exposure."

"A devastating loss. But, with the Three Hares out of the way, our future is limitless."

"We have lost a great deal of money on this deal, and it is time that we get our next project started," Ezra said. "The council will convene this evening to discuss our options. We'll be in touch."

The assassin departed, unsettled about the complexities of his future.

At 9:00 p.m., the council of the Red Fox came together at the palace—twelve members, including their leader, Ezra Reynard. They were the financial and social elites of the region. Bound in secrecy, with only one interest in mind—total domination.

"Council members," Ezra began, "we have lost our contract with Teumessian Industries, and we must begin anew. I have a plan on some "social restructuring" I would like to share, but before we get ahead of ourselves, Mr. Walker, what have you learned from our inside source within the Three Hares."

James Walker cleared his throat. "I have been informed that Ethan is alive and well, and that your assassin has lied to us."

The room erupted in rumbling discussions.

"Silence," Ezra barked as he slammed his hands upon the table, nearly losing his temper. He paused momentarily and took a deep breath to consider his options. "Interesting. Okay, so we shall allow our assassin to spy on us. He will share exactly what we intend him to share. No?"

James Walker, father of Liz Walker, said, "Brilliant."

The adventure continues:
The Three Hares: Reynard's Dream

Follow the series at -

www.geoffrey-simpson.com

# Acknowledgements

*The Three Hares* was conceived, nourished, and born during a wild and adventurous twelve-month period. Dozens of individuals, in one way or another, contributed to this novel, but there are a distinguished few who truly shaped the story within these pages. I give a heartfelt thanks to all, and a debt of gratitude to the following.

Jaidyn (10) & Mason (13)—It is your enthusiasm which inspires me to write. I will never forget my first fans.

Robert Sutton & Martin Schubert—Since the very first draft, your ideas for this project inspired each revision and each step closer to the now-released version. Sorry, Martin, but the horse made it through the final draft.

Gwen Wear—Your eye for design cultivated the aesthetics of *The Three Hares.* Not to mention, your unparalleled support for "Ethan rising."

Gary & Gloria Simpson—From the day I began typing the first chapter, your unwavering support and suggestions have carried me through. Mom, I wish I'd had an editor for High School English.

Janet Fix (thewordverve)—Where to begin… The voices of Ethan, Jacob, and Liz are intertwined between us. Whenever I re-read a paragraph, I remember our exchanges, lessons, and jokes, which pulled a manuscript from being a newbie mess to a novel of which I couldn't be prouder. Thank you for being you!

# About the Author

Geoffrey Drew Simpson

Born: February 1978, Cleveland, Ohio.
—The winter of the White Hurricane.

Geoffrey Simpson was born and raised in Avon Lake, just outside Cleveland, Ohio. From an early age, he connected with nature through camping, building forts, fishing, and treasure hunts.

After graduating from Kent State University, building a career in program management, and growing a family of two boys, Jonathan and Henry, with his beloved wife Lili, he took a breath. A breath to recapture the spirit of adventure so that it may never be lost. An adventure which can be passed down for generations, including to his own two boys. Now living in Minden, Germany with his family, he became a writer.

Geoffrey is the author of the young adult adventure / mystery novel, *The Three Hares: Bloodline*. He specializes in nature-themed, puzzle-solving stories driven by a pulsating grip of good versus evil. *The Three Hares* is his debut novel and is the first of a five-book series.

Checkout his website and sign-up for the newsletter.
www.geoffrey-simpson.com
www.facebook.com/The3HaresSeries/

CPSIA information can be obtained
at www.ICGtesting.com
Printed in the USA
LVHW020623221218
601183LV00019B/1142/P